About the Book

Brenda was a lonely child, resented by her sister and a disapointment to her Dad, she made her own fun losing hersellf in a dream world Introduced to a form of sex at a young age she became an observer of the way animals coupled together. Her sister was not kind to her. They moved to a new place where she had some contact with a lass from Dubbo.

Her first real pet taken by a snake in front of her and snakes were instrumental of leading to the loss of her next love, her dog D2. In her early teens her sister died in mysterious curcumstancies, She died of snake bite, causing her Mum to have a mental break-down and her Dad tp turn to alcohol. She ran away not caring where she was going. Here she got lucky as the truck she hitched a ride with turned out to be a decent bloke. He led her to a idelic life on a farm, he gave her a dog. A snake reared their ugly head again. Here a nasty man raped her. She went back to her Mum and became a nurse.

Finding out she was pregnant she again ran away to the ciity. A group of prostutes took her in where she lived while waiting for her babies. The bloke that had raped her saw her there and took tales of her working in a brothel home to the farm. The truck driver hit him and killed him. He did go to jail and saw some terrible events. A disgraced doctor saw her through her pregnancy, finding couples to adobt her babies. While getting over a tramatic birth of her babies she met with her friend from her previous home, and left to go to Dubbo with them.

She met a nurse friend who told her that her Mum and Dad were now working on the farm and about the truck driver being in jail. She went to see her grand parents at the same time as the truckie did when they both still had feelings and a quick marriage was arranged before they headed back to the farm and her parents.

ESCAPING SNAKES

BRENDA LOUISE

B L Wilson

BALBOA.PRESS
A DIVISION OF HAY HOUSE

Balboa Press books may be ordered through booksellers or by contacting:

Balboa Press
A Division of Hay House
1663 Liberty Drive
Bloomington, IN 47403
www.balboapress.com.au
AU TFN: 1 800 844 925 (Toll Free inside Australia)
AU Local: 0283 107 086 (+61 2 8310 7086 from outside Australia)

Because of the dynamic nature of the Internet, any web addresses or links contained in this book may have changed since publication and may no longer be valid. The views expressed in this work are solely those of the author and do not necessarily reflect the views of the publisher, and the publisher hereby disclaims any responsibility for them.

The author of this book does not dispense medical advice or prescribe the use of any technique as a form of treatment for physical, emotional, or medical problems without the advice of a physician, either directly or indirectly. The intent of the author is only to offer information of a general nature to help you in your quest for emotional and spiritual well-being. In the event you use any of the information in this book for yourself, which is your constitutional right, the author and the publisher assume no responsibility for your actions.

This is a work of fiction. All of the characters, names, incidents, organizations, and dialogue in this novel are either the products of the author's imagination or are used fictitiously.

Any people depicted in stock imagery provided by Getty Images are models, and such images are being used for illustrative purposes only. Certain stock imagery © Getty Images.

Print information available on the last page.

ISBN: 978-1-5043-2128-0 (sc)
ISBN: 978-1-5043-2129-7 (e)

Balboa Press rev. date: 09/15/2020

To all those who had faith in me and those who doubted me.

BRENDA LOUISE

FIRST ENCOUNTERS

THE BIRTH

Nurse Anna brushed the hair that had dislodged itself from under her starched cap. Matron would be making her rounds soon, and Anna needed to get away and tidy herself up. She already had several black marks on her record because of the unruly hair. Anna sighed heavily, and again tried to remove her hand from Nancy Willows's hand. Nancy hung on tight, really tight. Anna's fingers were almost blue form the lack of blood flow.

Nancy felt the nurse tugging at her hand, and taking a long, shaky breath, Nancy opened her eyes and looked at her. Anna placed her other hand on top of the one that was being held captive. "Please, love, I need to go for a minute." Anna gave Nancy a wan smile. "Matron and doctor will be here soon. Maybe they will get this baby out today."

Nancy gave a huge sigh, released the nurse's hand, and watched as the nurse hurried off, shaking her hand as she went. Tears streamed out of Nancy's eyes as another wave of pain engulfed her swollen body. How long had it been since she'd felt the baby move? She pressed her hands onto her belly. A moan escaped her lips. *Please, God, don't let my baby die.* How long had it been since she'd arrived? Time seemed to either stand still or rush past in wave after wave of agonising pain. "Hang on, little one," she whispered to herself as the pain abated.

Dexter Willows sat on the hospital steps, his head in his hands. The bloody matron wouldn't let him in to see Nancy. The old bitch had looked at him over her glasses and stated, "Birthing is not place for a man. It's woman's business. You will be informed in due course."

"Fuck me," Dexter said to the steps. "What is going on in there? Fucking what!" He thought this was worse than standing guard duty in the pouring rain for hours, when there was no enemy even in the country. *Pleased to be out of that bullshit show, anyhow.*

Dexter had rushed to town from his Dad's place, High Low. It'd taken four hours for the message to get to Dexter, and then four hours to get here. He'd thought it would all be over by the time he arrived. But no! The bloody bitch matron had shooed him away—and he'd been waiting for two days now. He was frantic with worry. Sandra's birth hadn't been like this. Dexter sighed. Giving his balls a bit of an adjustment, he looked up to find the matron peering at him, lips curled in distaste at what she had seen.

"Doctor wants to see you now," Matron snapped. She spun on her heel and strode off, stopping at the hospital entrance to look over her shoulder. "Come on now," she growled. "Doctor is a busy man."

Dexter followed slowly, working the stiffness out of his joints, refraining from any retort. He followed Matron into an office at the end of the hallway, past rows of waiting patients. Doctor Otto watched him enter and sit before leaning forward.

"Mr Willows, the baby is breach, and we had hoped it would turn it time. However, baby is now wedged very tightly in the birth channel." He paused and started to tap his thumbs on the desk. "Your wife, Nancy, is running out of strength, and the baby's heartbeat is erratic. We're going to remove the baby by using forceps. This may damage your wife, even render her unable to have more children. It's also possible that the baby may not survive. Your wife certainly will have a fifty-fifty chance of survival. I need your permission to proceed."

Dexter blinked and stared at Doctor Otto before nodding. Matron slid a piece of paper in front of him, indicating where she wanted him to sign. Handing the paper to the doctor, she motioned that Dexter was to leave. He hesitated before stammering, "Please, can I see Nancy?"

Both Doctor and Matron shook their heads.

"Will only delay the procedure."

They spoke together.

Dexter was ushered out to the steps again. *Fuck this,* Dexter thought. *I need a drink.* He jogged the nine blocks to the hotel, just making it in time for several quick tots of rum before the bar closed. He swayed a little on his way back to the hospital. *Hell, I think I may be drunk. Maybe I should have a feed,* he thought. But, by this time, he was almost to the hospital, so he shrugged his shoulders and plonked himself down heavily on the front steps. The drink took its toll, and he drifted off to sleep. He woke to a nurse poking him gingerly. "Sir, sir. Your wife is back from surgery."

He roused himself unsteadily to his feet. He clapped his hand onto the nurse's shoulder. "Is she okay? Is the baby okay? What is the baby?" The words stumbled over each other. His tongue did not want to work properly.

The nurse leaned away from him. "My goodness, sir, you smell of rum. Matron will not let you in smelling like that."

She stopped talking as he pulled away from her. He ran to the hospital, rushing through the doors and into the hallway. Dexter almost collided with several staff in the hall before he ran smack into Matron. *I'm for it now,* he thought. *Once she smells the rum, I'll be turfed out. Well, let her try!* To his astonishment, Matron took him to the toilet and handed him a toothbrush and comb. "Give yourself a bit of a tidy up, Mr. Willows. Your wife and daughter can wait a little longer. And after you see them, Doctor wants a word."

Another girl. Hope she's as cute as Sandra. Dexter came out of the toilet and smiled his thanks at Matron. He was shown to a room, where a very pale Nancy lay with her eyes closed. Nancy opened them as he gently took her hand in his work-rough ones. He kissed her fingers. "Have you seen her?" Nancy breathed. "She's very fair and tiny."

"I'll go and see her soon, Bunny," he whispered. She closed her eyes and drifted off to sleep.

"She's had a rough time, Mr. Willows." Matron touched him on the shoulder. "Let me take you to see your new daughter. Do you have a name for her?"

"Yes," Dexter said. "It was going to be Brenden or Brenda. So she will be Brenda Louise." As they walked to the nursery, Dexter thought, *This old bitch might not be too bad, after all.*

Dexter gazed at the bub through the window. He felt nothing.

SIXTH BIRTHDAY EVENTS

Brenda's head hurt. It'd been getting worse all day. Sandra had woken her up by pulling her out of bed by her hair, and Brenda had banged her head on the headboard. Sandra was nearly four years older than Brenda. Sandra was ever so clever at playing the sweet and innocent in front of others. Mostly, Brenda's head sort of hurt all the time. Her eyes were strange, with one eye wandering either right in towards her nose or right out. This happened a lot when she was upset or tired.

She often had trouble getting to sleep and wandered about a bit at night while everyone slept. She hated the way other people would stare at her when she was tired or had a headache, which only made the eye worse. When no one was about, Sandra called her names, like *cross-eyed fool* or other hurtful things. Brenda tried very hard not to be alone with Sandra much. Alvin, who lived on the property as well, didn't call her names, but sometimes joined in with Sandra's taunting. Really, the only people who didn't have anything to say about her eyes were Granddad and Alvin's dad, Horrie.

Brenda found it hard to join in ball games like catchie or cricket, as she couldn't focus enough to catch the balls. She was so bad at it that no one would play with her. She was good at other things like cards, dice games, or any games that relied on brain smarts to work things out. So much so that the other children didn't like to play these types of games with her, either. Brenda inadvertently won, or, if they did play with her, they would cheat or gang up on her. Brenda kept to herself for the most part. She found that made life simpler. Animals didn't judge her, though.

She especially avoided Sandra, who was very bossy and knew where to hit her. Sometimes, other visiting children wouldn't follow Sandra's lead on something. Sandra thought she always knew how something, anything, should be done. She was always sure her way was the only way. And she had all the rules. These rules sometimes changed if the games were not going Sandra's way.

Brenda and Alvin got caught every time they tried to get back at Sandra. Alvin was same age as Brenda. The last time they had ganged up on Sandra had been a beauty. They'd tied her hands and feet together and tossed her into the waterhole. Alvin had gotten worried and pulled her out before she'd drowned. Boy, oh boy, hadn't that gotten them into strife.

Brenda pressed her hands into her eyes. That seemed to help. She opened them as her mum sat down beside her, putting her arm round Brenda's shoulder. "You really should wear the glasses doctor gave you for your tired eyes." Mum ran her fingers through Brenda's hair "We'll see him again soon. He may want you to have the operation he talked about last time we were there. Now, come on, beautiful. It's your special day. Let's go make your cake."

Brenda nodded and headed towards the bathroom to wash her hands. She looked at herself and hated the way her right eye wandered about all the time. On her way back to the kitchen, she noticed Sandra's big doll on a chair; they had both gotten one for Christmas. So she grabbed Elsa, as Sandra called the doll, and bit her nose off. It felt so good to do it. Brenda knew she would get into trouble when Sandra saw the torn nose.

Nancy, Brenda's mum, was pleased to see Brenda had perked up a lot as she skipped into the kitchen, hopped up on a chair, and reached for a spoon. Nancy really hadn't been very well since Brenda's birth and often left Brenda in the care of Sandra. This operation for Brenda's eyes was putting a strain on money—or the lack of it—and now her doctor wanted to operate on Nancy too.

Nancy sighed. They couldn't afford both. Dexter was only paid a little amount, but he was expected to work up to eighteen hours a day. Nancy shrugged.

Sandra bounded into the kitchen just as the cake was put into the oven and Brenda was getting into the remains of the batter in the bowl with a teaspoon. Simply the best bit about making a cake was cleaning out the bowl. Sandra grabbed a spoon, and when Brenda protested, Nancy frowned at her and told her to share. Sandra kept pushing Brenda's spoon away from the batter, so Brenda gave up. *Wait till she sees Elsa*, Brenda thought.

Funnily, Sandra never said anything about Elsa all day, and Brenda found out why when she went to play with Jean, her doll, and found her nose bitten off too. To top off a really bad birthday, just before the cutting of the cake, Sandra brought out Elsa and Jean and cried what appeared to be real tears—and Brenda was blamed and sent to bed with no cake. The dolls were put away from the girls while Sandra smirked at Brenda from behind her hands.

Brenda did not cry, just lay in bed on her back stiffly, her hands beside her body. She had long learnt that crying only gave Sandra the pleasure of knowing she had really hurt Brenda. Brenda was disgusted at the way Sandra used tears to get what she wanted, always kowtowing to the adults by doing extra chores. Every chance Sandra got, she would involve Brenda in a prank, and Brenda would see her smirking as Brenda got a strapping and was shut away in the bathroom for what seemed like hours. Most of the time, the three children played well together. It was only when Alvin got called away that Sandra would start to lord over Brenda. Alvin hardly ever stood up for her. The only person who never failed to be kind was Granddad, and now he was feeling pretty sick and sometimes asked her to leave him alone.

Brenda crept out of the house and headed for the waterhole. It was still daylight, and the low sun sent pale spears of light darting through the leafy surrounds. Brenda loved it here. If she closed her eyes, she could listen to the water trickling over the rocks into the pool, Willy Wagtails flitting through the grass, kookaburras laughing in the tall trees just back a ways, and, several times, green budgerigars swooping through the foliage. They never stayed long, but Brenda loved the way their wings made a whirring noise.

Most of the time, frogs croaked at the edge of the pond, and dragonflies played Russian roulette with the speckled perch that inhabited the water. When hawks flew by or sat in the taller trees and made their screeching noise, the smaller wildlife became very quiet and still. All this familiar noise calmed her. Brenda always felt some sort of warmness inside herself as she watched the creatures interact with each other. She wished everyone could interact in such a harmonious manner. She gave a huge sigh as she thought about the widening rift between her and Sandra. She had overheard a visitor saying to her Mum, "Sandra has all the beauty, and Brenda has so much character in her face."

Her mind wanderings were brought back to earth as Alvin plonked himself down beside her. He reached over and took her hand gently in his, squeezing it and rubbing it with his thumb. The sensations felt very nice, and she leaned against his skinny little shoulder. They sat entwined for some time without speaking, until Brenda heard her mum clapping her hands, calling Brenda home. Alvin stood and gave Brenda a gentle hug and brief kiss on her cheek before she left. She smiled to herself as she meandered her way home. Nancy watched her as she stopped to look at something of interest in the grass along the way.

"You're such a dreamer, little one. I saved you a piece of cake." Nancy gave Brenda a squeeze. "What you did to those dolls was very naughty, and Sandra is beside herself."

Good, thought Brenda. *I bloody hope so.* She quickly apologised to herself for thinking the swear word. She'd used one of the many naughty words she had heard others use, but she was never game to reveal to her mum and dad she knew them. Nancy steered her to the bathroom to clean her teeth and brushed Brenda's fine, soft hair for her. Brenda loved having her hair brushed. It was nearly as good as

Alvin's hugs. She smiled and hoped Alvin would join her again soon. *Now, that was nice.* She shivered a little with anticipation. Nancy felt the shiver. "Let's get you into bed, little one."

"Carry me, please, Mum," Brenda asked pleadingly. It always made Sandra mad when her Mum carried Brenda.

Nancy hugged Brenda and picked her up easily, as she was a skinny kid, and carried her to the small room her girls slept in. As Nancy tucked her in, Brenda looked round her and poked her tongue out at Sandra before rolling over to receive her goodnight kiss and turn her back on Sandra. Brenda would need to get up before Sandra up in the morning, or the wake-up call would be rough.

PET, CITY, AND EYES

Sometimes, when Brenda sat gazing dreamily out of the window instead of doing her school work, she wondered what life would be like somewhere else. She was sure that this wasn't where she was supposed to be. Even Granddad was getting cross with her most of the time and did not want her sitting on him. That made her sad, as it really was the one place she felt safe. Granddad mostly treated her as though he liked her a lot. He had often put her in front of him on his saddle when he went for short rides. Now, he didn't ride any more, and the promised horse did not seem to be eventuating. She would have liked to have had a horse of her own. Sandra seemed to be content with small creatures for pets, like frogs and lizards. Brenda could not, would not, find them very nice. Once, Granddad had found a wild cat that had had kittens and brought Brenda one. She'd loved it and called it Dinky.

She'd loved the way it would curl up under her neck, and how his whole body had shaken when he purred. She'd been walking back from the waterhole one day when Bull, uncle Horrie's dog, had come up and barked at them. This had frightened Dinky, and he'd jumped out of her grasp, streaking up a tree, clinging there with Bull bouncing round the base. Brenda had screamed and screamed until her mum had come running and chased Bull away. After she'd calmed Brenda down, they'd looked up to see where Dinky was, and to their horror, they'd seen a large snake wrapping its self around Dinky. Dinky had made several little squeaks before going limp.

Nancy had dragged Brenda away as Brenda was yelling at her to save Dinky. Nancy had to pick her up and carry her home, with Brenda wriggling around to see if Dinky had escaped. Brenda had never felt such grief, and she had felt as though her heart was being squeezed by a giant hand. Dexter had come home just as Nancy and Brenda had gotten home, and he'd taken Brenda from Nancy as the story had come out in blubbering sentences. He'd held her ever so tight, with tears in his eyes, till Brenda had fallen into a hiccuping sleep. For the first time, he'd actually felt as though he could love this sad little girl.

After putting her to bed, Dexter had disappeared and returned with the remains of Dinky he'd cut from the snake's belly after he had killed it. He really hadn't wanted to kill it. Pythons were good to have about, as they ate rats and mice. He had wrapped the broken body in a rag before putting it into a shoebox. This, he'd taken out into the backyard and buried. Nancy had suggested that they wait for Brenda to wake up, but he'd said, "No. She would want to look at the body, and it's not pretty. She can help make a cross for the kitten later." They made a little cross, painted it white, and wrote *Dinky* across the top.

Brenda would go and sit beside the cross a lot after that. Even Sandra let up on being mean for a while. Brenda had felt as though all the best things in her life were leaving her, and she'd vowed never to ever get close to anything again. Dexter had brought home a baby possum out of a tree he had cut down. Brenda had looked at it and stroked its soft fur, but had left the cuddling and feeding to Sandra. She did not want to get close to anything again.

Nancy got word that a doctor had agreed to fix Brenda's eyes up, so they all went to the city to visit the other grandparents, as the operation was in December, and they would spend Christmas at Gran and Granddad Hay's in Brisbane while Brenda recovered. Brenda got totally sick of having doctors peering into her eyes and putting drops in them. Some of the drops hurt. She hated the crowds of people on the footpaths. She hated catching the buses and trams. She pretty much hated everything and everyone and found it difficult to like the grandparents. They were nothing like her beloved Granddad. But she stopped short of hating them. Sandra revelled in everything, which did not help Brenda's mood.

Brenda hated being in hospital after her operation, even though she got extra-special presents and quite liked the boy in the next bed. He had had his appendix out and had it in a little bottle. She even managed to smile at him a couple of times. Her eyes were very sore and had to have drops in them several times a day. She had to do exercises with them, like looking up or down or sideways. One morning, while waiting for her mum to come, she realised that her head was no long hurting—so maybe it had been worth the effort.

It was a bit hard to get back into the general humdrum of life when they returned home. Even sitting beside Dinky's grave did not fix how restless she felt. The one shining light at the end of it all was that she got a horse, Casey. He had been Granddad's, and she loved bringing him into the yard to pick on the green grass. He didn't mind her sitting on him, sometimes walking round the yard slowly.

"That horse has been good for her." Dexter smiled at Nancy as they watched Brenda sitting beside Casey's head and chattering to him. Brenda forgot that she had vowed never to love anything ever again. Sandra got a pony too, along with Alvin. They would ride off to bring in the milking cows together. Although Brenda would have liked to have gone with them, she rather liked it just being her and the horse alone. Sandra tried to make Brenda jealous, telling her of all the fun they'd had, but Brenda pretended not to hear or respond.

SEX AND SEX TALKS, TO AGE TWELVE

Sex was not talked about in general terms, but Brenda had seen all manner of animals mate and simply understood that that was the way it was. Granddad had once bought a pair of piglets that Brenda had found great to play with, and she'd loved the way their snorts would nudge at her hands. They'd gotten more aloof as they'd grown, and she was keen to have some little piglets again. She asked her Granddad when there were going to be more little pigs.

"Piglets, love?" he said. "That has to wait for the sow, the mama pig, to come in heat."

Brenda sat up. "What is *heat?*"

Granddad took a while to answer, so Brenda poked his belly, but before she could open her mouth, Granddad said, "The sow only wants to mate a couple of times a year, and those times are called *coming in season* or *in heat.*" He smiled at her, a sort of sad smile, and said, "Cows, horses, dogs, and cats are the same, love. But you should ask your mum or dad." He lifted her off the chair. "Run along, now." And he looked after her with a sad expression on his face, thinking, *She is so young to want to know that stuff.* Sex was generally not talked about, but breeding was mentioned from time to time.

Brenda took a while to ask any questions of her mum or dad, but she kept her ears open when the adults were speaking about breeding. She listened for the words *coming in season* or *in heat* and was rewarded with hearing mum tell dad that their pet dog was coming in heat. Mum asked if he could build a cage so the other dogs couldn't get to her. Dexter constructed a strong cage, and Flight was put into it. Brenda noticed the boy dogs on the property started to hang about the cage, tails wagging eagerly. Brenda couldn't help but wonder why the boy dogs were suddenly so keen to be with Flight.

Granddad explained that animals had seasons where their bodies were ready to produce babies. Every time she walked past, the boy dogs were laying up against the wire, tongues lolling out, panting. Every time Flight moved, they would jump up, tails wagging in an eager fashion. One day, she allowed one of the dogs in with Flight and bolted before she saw what happened, as she could heard her granddad coming to feed the pigs. She raced off to meet him. At dinner that night, Dexter said to Nancy that one of the dogs had gotten to Flight today, and that he'd managed to separate them and hoped all would be okay.

Brenda was not unhappy when told her mum and dad were moving to a new home. She told Casey in gulping sentences that she would need to leave him, and that it wasn't her fault, and she didn't want to go away. She patted his cheeks and looked into his brown eyes, and he seemed to understand. When she told Casey about that, he shoved her with his nose and snorted a little before turning his head away. She was happy to be getting away from Alvin, as his stories were getting a little off-putting. He'd made it easy to listen the stories, and his hugs made her feel warm inside. No one else had held her like that, and it was nice in its own way. Still, deep down, she knew it was not really right. She made another vow to herself that no one would do that to her again, forgetting that she had already broken one vow. Granddad rubbed her back when she tearfully confided to him that she was sad that Casey wouldn't get any more green grass. Granddad said that he would keep letting him into the house yard for the green grass "After all, he has been my best horse," he said. That made Brenda feel a little bit better.

Nancy sighed and sat down beside Brenda at the table. "You go and feed the chooks," she told Sandra, who "accidentally" kicked Brenda in the shins as she got off her chair. It really hurt. "For anyone or anything to have babies, there needs to be a boy and a girl. When the time is right, the boy puts some seeds into the girl so she can grow the baby in her tummy." Nancy hesitated, wondering how much she should tell Brenda.

"What about hens and ducks?" Brenda asked. "They don't have babies like that."

This should be a bit easier, Nancy thought. "They still need the rooster, or drake, to put seeds into the hen or duck so they can build eggs around them." Brenda had her thinking face on and had a tiny frown between her eyes. Nancy got up to take the eggs from Sandra as she returned to the table. "Come now, girls. Let's get into some school before lunch. If we can get this school paper finished, that will be it till after we move." Nancy placed the correspondence-school papers in front of the girls. "By the way, Flight is going to have puppies." Brenda kept her eyes on the school work, but she felt a little guilty.

Brenda missed the birth of the puppies, but she heard Dexter say he had done away with all but one of them. "Horrie wants the pup for Alvin." Brenda could sit and watch Flight and the puppy for ages and liked to hold him close to her chest, feeling him breathe with her. Flight got very sick a few days after the birth. Her teats got swollen and hard, to the point where the she wouldn't allow the puppy to suck at all. Alvin took the puppy away, and the next day, Flight was gone too.

Brenda asked where she was, and Sandra snapped at her before anyone else could say anything. "She's dead! Having the puppies killed her."

As Sandra ran out of the room, Nancy said, "Her udders got infected, is all. Nothing to do with having the pups." Still, Brenda thought having the pups and Flight's dying was her fault.

NEW BEGINNINGS, YEAR TWELVE

Brenda loved the new place, Bemerside. There were lots of buildings. The big house, facing a waterhole, plus two duplex buildings, a set of four room quarters, butchering building, and a storeroom with office, all set in a semicircle behind the main house. Behind these structures was a workshop and sheds (feed and saddle rooms), and, behind these, a yard with five stables attached. Brenda later found out that these were horse yards only, and the cattle yards were quite a long way from the main house. Off to one side was an area planted with fruit trees and a vegetable garden. Between the houses and the shed, there was a pen for chooks. There was a fence round all the buildings, except the horse yard, with large trees planted along the fence line.

The manager, Steve Hasting, and his wife, Holly, had two sons—one older than Brenda and one close to Sandra's age. Fred was fourteen, and Harry was sixteen, and they were at boarding school. They had had a daughter who had died very young, and she was buried in a corner of the main house yard.

The quarters were only used when mustering was on. Sam, the store man, and Albert, the gardener, lived in one of the duplexes. Albert was an aboriginal and the first black man, though he was more brown than black, who Brenda had ever seen. Dexter was to look after most of the outside maintenance like fences, roads, and pretty much where ever he was needed. Brenda found Sam a bit different, as his pale-coloured eyes seemed to look right though her. He made her feel a little uncomfortable when he called her *little darling*. Brenda avoided going to the store for her mum as much as possible. Sandra, crawler that she was, would ask sweetly most days if there was anything her mum needed.

Holly, a tall and willowy lady, painted watercolours and had had exhibitions of them in the city. Brenda thought some of the pictures were nice, especially the ones of scenery round the homestead. Holly had a painting of her daughter in the lounge. Brenda had seen it when they'd first arrived and had been invited to the "big" house for smoko. The little girl had looked a lot like Brenda. Holly was often seen behind her easel, roundabout, and she always waved. She encouraged Brenda to draw and even gave her some coloured pencils. Brenda was not very good at drawing, but she tried, and she wrote little stories about the crude pictures. Holly said the stories were good.

Steve, or Boss as he was referred to by everyone, including visitors, was a head shorter than Brenda's dad, and very skinny. He always seemed to be in a rush. Once a month, all the staff were invited to a cook up at the big house. This was the only time he did not seem to be in a rush. He had a very deep voice and would sing at these occasions. Brenda was surprised to hear her mum join in with the singing—and that she had a very strong voice.

They moved into one side of the other duplex (no one lived beside them). It was freshly painted and had huge windows on all sides of the house, with a little laundry lean-to off the back and veranda off the eastern and northern side of the house. Best of all, Brenda had her own room. It was really tiny and had been used as a storeroom-come-pantry. Brenda begged and begged to be allowed to have it. It was the only room in the house with a lockable door. This, Brenda found very enticing. Imagine not having to beat Sandra up every day to avoid the rude wake-up calls! Dexter finally said, "Oh, for pity's sake, let her have the room. I'll build a pantry cupboard in the laundry or kitchen—or both. For the sake of peace, give it to her." Sandra seemed pleased enough not to have to share, as well.

The large waterhole in front of the big house was fed by a spring, and so it never went dry. Huge gum, box, and ironbark trees lined the banks, which were also littered with logs and blackberry bushes. It was not like the protected waterhole Brenda had left behind. Swimming was not allowed, as it was used for water for the houses, but fishing was allowed. Brenda loved fishing and could sit for hours, line in hand, observing the ground creatures and different birds that came to drink there. One day, she saw a dingo come in for a drink and marvelled at how beautiful it was. She hardly breathed for fear it would see her and become frightened. As the dog turned to go, it seemed to look straight at her, and Brenda noticed the dog must have been a female, as her teats were hanging down like Flight's had before she'd had her puppies and her belly was quite round.

Dexter was away a lot driving bulldozers and grading roads. Sometimes, when he was camped away for more than a week, they would visit him for a couple of nights. Brenda loved these times, as the family would lie in their beds in the open and look at the millions of stars. Dad liked to point out certain stars and give them names, like Venus and the various constellations. He was very clever and knew so much. Brenda loved listening to him talk about the stars, even though she had heard it all before. Sandra would yawn and got to sleep. Before Brenda drifted off to sleep, she'd notice that Dexter and Nancy would be holding hands.

Mum was a good camp cook, making lovely dampers in the camp oven. They ate them warm, dripping with syrup. It was so yummy. Dampers cooked in the stove at home were never quite the same. Brenda found it hard to concentrate on the school work while in the camp, as there always was so much to look at and discoveries to be made. She would watch ants scurrying along, always so busy, and it amazed her the size of some of the food they would carry. Sometimes, the ants would need to work as a team to carry extra-big things like grasshoppers. She would shut her eyes and listen to the songs of the birds, particularly the butcher birds. They had so many songs. Sandra would smirk at Brenda as Nancy tried to get Brenda to do her paper. Sandra was always a good student.

During her regular visits at the waterhole, Brenda noticed that the dingo came round at the same time just at dusk. She tried so hard to be there, as she felt that the bitch didn't mind her being there. Once, Brenda followed her a little way when she left. The dog stopped and looked back over her shoulder before racing away. Brenda did notice that she always went the same way, though. The dog's tummy got bigger, and her teats almost touched the ground. Brenda did not see her for a few days and worried that one of the men had shot her or given her a poison bait. On the third day, she came back, and it was clear that she had had her puppies. Brenda thought the bitch winked at her and smiled. She was sure that the tail wagged when the bitch looked at her. *Golly, I wonder how many and where they are,* Brenda mused, wishing she could see them.

As it was coming into the cooler time of the year, and the days were getting shorter, it was sometimes almost dark before the dingo appeared. Brenda kept ignoring Nancy's clapping that was calling her back home, and she would get a scolding, but she felt compelled to wait for the bitch. About six weeks after Brenda had noticed that the bitch had had the pups, she sat lost in thought as the dog drank—and was brought out of her daydreams by a loud rifle shot. The bitch jumped, ran a few steps, and fell over. Brenda was stunned into silence as she turned to see Dexter lowering his rifle.

Before she could find her voice, Dexter said very softly, 'Those dogs are a menace, baby. Sandra told me she had seen her here. Come home now, love. We will get the scalp in the morning." Brenda couldn't speak for the lump in her throat, and she went with her dad, holding tightly to his hand. *Bugger Sandra*, she thought, and she didn't even offer any apology for the naughty word. At dinner, Sandra kept giving Brenda little self-satisfied smiles. Brenda felt real hatred for her.

As Brenda lay in her bed, she wondered about the puppies and how hungry they would be. She knew that when Dexter went to get the scalp, he would notice that there were puppies somewhere and would most likely go to find them and kill them too. Brenda pushed her face into her pillow and cried long and hard. Being exhausted from the crying, she missed getting up with Dexter for the morning cuppa. When she woke, she gasped, as the sun was already up, and she could hear Sandra and Mum getting breakfast. She ran out the back door and raced to the waterhole, slowing down as she got there. She crept round the water's edge without the men who were working on getting the pelt off the dead bitch's back noticing her. She heard the boss say, "Puppies for sure, mate. Can you try to find them after breakfast, Dexter?" Dexter nodded.

Brenda was horrified and snuck off in the direction the bitch had always gone after her drink. She tuned her ears to the surrounding sounds to see if she could hear any puppy noises. She knew that dingos did not bark, but was sure by now that the pups would be hungry, and they may be whining for their mum. She looked into hollow logs and under bushes. Frustrating tears ran down her cheeks, and, as she heard the clapping calling her home, she sat down, gulping for air. She squeezed her eyes closed and pushed her fists into them till they hurt. Sitting on a rock, with her head in her hands to gather herself before going home, she thought she could feel something scratching the rock behind her. *Must be a twig,* she thought, and glanced behind her. There was no bush there.

Then, she heard a tiny sound, and she jumped up and looked behind the rock. There was a hole going under the rock, so she laid down and peered into the hole before reaching in as far as her arm would allow. She touched a warm body covered in fur. Gently, she got her hand under the creature and slowly withdrew her hand from the hole. The puppy was beautiful, but shivering with fear. Brenda put it down and reached back into the hole, but couldn't reach the other pups. *I'll need a shovel,* she thought. Tucking the puppy into her blouse, she ran towards home as fast as she could. She hoped that she could get home and back before anyone else found the puppies. She had no thought as to what she was going to do with them, except rescue them.

She ran head first into her dad. "What are you doing, little one? Get on home. Your mum is getting cross at you not coming when you were called." Brenda noticed he was carrying a tomahawk. She stared from the weapon to her dad's face and opened her mouth. "Go now, girl," Dexter snapped at her. He turned and walked back the way she had come.

Damn, he will find the other pups. She patted her bundle of fur, saying to it, "I'll care for you, puppy." She walked quickly homeward. She made it into her room and hid the puppy under her covers before Nancy saw she was home

"No breakfast for you. Now, have a wash, and we need to finish the school paper before the mail goes tomorrow." Nancy did not wait for an answer.

"I'll feed you at lunch," Brenda whispered to the pup. How and what she hadn't worked out yet.

Brenda found it hard to concentrate on the school, and she kept telling her mum that she felt crook and maybe she should lie down for a while. Finally, Nancy agreed, so Brenda got a glass of milk and went to her room, firmly locking the door. She put her finger into the milk and put it in the puppy's mouth, but that didn't work well. She tried putting the corner of her hanky into the milk and putting that into the pup's mouth (she had discovered the pup was a girl), which had a better result, with the puppy sort of sucking at the hanky. Brenda snuggled down with the puppy. *What shall I call you?* she thought, finally settling on Dinky Two. This later got shortened to D2.

Nancy banging on the door woke her with a fright. Brenda went out, trying to look calm. "I feel better, Mum. Let's get this school down." Both Nancy and Sandra looked at her with their eyes wide. She'd never, ever volunteered to do school work before. To their amazement, Brenda got right into the work and finished all the paper in record time *and* got it alright. Nancy let Brenda have a biscuit for her efforts.

Brenda wandered over to the station storeroom and got a box off Sam the store man. "Glad to help, little darlin'," he said. It was a big box with high sides. Then, she pulled up some grass from under the fruit trees. Albert startled her while she was gathering the grass. "What you up to, young lass?" Albert had such a soft voice that Brenda hardly heard him, and she stammered, "Making a nest."

Albert looked at her with his head bent over to one side. "No hen's gone clucky."

Brenda felt herself go red, as she really wasn't a good liar, and she said, "I have a dingo puppy." The words came out all in a rush.

"Come, lass. I'll get you some rags. They be better than the grass, and I think I have a bottle somewhere. The pup belonged to the bitch shot yesterday, yes?" Albert put his hand on Brenda's shoulder and gave it a squeeze. "The pup's dad will be one of the boss's dogs, most likely, and we might be able to get away with saying it's a Kelpie later." Albert went on to say, "Kelpie are known to have a little bit of dingo in their breeding, anyway."

Brenda felt tears well behind her eyes, and she blinked hard to keep them back and followed Albert silently. She hoped Albert was right, that she could pass the puppy off as a Kelpie. After collecting the rags and bottle, she snuck the items into her room while Sandra and Mum were hanging washing out. Nancy couldn't get over the change in Brenda. She kept her room spotless and did her school without being hassled into it. Sandra pinched Brenda's arm and snarled into her ear, "You're up to something. I know you are, and I'll find out." It amused Brenda that Sandra followed her about outside, never twigging that her secret was right under her nose all the time.

The puppy was so good, never making a sound, and as D2 started to move about, she would wag her tail when Brenda came into the room. Albert suggested that she should move the puppy over to his place so she could move about more freely. Brenda had worried that Sandra might catch on to what she was up to with having the puppy in her room, but Fred and Harry had come home for holidays, and Sandra forgot all about following Brenda. Albert told Mr. Hasting that someone had given him a pup, and then he asked Dexter and Nancy if he could give Brenda the puppy. They both agreed.

Brenda forgot, again, that she would never love anything again. She spent as much time as possible and heeded Albert's words that D2 was a hunting dog, and she must keep D2 away from the stock and train her to come to Brenda when she called. Brenda worked so hard at this training, knuckled down at school, and never gave anyone any trouble so she could get all the free time she needed. Even Sandra couldn't find any faults to catch her out on. Brenda couldn't forgive her for the killing of D2's mother, though.

BOYS AND GIRLS

Brenda hated herself. Her belly often cramped constantly for days from menstruation pains. She wondered if animals got these pains before they mated. Nancy had explained to her that this was her body getting rid of unused eggs that were not used to make babies. She doubted it, as they were always keen to get on with it, and, at these times, Brenda certainly did not want herself or anyone else to go near that part of her body. Her menstruation had started over two years ago, when she'd been only twelve years old.

"Oh, it'll get better as you get older," Nancy had said to her. Well, it didn't! *Maybe what I need is to have a baby*, she thought. She'd suggested that to Nancy and gotten a very big lecture that good girls did not have babies till they were married and would never let boys touch the private areas of their bodies. Brenda had cast her eyes down to the floor.

Brenda loved patting D2. D2 was fat and shiny, and her eyes were bright when she would look up at Brenda, her tail thumping the ground. She had trained D2 to never hear anyone else's voice except hers, something that really irked Sandra. "You have been a good friend, D2," she would whisper often. It could have been ever so different. Sandra had got tired of waiting to find something to pick on Brenda about after she'd gotten D2, but every so often, Sandra would sneak down to watch Brenda training the pup—but only when the boys had returned to boarding school and she was bored. Sandra would hide and try to confuse D2 by whistling at her.

Early on in the training process one morning, Sandra bounced from behind a bush as Brenda was teaching the puppy to sit and wait to be called before moving. "I've got it! That pup is a dingo," she yelled, startling both Brenda and D2. D2's bristles came up, and she growled deep down in her throat and would have attacked Sandra if Brenda hadn't been close enough to grab hold of the pup. Brenda had always worried that someone would twig to the fact that D2 was, in fact, half dingo. She resembled the dingo more than the working dog part of her. Brenda had been very careful to keep D2 away from others as much as possible. Brenda stood very still, holding the pup, looking wide-eyed at Sandra, tears streaming down her cheeks.

"Yep, she is most defiantly a dingo." Sandra rubbed her hands together with glee. At last, she had something on Brenda.

"H-how would you know that?" Brenda's voice sounded very squeaky, and she stuttered. She felt tears welling behind her eyes, as she had so been afraid of someone finding out about the pup, she hadn't prepared for it to be Sandra.

Sandra snorted. "You think you're so clever, don't you? Crawling to Mum so she lets you off chores. Getting all those awards for your school work." Sandra's voice was dripping with venom, and her face went very red. "I heard Albert talking to Sam, telling him how well the pup was going, seeing as her mother was a dingo. So there! Gotcha!" Brenda knew that both Sam and Albert had been aware of where D2 had come from right from the beginning.

Sandra made to turn away as Brenda spoke through her tears. "No, no. Please don't tell anyone. Please, please!"

"Right," Sandra said. She stood with her chin up and hands on her hips. "What is it worth, hey? What will you give me to not tell?" Sandra glared at Brenda, as the pup was still growling. "I want your room so that savage animal won't rip my throat out one night." Sandra could hardly contain her glee now. "And you will do my chores, and brush my hair, and polish my shoes." She hesitated, giving Brenda a scornful glance "Might even get you to do my essays. You're good at them. Oh, and you're to stop going to the store. If Mum asks you, tell me, and I'll do it." That last bit was a bit puzzling, as Sandra had always been keen to do that chore.

Brenda gulped, as she just loved her little room and the privacy it had given her. And so it was—for a time. The girls had swapped rooms, much to the amazement of Nancy and Dexter. They were also pleased to see how the girls seemed to be getting along, doing nice things for each other. They didn't notice that it was all one-sided. Sandra was very clever at offering to do things for Brenda in front of Nancy or Dexter, and somehow would always get distracted before completing the offered tasks. Sandra again tried to beat Brenda up so she could drag her out of bed, but got a rude shock when D2 snapped at her from under Brenda's bed—so that bit of fun was taken away from her. She hated the pup for spoiling her fun. After that, Sandra had no reason to get up early and became a bit lazy and hardly ever got up before she needed to. She used the excuse that, as she was now into her high school, she did study at night and went to bed late. Sandra never gave up on getting Brenda to do her chores whenever she could get away with it. Brenda did not care too much, as D2 made it all worth it.

Brenda did her level best to keep Sandra satisfied so she wouldn't tell on D2. Brenda hated going to the store, as Sam would touch her as he moved about to get the things she had come for. He constantly asked her if she wanted to see the animals he was caring for at the time. Sam volunteered to look after injured babies, anything from lizards to native animals and birds. Even calves, sometimes, and, once, a brumby foal. Brenda had liked that little horse—till it got sick and died. He always had a few snakes in glass cages. Brenda hated the way their eyes looked dead. If she did go to see what he was caring for, at first, Sam would stand very close to her. Brenda stopped looking at the baby things after he tried to get her to hold a snake he'd caught. *Sandra can have the trips to the store*, she thought.

The stalemate with Sandra went on for several months till the boys returned for the Christmas break and Sandra's attention was directed elsewhere. Sandra shadowed the boys a lot, particularly

Harry. Harry was tall like his mum, and Fred was the image of his Dad. Sandra, who had developed breasts by this time, would giggle and ask ridiculous questions all the time. Brenda once overheard the boys talking about Sandra saying that "she was definitely asking for it." Brenda grinned to herself, as she was sure they were talking about mating, or *sex*, as Nancy referred to human mating. Brenda never let an opportunity go by to tell the boys that Sandra liked them. The boys often came to watch Brenda working on D2's training. They commented that she was a really pale red for a Kelpie.

Nancy had gone to take some stores out to Dexter's camp when Brenda got her chance to get back at Sandra. Brenda was playing with D2 when she saw the boys approaching their duplex. Sandra let them in, so Brenda crept round the side of the house after the boys had disappeared inside and stood underneath the dinning room window for a time. There seemed to be some murmurings coming from inside the house. She pulled over a drum and climbed up to see what the trio was up to and almost gave herself away as she jumped down with a gasp. The scene was unbelievable and indescribable, which she couldn't come to terms with in her mind. This was nothing like she had ever encountered before, nothing like she had seen in the animal world. Before she could get her head around the happenings between the trio, the boys were heard laughing as they left. Brenda scurried round to enter by the back door. Sandra was sitting primly on the dining room bench seat—the same one she'd been laying on a few moments ago. Her head jerked up as Brenda burst into the room, yelling, "I saw you and the boys! I want my room back, and you will do all my household chores for a week." Sandra had gone bright red and simply nodded.

Brenda drew breath and repeated, "I want my room back. And no more about your bloody chores or my dog, you hear?" Brenda walked away before Sandra could answer, and when she came back after her mum got home, she found that her things were back in her room. Sandra was telling her mum that the room was too small, anyway.

... ...

After the incident of seeing Sandra with the boys, Brenda began to feel strange sensations round her pelvic area and had bouts of abject sadness. She wondered if the act had felt as good for Sandra and the boys as it appeared. She also wondered about the fact that Sandra had had both boys at the same time, and if that was normal. She wondered about her mum and dad and all the other married folk she knew—if they got in an extra person as well. After pondering this for some time, she blurted out at the dinner table, "Mum, when you and Dad have sex, do you get in another person?"

Sandra gasped and coughed really hard while her Mum and Dad looked at her and then at each other. Both of them opened and closed their mouths several times. Dexter managed to speak first. He slapped his hand down hard on the table, causing all the things on the table to bounce. Sandra and Nancy jumped up as he roared, "What in the heck does that mean? Go to your room, Brenda!"

He sounded so angry that Brenda leapt away and bolted to her room. She left the door open a little so she could hear the ensuring conversation. As she peeked out from her room, she saw Sandra slowly backing away. Her face had gone as white as a sheet as Dexter snapped at her. "You know what has brought this on?" She shook her head.

Dexter slumped down and put his head in his hands. "Sorry, Sandra. I knew you wouldn't, as you are the good and kind, never giving us any grief." He reached out and gave Sandra a hug and told her to go for a walk while he and Nancy discussed matters. Sandra bolted out the door, passing Brenda's room and giving her a begging glance.

Brenda heard Dexter say, "That girl has been trouble right from the start! It's her fault you couldn't have more children." Then, the parents sat and spoke in voices so low Brenda couldn't hear what they were saying, so she lay down and pondered her mistake for asking the question. There were so many things that she wanted to know, like, when people did the mating thing, why did it not always end in a baby? Or, like animals, did they only do it when they wanted to have a baby? Maybe the seed had to go inside for there to be a baby made. She was sure Sandra didn't want to have a baby, but she had certainly done *it*, and by the looks of it, the act hadn't been the first time. Why was that? She wished Granddad were here to talk to, as he never overreacted like Dexter had.

After what seemed a long time, Nancy came in and sat on the edge of the bed. She'd been crying, and Brenda felt sorry she'd upset her. Nancy stopped her from speaking by holding up her hand. "Let me speak first, little one. That was an odd question, and not one that should ever be asked at the dinner table. Thank goodness there was no one else here. I would have been very embarrassed. Now, you can ask me anything in private, and I'll try to give you an answer. Now, where did that question come from?"

Brenda opened and closed her eyes a couple of times, and, taking a deep breath, said, "Well, the cows often have more than one bull after them, and the stallions have lots of mares. The roosters have lots of hens, and—" Brenda let her voice fade away as she saw the look of relief on her mum's face.

Nancy sighed. "That's true, little one. But they're animals, and it's different with humans. When you love someone and get married, it's okay to do"—she hesitated— "mating. Or, as we call it, making love. Then, and only then, is it okay to"—she paused—"make love. But you're too young to worry about these things yet, Brenda."

"What about kissing?" Brenda blurted out. "I have seen you kiss other people, and you hardly ever kiss Dad."

Nancy sat for quite some time before answering. Dexter was a man who kept his emotions and feelings inside himself and did not show his feelings in public, aside from a squeeze of her hand or brief peck on the cheek if they had been apart for a bit. How could she pass that on to Brenda, as not all men were like that—or as honourable? Some liked to hug and hold hands all the time, and how could she convey to Brenda that what was expected might vary from couple to couple? As she would never have thought of involving another person into her and Dexter's lovemaking, she fully accepted

Brenda explanation of the animal theory. "Kissing is a little different. You might kiss those you know as a greeting, and, later on, you may find you want to kiss a boy you like, or he may kiss you. Kissing is okay as long as both people want to do it to each other." Nancy looked deep into Brenda's eyes and noticed there were still questions lurking inside her head. "Tell you what, Brenda. When you think of something you want to ask, write it down at that time, and we will sit and talk about them, yes?" She leaned and gave Brenda a kiss on her forehead "Enough for now, love." She tucked the blankets in round Brenda's thin body and made her way out of the room with a heavy heart, not sure if she'd answered all of the issues successfully.

Brenda watched Nancy leave and, tucking her hands behind her head, thought long and hard about all the mating stuff she knew. Yes, she had enjoyed Alvin stroking her hand, and for the most part when he hugged her, and she guessed that was part of the lovemaking process. Sandra had definitely seemed to enjoy the touching of the boys, judging by the *mmm*s she'd made. Brenda was amazed that the boys had seemed to enjoy the exercise so much. Her mum and dad never seemed to touch each other at all. Still, she wondered about the baby issue. *Have to ask about that soon*, she thought as she rolled onto her side and, wrapping her arms round herself, lulled off to sleep with some gentle patting.

Dexter did not know how to treat Brenda after that and hardly ever spoke to her, only addressing her in cases of absolute necessity. Brenda noticed, but thought very little about it, as he had always a bit aloof with her and Sandra. Sandra, on the other hand, went through a stage of being very nice for a week or more before slipping back into her usual selfish self. Brenda did notice that the boys also kept their distance from her, and she supposed that Sandra had told them Brenda had seen them. "It's all very confusing," she confided in D2. She did get to find out that her mum had had trouble giving birth to her, as Brenda had come out backwards, and Mum had been damaged inside, so she couldn't have more babies after that. Nancy said that that sometimes happens with creatures as well, and Brenda shouldn't concern herself with it.

Brenda forgot that D2 should be kept away from stock, and had asked Albert to teach her to milk the house cows. She enjoyed going with him to bring them home in the evening so the calves could be shut away from the cows, ensuring there was plenty of milk in the morning. D2 was really good at finding the cows in the big paddock they were in during the day. Steve saw D2 working the cows and complimented Brenda on how well the dog worked. Albert said D2's tracking skills made his job so much easier. Albert told Brenda about native foods and what was good to eat in the bush. He told her his dreamtime stories about Min Min lights that floated at night and were thought to be lost souls looking for their homes. Brenda wanted to know more about this giving birth. She so wanted to see something give birth, so she asked Albert if any of the station animals were going to have babies soon.

Albert became a little worried about answering these questions, so he mentioned to Dexter that she'd been asking. Dexter was furious and told Nancy to ban her from asking Albert about these questions. Nancy thought for a while, and then, after a heated discussion, got Dexter to agree to allow Brenda to see the boss's dog have her puppies if Steve and Holly would agree to it. Steve said it would be okay, and they would give them a call when it happened. Brenda was a little worried about this, as she remembered the fact that Flight had died after giving birth.

Brenda got to see the puppies born and was amazed to see them come out in a little bag. *Sort of like a present*, she thought. Sandra had been asked if she wanted to watch as well, but she'd shuddered in disgust at the thought. Sandra hated blood. Sandra was horrified to see the bitch lick the wrapping off the pups, and hoped that that did not happen in humans. The five puppies, all pre sold, were kept till they were round six weeks old. Running about, they were so delightful to watch as they had their squabbles, growling fiercely. Dexter told Albert that he could allow Brenda to be in on any births he was in charge of, but not to answer any questions, and tell Brenda to go and ask her mum. He agreed to this, but he knew the child would be full of questions—and he would be careful not to go too in-depth with his answers to her. He liked Brenda and admired the way she was handling D2. The boss commented that the young dog looked a bit like one of his working dogs and wondered how his dog could have gotten near Albert's mate's bitch.

LIFE AND DEATH

Albert alerted them to the births of horses, cows, and also showed Brenda how to peel the shell off chicks. Brenda loved the way the chicks went from slimy and wet to fluffy so quickly. Albert told her that the animals licked their babies to warm them up. Brenda noticed that the births were all practically quiet occasions. She never tired of watching this new life come into the world. *That is what I am going to do when I grow up—look after babies,* Brenda vowed to herself. Brenda wanted to know why the animals all seemed to eat this wrapping. Nancy assured her that was not the case, and the wrapping was called afterbirth and protected the baby while it was inside the mum's tummy. Brenda asked, "Protect it from all the food in there, Mum?"

Nancy heaved a huge sigh and thought for a moment before answering that question. *This is getting very deep,* she thought. "There are two sacs in there, love. One for food, and then one for the baby. The baby's one is tiny and grows with the baby." Nancy hoped that that would be the end of it for a while, as Brenda stopped talking and sat staring at her hands.

When Nancy told Dexter about that conversation, he decided that she could go and watch next time Albert killed anything for their meat. He said he would arrange it with Albert. Albert was not real happy with the responsibility and asked if he or Nancy could be there to answer the inevitable questions. Nancy agreed to attend the next dressing, as this procedure was called, and so Nancy, Sandra, and Brenda trailed behind as Albert dealt with chooks, ducks, pigs, goats, and cattle. Nancy thought that it would be a good lesson for the girls. Sandra had never shown and interest in this sort of stuff, or asked the many questions like Brenda, and it would be a good education. Sandra was becoming quite beautiful and should know about this stuff too, so Nancy insisted she should be in on this educational project.

Brenda asked so many questions that Nancy wondered if she would ever get tired of asking. *She's testing my knowledge,* Nancy thought. Brenda was shown the sac and the *foetus,* as the babies were called in the bigger animals. Nancy told her the proper names for body parts. Brenda was amazed to see lots of eggs inside some of the poultry. Nancy explained if the rooster or drake did not put seeds in, there would be no chicks or ducklings. Nancy explained the different times it took for each animal to grow their baby. It was all a bit confusing, as one answer only led to another question.

Sandra hated going with them and was very embarrassed by all of Brenda's questions as she poked at this and that in the animal of the time. Albert kept very quiet, but found Brenda's quest for knowledge amusing. After the first few times, Sandra refused to go with Nancy and Brenda. Nancy wondered if the questions would ever stop and decided to see if she could get some simple books for Brenda. After watching several births and hatchings, Brenda posed a question to Nancy. "This birthing thing does not seem all that bad, Mum. So why was my birth so bad?" She stopped, as Nancy seemed to be going to cry. "I heard Dad say that I damaged you, so that's why I don't have any smaller brothers or sisters."

It took Nancy a while to gather her thoughts before answering. "Well, you were coming out backwards, and some of my tubes and things were torn."

Brenda was watching Nancy closely and eventually said, "Heck, Mum, that would have hurt." To which, Nancy nodded. Nancy had had enough of the questions by this time and told Holly how Brenda's questions were getting her down. Holly loaned them an encyclopaedia that had diagrams of reproductive systems and body parts that she thought might help Brenda. It did seem to satisfy Brenda for a time. After a bit of study, Brenda came out and announced she had decided to become a nurse. Try as she might, Nancy couldn't get Sandra to look at the book. *All in good time*, she thought. *Maybe Sandra is not as advanced as Brenda in the area of sex and babies.*

Not long after Nancy had given Brenda the book, one of the milking cows had a lot of trouble giving birth, as the calf was breach. It was the first time Brenda had seen any animal have trouble with the birthing process. The poor cow strained and kicked her back legs, giving out loud moans. Albert got Steve and Dexter to hold the legs, and he stuck his arm up inside the cow to try and turn the calf around. Steve had asked Dexter if he thought Brenda should see this, to which Dexter snapped, "Do her good to see it's not always pretty."

It took a long time before Albert grunted and sat back, heaving on something inside the cow. The calf plopped out onto the ground. It was dead. Albert was covered in blood and slimy stuff. He did not smell nice. The poor cow sighed and went very still. Albert said, "We'll give the cow a bit before we go back in for the afterbirth, hey?"

Before they could do that, the cow rallied and scrambled to her feet, sniffing at her dead calf. The cow licked and licked, but it was useless. The men returned later to take the body away to use as bait for dingos. In the morning, when Brenda came to assist with the milking—she liked milking—the poor cow had a protrusion from her back end. It looked terrible. Albert took her to go home. Brenda raced home and dragged Nancy to the yard, screaming at her, "What is that? What is that, and why?"

"That, love, is a prolapsed uterus. The cow has torn her insides because she had so much trouble giving birth. That cannot be fixed in animals, and she'll need to be shot. Now, come away, love. Come away." Nancy felt exhausted and watched Brenda digest the comments.

Brenda turned and gazed at her mum. "That's what I did to you, isn't it, Mum?" Without waiting for an answer, Brenda took off for the waterhole, D2 racing beside her. Nancy looked after her with sad eyes, shaking her head slightly. Brenda was late getting home and had done none of her chores that day, but Nancy never chastised her and stopped Sandra from complaining about that fact. Brenda never asked any more questions, but she read and reread the encyclopaedia.

....

It was coming up to Christmas school holidays, and Sandra spent a lot of time doing her hair up in different styles and even was a little distracted with her school work. Nancy had had to speak sharply to her to get her mind into the work. Brenda smiled to herself, as she was sure she knew that Sandra was thinking about. Sandra had alternate moods, swinging from irritable to happy. Brenda kept well out of her way, spending as much time with D2 as she could. She loved D2 and told her all of her troubles and thoughts. D2 listened, never taking her eyes off Brenda when she chattered.

Ever since Brenda had started to menstruate, she'd not had an easy time of it. She often complained to D2 that life was not fair. Sandra was very scornful of Brenda laying down when she got her monthlies, saying she was putting it on. Once, Nancy had asked Sandra to take Brenda a cup of tea, as the hot tea seemed to help with the cramps. Sandra had accidentally spilled some onto Brenda's tummy. It had burnt the skin, and when Brenda had cried out, Nancy—for the first and only time—had snapped at Sandra to be more careful. Sandra had been so shocked that she'd put the cup down and, after giving Brenda an evil look, had left without a word.

The boys arrived home during the night, and Sandra rushed her morning chores so she could get over to see them. One chore was washing up, and she gazed out the window above the sink to see if she could catch a glimpse of the lads. Brenda was sweeping out and heard Sandra gasp as she dropped a plate, smashing it onto the floor.

Darn. Now I'll have to clean that up too, she thought angrily. Brenda glanced at Sandra and saw she had become very pale and was holding onto the sink as if to hold herself up as she gazed, wide-eyed, out of the window.

Brenda went to the front door and saw Fred and Harry walking up to the horse yard with two girls. They were holding hands, talking, and smiling at the girls and each other. Sandra gulped as tears started to stream out of her eyes, running unheeded down her cheeks. Nancy had come in to see what had been broken, and she saw Sandra crying. "Did you cut yourself, girl?" Nancy spoke sharply. Sandra shook her head.

Nancy looked out of the window and saw the four young people disappear behind the shed. "Holly said the boys were bringing their girlfriends with them this holiday. Be nice to have some female company, don't you think?" Nancy put her arm round Sandra's shoulders. Nancy's heart went out to Sandra, as she thought that Sandra's tears were for loss of her first love.

Sandra pulled away and bolted out the door, swiping angrily at her cheeks, running after the boys and girls. Brenda thought that this could be interesting, but as she had to clean up the broken plate, never got to see what went on when Sandra caught up with the boys. After that, Sandra became very quiet and sullen, only answering when she absolutely had to. Nancy assumed, and part correctly, that Sandra had had a crush on one of the boys and was sulking over the girlfriend, and so she left her to get over it. *First love is always so intense,* she mused, thinking it was sort of cute.

Brenda met up with the new arrivals when she went fishing that afternoon. Fred's girl was Sharon, and Harry's was Jewel. Brenda found them both very nice. D2 seemed to like them, so that was enough for Brenda. Jewel was only a year older than Brenda, and they got on really well whenever they met up round the place. Jewel was very down-to-earth. She told Brenda that her parents had a small cropping farm near a place called Dubbo, and as she was keen to carry on at the farm, she was going to the same college as the boys to learn about agricultural crops. Brenda often brought up how nice the girls were at the dinner table, knowing it would bug Sandra.

Sandra became more and more morose and took to taking long walks. One day, Sandra was not home by dinner time, and both Dexter and Nancy became first cross, and then worried. Dexter went round the houses, but no one had seen which way Sandra had gone that day. As she had been gone most of the day, she could be quite a long way from the station. Dingos could be heard howling in the distance. Dexter hoped that the dogs hadn't frightened Sandra, and she wasn't stuck up a tree to get away from them. Brenda was sent to bed, and Dexter gathered Albert, Sam, and Steve to commence a search towards where the dingos could be heard. D2 answered with his own howls, something she had not done before. Nancy yelled at her to "shut the bloody dog up."

Brenda dosed off, only to be woken by Nancy screaming, "No, no" over and over again. Brenda came sleepily out of her room, blinking in the light. There was a bundle on the table that Nancy was clutching at, and she screamed. Dexter noticed Brenda and reached out and drew her to his side. "Sandra"—he hesitated—"is dead, love." It took a while for the words to sink in, and a while before she realised that the bundle on the table was Sandra. She pulled away from Dexter and backed away till her back found a wall. D2 pushed at her hands with her nose, giving them a lick. Brenda sank down to the floor and pressed her face into D2's soft fur. She did not know what to think or do. She wished Nancy would stop screaming. D2 lay down beside her and placed her head on Brenda's lap.

Other people kept coming and going. Brenda heard snatches of words—*snakebite, police are on their way, ambulance and doctor are on their way.* Amid all of the confusion, Jewel came and sat beside Brenda, hugging her. Brenda started to let the impact of what was going on sink in, and she was unsure as to what she was feeling. No more Sandra had some sort of appeal in a way, and though fun times were very few, she would miss them. Like watching her face when she struggled with school or helping Nancy in the kitchen. Brenda and Jewel looked at each other and nodded before getting up and leaving the noise and hubbub, going into Brenda's room, where they sat quietly till things quieted down. Jewel kissed Brenda on her cheek and left Brenda alone. Brenda did not know what to do, so she lay down, letting her hand lay on D2's ears, and went to sleep.

The next morning, Brenda found her mum and dad sitting quietly at the table. They pointed to the cereal and went back to sitting. Brenda ate her breakfast, watching her parents. It was all very strange. Her mum's eyes were very red, and her hand trembled. When she caught her dad's eye, he quickly looked away. Brenda went to her mum, putting her hand on Nancy's shoulder. This caused Nancy to burst into tears, but she hugged Brenda tightly. "Mum?" Brenda asked when she could breathe again. "What happened to Sandra?"

Her dad jumped up and strode out of the room. Brenda was sure she heard him mutter. "It should have been her." Nancy took several huge breaths and whispered, "Sandra got bitten by a snake, love," before she started weeping again.

"What happens now, Mum? Please, I want to know." Brenda pulled away from her mum and sat on the other side of the table so she could see her mum's face. She had found her mum crying, and it seemed so awful and was very distressing, as she had only seen her cry when she was happy before. Brenda simply felt numb. Actually, if she was truthful with herself, some little bit of her was sort of glad she would no longer have to put up with Sandra's spite. There was a dull, lumpy feeling in her chest and tummy she did not know how to address, but she certainly didn't feel like crying like her mum.

Nancy gazed across at Brenda for a long time, and Brenda didn't think she was going to speak. D2 poked her nose into Brenda's hand, and she absently rubbed her ears. "Yes, little one, you do need to know. The doctor took Sandra to the hospital last night. Dad and I are going in to speak to the church people. Holly and Steve say we can bury her here. Over beside their little girl. She was bitten by a snake too." There was a significant pause between each statement.

"Do you want to come with us to town?" When Brenda shook her head, Nancy went on. "Thought not. Well, keep out of trouble, and we will be back before dinner."

Brenda was still confused, but said nothing as her dad called out for Nancy to get ready and said he would be back to pick her up soon. As Nancy went to have a shower, Brenda gathered her fishing lines and headed for the waterhole. *Maybe I can catch some fish for dinner,* she thought. *Besides, I need to think, and fishing will give me plenty of time to think.*

This was where Jewel found her, just sitting, looking blankly across the water. She hadn't even cast out her line. Jewel put her arm round Brenda's shoulder and sat hugging her as unbidden tears rolled silently down Brneda's cheeks.

"Sharon and I are going back to our homes for Christmas tomorrow. Mrs. Hasting wants to do Christmas shopping as well, so she's taking us in to meet the bus." Jewel dropped her hand off Brenda's shoulder, and, after glancing sideways at Brenda, sighed and added, "I've enjoyed coming out here, though. It has been fun."

Brenda sniffed and wiped at her wet cheeks and leaned into Jewel. "I'm sorry you're going to miss my fifteenth birthday." Here, she hesitated. "Guess there will not be a party now, anyway." After a brief pause, she went on. "Sandra was bitten by a snake."

Jewel, her face very serious, nodded. "Yes, everyone knows now. Mr. Hasting and the boys are digging a grave now. Apparently, the funeral will be a couple of days away, since all the bits and pieces are being sorted out. That's another reason we're leaving earlier than planned, as Mrs. Hastings doesn't want to be here. And, besides, the boys are quite upset about Sandra passing away."

"Passing away? I wouldn't have thought about it like that," Brenda whispered.

Jewel gave her another hug and kissed her cheek. "We're off early in the morning. Hope to see you again one day. We should write to each other." Brenda nodded her acceptance to that idea and watched Jewel run back to the big house. Jewel turned and waved as she went through the side gate into the house yard. Brenda gathered her things and made her way home past the big house yard where Mr. Hasting and the boys were digging a big hole. It must need to be very deep, as she could only see the tops of their heads. She didn't speak to them, just watched for a few minutes. D2 pushed her nose into Brenda's hand, and they walked slowly home. *Best I do something about dinner,* Brenda thought.

DEATH AND CONSEQUENCES

It was very late when Nancy and Dexter got back from town. Brenda got up to tell them that she had put dinners in the oven. Both of her parents looked completely exhausted. Nancy had stopped crying even, though Brenda felt a little frightened of her strained and colourless face. Her eyes looked dead. However, she gave Brenda a gentle pat on her back and said, "Thanks, little one. We will talk in the morning."

When Brenda got up before Nancy and Dexter, she found the meals untouched, so she gave them to D2. *Got to keep busy,* she thought, so she filled the kettle and got the stove going while she waited for whatever was going to happen next. Dexter got up, put on his hat, and left, mumbling, "Got to see the boss about the grave." Nancy followed, and after tea was made and poured, she indicated to Brenda to sit with her.

Nancy sighed a huge sigh and took a deep breath. "Well, little one, the funeral is tomorrow. The funeral people will bring Sandra out tonight so we can all have a private moment with her before we put her in the grave. There will be a short service by the minister on the big house veranda before we all walk Sandra to her last resting place." All this came out in a bit of a rush, and, after a short break, she went on, her voice a dull monotone. "Today we must make some little cakes and biscuits to give to the people who attend the service afterwards. We must make sure our best dresses are pressed."

Brenda got busy making the cakes and things, watching her mum and dad have several whispered conversations—some of which sounded very angry. She heard words like "It has to be one of them," and "The boss needs to know" from her Dad, and "Please, just let us get through this first," and "I do not think it is one of the boys," and "The dates are wrong" from her Mum. Dexter ended up disappearing to the shed to make Sandra a cross. Nancy spent most of her day simply sitting and weeping. Brenda felt quite grown up, flitting about in the kitchen and ironing their best outfits. She kept refreshing her Mum's teacup when the tea got cold and took her dad over a sandwich for his lunch. Dexter merely grunted his acknowledgement of the offering.

Brenda noticed he smelled of rum and almost ran into Sam the store man coming into the shed with another bottle. She found it odd that her dad was drinking—and with Sam, of all people. She couldn't recall any time when they had spoken more than a few words. Dexter sometimes had a beer with the boss, but mostly only drank anything if they went to a rodeo or the like. Brenda wandered home, pondering all the odd activities occurring around her at this time. Dexter hadn't arrived home when Nancy and Brenda went to bed. Brenda was tired from all the cooking and stuff. She felt kind of melancholy. She was happy when D2, for the first time, hopped onto the end of her bed. She kept her feet against the dog's warm body, and it seemed comforting.

The day of the funeral started quietly enough. Dexter and Nancy got dressed in their good clothes, so Brenda followed suit. The funeral people, *undertakers* she found they were called, arrived with Sandra's coffin round 9:00 a.m. and brought it into the dining room on a trolley and said they would be back in an hour, just before the service. During that hour, the minister came and spoke quietly with the three of them as to what was going to happen next. Dexter sat, stone-faced, looking out the window, hardly acknowledging anything or anyone around him. Nancy sat so she could have her hand on the coffin, quietly weeping but nodding to the minister's words. Brenda was very overwhelmed by it all and sat holding tightly to Nancy's free hand, letting it go only to give Mr. Hasting the cakes and biscuits she had prepared. She was aware of some traffic movement about the place.

They all walked slowly behind the funeral car as it drove over to the big house. There were chairs lined up on the covered barbecue area, and the minister led them to the front row of chairs. Brenda was amazed at the number of people in attendance and recognised several faces from town and nearby properties. Sam and Albert sat right at the back. As Brenda sat gazing at the coffin, she had a brief moment of pleasure at the thought of never having to watch her back again, and even as she thought that, she still had the terrible feeling of emptiness inside herself. She slipped her hand into her mum's hand and felt her fingers squeezed so hard that she had to drag them away. The rest was all a blur of words, hymns, and following the coffin to the grave, where everyone dropped a leaf or handful of dirt onto the coffin. Brenda backed herself out of the folks hugging Nancy and shaking hands with Dexter. Albert gestured for her to come and sit with him, where he patted her back gently and sat silently beside her.

Dexter burst out of the melee when Mr. Hasting and some of the other men started to fill in the grave, chasing them away and filling in the grave by himself. The womenfolk headed back to the veranda where tea, cakes, and biscuits were laid out. Dexter grabbed a shovel and snarled at the others to leave so he could do one last thing for his daughter. Brenda joined the throng round the tables and watched in fascination as her dad frantically shovelled the earth back into the hole before finally—savagely—jamming the cross into the loose ground. She noticed he had tears running down his cheeks as he put in the cross. Mr. Hasting and Sam walked quietly over to him and produced a flask, from which Dad drank thirstily before he came and stood beside Nancy. Brenda stood close to them, and she heard Nancy whisper, "Not today. Please, not today."

Eventually, people drifted away. Dexter had continued to sip away at the flask, causing Sam to refill it several times. By the time everyone had left, he was very wobbly on his feet. Steve offered to grill some steaks for the Willows family for dinner, but Nancy, who had a firm grip on one of Dexter's arms, declined quickly. "Thanks, but we'll go home now. And thank you for everything today."

Nancy nodded to Sam, who took Dexter's other arm, and, between them, they got Dexter home, where he collapsed onto the bed and immediately commenced to snore. Brenda loitered at the table, filling her pockets with biscuits and cakes. Some for her, and some for D2. Albert touched her gently on her shoulder. "You okay, Brenda?" he asked in his soft voice. Brenda did not speak, but she nodded and headed away home, wondering why she still had that empty feeling, still feeling guilty about her thought during the service. *I am a bad person*, she thought.

D2 nosed at her pocket, bringing her back to earth. She knelt down and hugged the dog, whispering into her ear, "Well, you still like me, anyway." And girl and dog went off towards the waterhole, where they shared the food and watched the sun go down. As darkness fell, Brenda heard Nancy clap the summon to come home, so she jumped up and raced D2 home. She found Nancy curled up on Sandra's bed, so she and D2 crept into her room. Brenda allowed the dog to curl up on the end of her bed again.

D2 woke her, jumping off the bed early in the morning, but as she went to let D2 out, she saw her parents sitting at the table. She put her hand on D2's head to stop her whining. Nancy and Dexter's voices carried to her, and she stood wide-eyed, hearing what they were talking about.

Nancy said, "But she was at least four months along, so it couldn't have been the boys, love. I know she was hanging about with them, but I'm sure nothing happened with them. She was hardly ever alone with either of them." Brenda blinked rapidly, remembering what she had seen. "Besides, if it was one of the boys, she would have been only three months in." Brenda had to stop herself from audibly gasping as she realised the fact that they were discussing that Sandra had been pregnant.

Dexter, who was sitting with his head in his hands, replied, "Okay, so it wasn't one of boys. Who, then?" And after a brief pause, he went on. "There was that insurance bloke and auditor here. That would suit that time frame." He sighed. "If it was consensual, they couldn't do anything, as she was past sixteen. Guess I'll still need to tell Steve and report it to the police, as it could have been rape. Sandra was a good girl and wouldn't have done it willingly." He looked up. "She ever talk to you about sex, Bun?"

Nancy shook her head. "The little one asks about all that. Sandra said all that stuff was very disgusting."

Dexter stood and walked slowly out of the door, heading towards big house. Brenda crept back to her bed and made getting up noises before coming slowly out of her room. Nancy glanced up, and seeing D2, shook her head before lowering her head onto the table. Brenda touched her and told Nancy she was going to help with the milking. She got no response from her mum, so trotted off to the milking yards, where Albert handed over the milking to her while he raked out the calf pen. She felt a sense of comfort as she snuggled her head and shoulder into the soft, furry flank of Vera the cow and let her mind go off to faraway places. *Don't know why Sandra doesn't like this*, she thought, then stopped squeezing the teats for a couple of seconds before sighing deeply and continuing.

After Brenda and Albert had separated the milk and put the cream and milk in the cold room, fed the stallion, pigs, and chooks, Brenda walked slowly home. Nancy was still in the same position and did not respond to Brenda's question of if she required Brenda to do anything before school. Yesterday's dishes were in the sink still, so she washed them and swept out before making her mum a cup of sweet tea. Sweet tea had always been the cure-all for everything. Her mum sat up and sipped at the tea while Brenda got out the schoolbooks. As she retrieved the books and placed them on the table, Nancy gasped and reached out to touch Sandra's workbook.

"Have to let them know, I guess." She breathed, her face going even whiter, if that was possible. Brenda felt a shiver of fear.

Dexter came in at lunch and made himself a sandwich. Nancy roused herself briefly as he told her he was going to town to report matters to the police. He hardly gave Brenda a glance, but said, "You get tea on for your mum, girl," and strode out, not waiting to hear Brenda's answer. Nancy retreated over to Sandra's bed after he had left. She laid down, sobbing silently. The only indication was her shoulders shaking. Brenda finished her school paper and put it in the reply-paid envelope the correspondence school provided, and she went to take it over to Sam so he could put it in tomorrow's mail.

Holly and the boys had returned, and the boys caught up with her as Brenda and D2 headed to the waterhole to think. The boys' questions came at her all garbled together. "Is it true she was pregnant?" "Do they think it was us?" "Did they know what we did?" Brenda raised her hands, backed away from them, and, for the first time, swore out loud. "Bloody hell, and bugger me! Give over and be nice, hey!" Her voice had a hard edge to it "Yes, she was. And, no, it wasn't yours! Now clear off, and leave me alone." Brenda and D2 ran away from them. They did not follow.

When Brenda got home—just as she saw her dad drive back in—her mum was still on Sandra's bed. Brenda leaned over her and noticed Mum seemed to be sleeping at last. She busied herself putting together a meal of sorts. Dexter walked heavily into the unit. He smelt of rum and sat silently at the table till his meal was placed in front of him. It was a very silent meal. Nancy got up just as they finished and sat picking at her plate while Brenda washed up. After Nancy had pushed her plate away, she got up and went to sit with Dexter out behind the laundry.

They did not even try to keep their voices low as they discussed how Dexter had got on at the police station. Seemed to Brenda that that hadn't gone well, and the police had shown very little interest in filing a report or attempting to locate the two men that were on the suspect radar. Seemed that it had to do with Sandra being over sixteen, and only after Dexter had gotten really cranky had they agreed to file the report. Dexter was upset with Steve. It seemed as though he did not think either of the two men in question would be involved with rape. All the conversation ended with Dexter striding off to drink with Sam and Nancy dissolving into tears again and returning to Sandra's bed. Brenda felt frightened by it all. *Bugger Sandra*, she thought.

This became the pattern of the next few weeks. Nancy was almost like a ghost in the house, taking no part in any of the day to day running of the house. Nancy did not even remember Brenda's birthday, and when Brenda tried to remind her, Nancy stared blankly at her. That was very hard to take, as Nancy had always made an effort for the girls' birthdays. Dexter, like a mobile, silent statue, mechanically arrived for meals, never commenting on anything, disappearing at night to drink with Sam. Brenda slowly worked herself into a routine of housekeeping and school work. She didn't like going to the store, as Sam made some odd remarks and had gotten into the habit of coming up behind her and touching her on her shoulder before she knew he was there. She didn't like his touch, as it always felt too personal somehow. Once, she even told him to bugger off, which seemed to amuse him.

Sam told Dexter that she had sworn at him, and for the first time since the funeral, Dexter acknowledged Brenda as he growled at her and slapped her face hard, saying, "He's been a great support through all of this, and do not ever let me hear of this sort of nonsense again, you hear!" The last words he spat out, his face very close to hers. The physical and verbal attack frightened her, as she had never been punished this way previously. Sandra had been the only one to be really mean to her.

Brenda's birthday came and went, as did Christmas, with little change in the situation she found herself in. She wrote long, sad letters to Cindy and Jewel, only to later burn them and write short notes without really saying anything. Her school work finished for the summer break, so Brenda had little to do except cook, clean, and work with D2. There was still the early mornings helping Albert with the feeding and milking too. They worked for the most part in silence each knowing what needed to be done and when to help each other without being asked. It was the closest she got to feeling happy. Albert would give her a nod when she arrived, and her shoulder a squeeze when the jobs were done. His shoulder squeeze did not feel anything like Sam's touch.

Nancy watched all this and said nothing. In fact, she had become more and more morose and no longer slept in her own bed, choosing to sleep on Sandra's bed. She sipped at the sweet tea Brenda made and only picked at her meals. She made absolutely no effort to do any of the household chores, so Brenda quietly went about doing everything except the mending and ironing. Brenda only heard voices when she went to milk. Her Dad ignored her, as he just came, ate, and left, only to arrive home drunk and flop onto his bed. He never took any notice of Nancy, either. Brenda was so confused, as none of it seemed real. She would have been completely lost without D2, and chatted to her, telling her how frightened she was for her mum, who was losing weight, and about her dad's drinking—plus Sam touching her more and more often.

Occasionally, Nancy would come to life and wander through the rooms, muttering, "Where is Sandra? She should be back by now." Then, she would go back to sit on Sandra's bed. If Brenda was there, and quick enough, she could get Nancy to eat a sandwich. Eventually, Brenda told Holly how worried she was about her mum, and Holly came over to see for herself.

Holly was shocked at the decline in Nancy's appearance and at fact that she only answered in monosyllables. "You were right to come to me Brenda." Holly had taken Brenda outside. 'None of this has been easy on you, has it? I'll talk to Steve, and we'll come up with a plan."

The next events happened so quickly that it made Brenda's head spin. Dexter was called in from his grader as Holly came and packed a suitcase for Nancy. Nancy looked confused but went with them.

Dexter and Holly returned late that day without Nancy. Holly sat beside Brenda, telling her that her mum needed to stay in hospital for a while. Holly frowned as Dexter simply silently ate his dinner before muttering to Holly, "Going to have a drink with Sam."

Holly looked at Brenda with her eyebrows raised in question, and suddenly, Brenda felt very angry and spat out her reply. "Every night. Every bloody night!" Then she felt so ashamed of herself for the swear word.

Holly gave a hug, which only made her feel worse. Hot tears spilled out of her eyes, and she gulped loudly. Holly held her till the tirade stopped. "Come now, Brenda." Holly spoke softly. "The boys will be home for their first school break soon, and Jewel as well. You got on well with her, yes?" She hesitated, giving Brenda a glance, and went on after Brenda nodded. "Keep your head up till then, hey." She gave Brenda a final squeeze before leaving, thinking that something must be done about Dexter's drinking. Brenda felt really tired and went to bed without clearing the dishes away.

When she got up, she found D2 had done a reasonable job of cleaning the dishes. Over the next few weeks, Dexter stopped going out every night, but he would just sit outside after dinner before retiring. He hardly ever spoke to Brenda. The trips to the store were becoming a nightmare, with Sam's touching becoming very embarrassing as his hands became very close to her private places. Brenda's breasts were developing, and while he never actually touched them, she could feel his eyes on them. After Dexter had slapped her for telling Sam off, she became very good at watching for Holly to head to the store and arriving at the same time. Sam noticed and would frown at her.

It all came to a head when Holly was away collecting the boys and Jewel. Brenda found herself alone with Sam at the store. She had crept in and had almost got all her stuff. Sam, who had been doing whatever with the snakes he kept, cornered her as she was about to leave. He blocked her way and just stood there, looking her up and down. Brenda felt her pulse quicken and colour infuse her face.

"Ah, you will come around." Sam's breath came in short puffs "Come out the back. hey?" He leaned in close to her, so close that she could smell his breath. Brenda took a chance as he adjusted his balance to move closer to her. She ducked under his arm and out the door. She could hear his high-pitched laugh behind her.

Brenda was really upset at the incident. Who could she ask for help? Certainly not Dexter. He wouldn't hear any bad words about his so-called best friend. Albert was out of the question, though he had noticed Brenda had something bothering her. Holly, maybe. Perhaps Holly and Steve together would be the best plan. She decided that that would be the best plan, but Steve and Holly got called away to attend a funeral before Brenda got the chance.

A lady friend of Albert's, Linda, came in to do for the boys and Jewel. She had a young lass with her round Brenda's age. A pretty girl with skin paler than Albert's, but she had the same lovely, soft voice and ready smile. Her name was Cindy. Cindy, Jewel, and Brenda spent a lot of time together just sitting and watching the birds and wildlife round the waterhole. Cindy confessed that her mum, Linda, was a sort of auntie who helped her mum out from time to time, and she was also a sort of medicine woman among her folks round Dubbo. Cindy had decided to follow in her footsteps in a different way and become a nurse. Jewel still had her heart set on running her family farm, and so far was happy with her studies, but she listened as the other girls talked about such a different avenue.

Cindy pointed out some of the medicine plants that her mum used to treat ailments. It transpired that, although Cindy and Jewel did not go to the same school, Jewel did know about Cindy's family, particularly her mum's natural medicines, and found the use of plants and roots interesting, as she wondered if they too could be incorporated in animal husbandry somehow. The girls all exchanged addresses and vowed to keep in touch.

Brenda made an effort to go to the store whenever she saw Linda heading over—to avoid having Sam touch her. She really was unsure how to deal with Sam, and if she tried to tell to Dexter that she didn't like Sam, he would yell at her, say Sam was being a good mate, and tell her to shut up. Brenda was happy to reunite with Jewel, who had bought her some lovely soaps on a rope for her birthday, and Brenda confided some of her problems and how lonely she was. Somehow, she couldn't talk about Sam. In fact, she felt a little guilty about it. Jewel listened and then chatted gaily about happenings in her life.

Brenda wondered if anyone really cared about her, but she was happy to have Jewel and Cindy filling some of her lonely hours. Eventually, Sam tried to touch Jewel as well, who was horrified and pulled Brenda aside to ask if Sam got too close to her too. They then confided in Cindy, who didn't really understand, as she never went to the store without Linda. But Cindy agreed to keep her eyes open. One day, she confessed that she had come in behind Linda and had seen Linda wallop Sam really hard across his face—so hard that his lips split and his nose bled. Linda left on the next mail truck, stating that she was needed at home to treat an elder of the tribe. Holly and Steve were nearly due back, so the boys and Jewel had to cook for themselves for several days. Brenda found they were useless at it and gave them some pointers. It gave her sad life some amusement.

She saw Jewel rushing out of the store one morning and wondered if Sam had tried it on with her again as well. That arvo, when she and Jewel were walking to the waterhole to fish, which was just an excuse to talk, Brenda got up the courage to ask Jewel about Sam. Jewel shuddered and replied, "Yes, the old bugger (they used swear words when they were alone) touched my bum."

Brenda told on the latest incident, and, after the initial shock, they discussed what could be done. "You go and flirt with him, and I'll wait outside and come in and catch him molesting you." Jewel smiled wolfishly. Brenda stared at her, wide-eyed, for a while. Then, she nodded slowly. Jewel went on. "Mr. and Mrs. Hasting will be back in a couple of days. So you lead him on a bit, and we'll set up the pounce when they get back. He will not have a leg to stand on then." Her eyes gleamed with excitement.

Brenda made a couple of lone visits to the store and smiled at Sam, allowing him to stand close to her. Sam got quite thrilled. He assumed that she had come round to his way of thinking. He tried to hold her hand, and his hand felt heavy when he touched her shoulder. Out of the side of her mouth, she whispered, "Stop! Someone may see us." As she left the store, she thought she heard him mutter to himself, "She'll be the best yet." Brenda wondered what he could have meant by that.

Jewel came and got her as soon as she got the phone call that said Holly and Steve were on their way home. "Come on, Brenda. This is the day to do it!" Jewel sounded so excited. "I'll stand over by the big tree, and, as soon as I see the car coming, I'll give you the nod. Okay?"

Brenda felt very frightened, but nodded silently and sat watching Jewel as she pretended to be reading beside the trees. All too soon, the nod came, and Brenda ran to the store before she could think of a reason not to go through with it. She arrived quite breathless as she burst through the door. Sam totally mistook her demeanour as excitement, rushing to her side and trying to touch her. Brenda, who was still a little out of breath said, "Let's go out the back, hey." Sam went to shut the door, but Brenda grabbed his hand and yelled, "Now! Now, while there is no one here to catch us."

Sam followed her meekly while Brenda kept up a chattering to hide the sounds that she could hear of a car arriving and Jewel's soft steps as she came into the store. Brenda shuddered as she glanced at the snakes in their glass cages at the back of the room. Brenda turned round and faced Sam, pretending to undo her blouse. "Did you do this to Sandra too?" Her voice was quite low and husky.

Sam nodded, his breath coming in short gasps as he saw the outline of her breasts emerge from her blouse. "Sandra, she liked it." He paused as his hand went to undo his pants. "What about you?"

Brenda shut her eyes tight, took several deep, shaking breaths, and turned away from Sam, who reached out to touch her. Brenda screamed and flung herself at Sam, pushing him away with all her might. "Get away from me!"

Brenda started screaming and couldn't seem to stop. Jewel, Holly, and Steve came rushing in to see what was the matter. Sam lay stunned amid broken glass and snakes. Sam saw the new arrivals and fumbled with his pants. As he moved to do that, one of the snakes struck, affixing itself to his hand before slithering off under some boxes. Sam added his screams to Brenda's, which then bought Albert and Dexter running from the back shed. "Jesus! God help me!" Sam screamed. "That is a western brown. I'm as good as dead."

Everyone was stunned to silence as Brenda found her voice and yelled, "He interfered with Sandra." Holly got to Brenda and held her, shushing her. Dexter, who had just entered the store, heard that and stopped in his tracks before reaching for a shovel and advancing towards Sam, who was clutching his bitten hand between his knees. Sam raised his other hand to ward off the expected blows. Steve managed catch hold of the shovel before Dexter could successfully smash the implement down on Sam's head.

Dexter added his screams to the bedlam. "You got her pregnant!" To which, Sam nodded. "And you pretended to be my friend?" The last bit was said with his voice dwindling away to a whisper. Dexter slumped against the shelves.

Steve stood in the middle of everyone. He sent Albert to phone for the police and ambulance. He was not sure how to proceed. Sam grunted when he heard the request for an ambulance and spoke very calmly. "I'll be gone before they get here. That snake delivers a huge amount of venom when disturbed. And that one was quite disturbed, I'd say." Sam gave a half smile. "I'll bleed to death, as the venom stops the blood from clotting, and I'll suffer, but not for too long. Guess I should confess."

Sam finally raised himself to a full sitting position. "Couldn't help it, really, as I like young girls. And if they hadn't wanted to squeal, they would have been okay. There were others before I came out here, and I managed to not get caught. Your little girl," he nodded at Steve, "was my youngest." Holly and Steve gasped before he went on.

Sam glanced at Dexter. "Your girl was the most demanding girl I've had. By the way, she did tell me she was pregnant, which is why she had to go as well. That bit was so easy, as this snake," he flipped his hand in the air, "has small fangs and a painless bite. So it was just a matter of getting them near enough for the snake to bite them. Neither of the girls knew they had been bitten." Sam winced as pain began to engulf his body. He glanced again at Dexter. "This one led me on to a set up this trap. Suppose I deserved the snakebite. And her dog is a dingo!" Sam slumped back and closed his eyes.

Dexter was the first to move after he and Steve exchanged glances. Brenda still had her head buried against Holly's shoulder and watched him go out. He was still carrying the shovel. There was a dull thud, a yelp, and another thud. Brenda jerked away from Holly and ran outside to find D2 with her head smashed in, her body quivering. The shovel was tossed to the side as Dexter strode off back to the shed. Brenda sat and held her friend, blood seeping into her clothes. After a brief conversation with Steve, who stood looking from Brenda to Dexter, shaking his head in disbelief at what had happened.

Brenda sobbed. Her body shook. The sob became a scream. Holly, who had followed her outside, had to physically shake her to get her to stop. Brenda's hands clutched at D2's body. She swayed from side to side, her face very, very pale. Her breath came in gulps. Holly and Jewel disentangled Brenda from D2 and took her back to the big house.

Holly went back in to take Steve by his hand and drag him away from where he stood staring at Sam, whose fingers were now clutching at his stomach. Sam looked up as Holly re-entered the room, his eyes begging for help. Holly, who was a very gentle woman and very much a lady, looked at Sam and spoke softly, her voice trembling. "Fuck you, you miserable cunt. May you die a slow and painful death." Even in his painful situation, Sam looked surprised at the outburst. Steve allowed her to take him outside, looking a little shocked as well.

They were met by Dexter returning from the shed and only just stopped him from storming back into the store with a bloodstained shovel. "He deserves to die. He deserves to die," he kept muttering. Steve caught hold of him and had to punch him hard, knocking him to the ground. As he fell to the ground, there was a loud *bang* from inside the store, making everyone jump.

"Guess he has looked after that himself," Steve said as he helped Dexter to his feet and led him away, gesturing to the gathered people to leave as well. "Leave it all for the police, folks."

Brenda had torn herself from Jewel and had just made it back to the store. The sound of the shot caused Brenda to take a sharp intake of breath and stop sobbing. She looked past Steve, at Dexter, with such venom in her eyes that Holly felt afraid for her. *Poor child*, thought Holly. *She has been the real victim in all this, and her feelings have not been considered.* Albert and Holly disentangled Brenda from the body of the dog again, gently lifting her to her feet. Jewel stepped in and took one arm as they walked Brenda back to the big house. Brenda looked back over her shoulder and gave a little cry before shaking off the helping hands and walking straight and tall between Holly and Jewel, her head held high. Holly felt the change happen and wondered what it meant for the child. Brenda whispered, "I want my mum." It was only just loud enough for Holly to hear.

Albert wrapped D2 in some canvas and carried her towards the waterhole, where he buried her close to Brenda's favourite spot. Dexter never spoke to Albert as he made a cross for D2's grave. He was seated on the anvil while Steve talked quietly to him, trying to get him to talk about his feelings. Steve asked about what Dexter wanted to do. Did he want to go to visit Nancy? And what about Brenda? Steve was sorry he had been so adamant about dingos. He had thought that D2 had been part dingo all along, but hadn't said anything, as Brenda had trained the dog very well.

Finally, Dexter broke down and admitted that he hadn't been kind to Brenda through all the past events, admitting that she had actually been very helpful under difficult times. He showed great distress with the realisation that he had killed the dog. He alternated between anger at Sam for pretending to be his friend and ager at the fact he hadn't shown Brenda any support. He could now see that Sam had wanted him to leave her to herself so she would get lonely, and so be more easily seduced by him. After a lot of alternating between sadness and anger, Dexter agreed to take some time so he and Brenda could go and visit with Nancy. He agreed to leave on the next weekend.

Brenda stayed in the big house, only returning to the home that held so many sad memories for her to pack. She snuck back once and sorted through her mum's things, packing her make-up, jewellery, and perfumes, thinking she may want them now, as surely by now she was much better. At the bottom of the jewellery box, she found quite a bit of money. This she also took without mentioning it to anyone. She also riffled through Sandra's drawers and got out her bras. Whenever she encountered her dad, she kept a cold distance and flinched if he tried to touch her, her eyes and face showing no emotion. She took the news that they were to go and visit her mum without comment. She didn't even cry when Albert took her to show her D2's grave. She felt completely devoid of emotion and just numb.

Brenda hugged Holly tightly as they said goodbye. Jewel whispered, "See you next holidays" as she wrapped her arms round her friend. Brenda returned the cuddle and turned quickly, getting into the car Steve had loaned to them for the trip to the city, where Nancy was living with her mum and dad. Brenda didn't look back, sitting as far away from Dexter as she could.

BRENDA LOUISE

SECOND ENCOUNTER

DOWN THE LONG ROAD

Dexter drove straight through, stopping only for food and fuel. Brenda accepted the food but didn't speak a word for the entire trip. They arrived at 38 Golda Avenue in a suburb of Brisbane just as the sun was rising over the multitude of houses that seemed to go on for ever. Brenda thought how dreadful it must be to live so close to each other and not be able to see past the house next door or across the road. They were both tired and stiff from the long drive. Granddad Hay greeted them warmly. "Kettle is on. Nancy is having a shower, so come on in to the kitchen where Mother is cooking eggs for breakfast."

Gran Hay, a big woman, wrapped her arms round Brenda, giving a warm hug. For some reason, it made Brenda want to cry again, but she took a deep breath, squaring her shoulders before sitting at the table, hungrily munching on her eggs and little soldier fingers of toast. She was almost finished when Nancy rushed into the kitchen, her hair still wet from the shower. Nancy didn't even look at Brenda, who sat, her fork halfway to her mouth, holding her breath. Nancy stood in front of Dexter, her face anxious. "Did you bring Sandra? Did you?"

Brenda dropped her fork. It made a loud clatter, breaking the silence. "Mum. Mum," Brenda whispered, at which Nancy glanced at her and patted her shoulder in an absent kind of way, never taking her eyes away from Dexter's face. There was a look of expectation on Nancy's face. Gran watched as Brenda wilted and seemed to halve in size. Gran's heart went out to her. Brenda quite deliberately straightened the cutlery before excusing herself from the table, looking up at Gran, asking, "May I go and lie down, Gran, please?" Brenda's face showed absolutely no expression. Gran took her hand, leading her off to her room.

Brenda slept for many hours and woke to the afternoon sun shining weakly into her room and birds singing in the trees near the window. *If I don't look outside, it's almost like I'm still in the bush,* she thought. She lay on the bed for a while before getting up to go and have a shower. The house seemed to be very quiet, however, she heard Gran and Granddad talking in the kitchen. Gran was saying, "Maybe now she will start to get better and realise Sandra is truly gone." The conversation stopped as they heard Brenda open the bathroom door. Gran had a cup of tea ready for her when she went into the kitchen. Gran gave her a huge hug before she sat down. "Do you want to talk about your mum, love?"

Brenda glanced up as she stirred sugar into her tea and shook her head. Nothing else was said as Nancy and Dexter came into the kitchen. They were holding hands, and both appeared to have been weeping. Neither of them acknowledged Brenda. Brenda noticed Granddad touch Gran as she opened her mouth to speak and shake his head at her. The conversation flowed on round Brenda, talking about nothing in particular. Brenda did notice that Nancy took part in the chatter, and that she never let her gaze land on Brenda's face, only just slid past her. Nancy's eyes had no real life or expression in them. Brenda ate the meal placed in front of her, hardly tasting it. Gran followed her back into her room afterwards, making suggestions as to what they could do during the visit. She sat on the bed, rubbing Brenda's back till she fell asleep.

Over the course of the visit, Nancy would simply give Brenda a pat on her head several times. Gran and Granddad took her to the zoo, where she got to hold a koala, finding the animal's fur so very soft. They also went to the beach several times. Nancy and Dexter even came one day. Nancy even laughed as Dexter splashed water at her. Nancy talked animatedly to Dexter after the first day, but never actually spoke directly to Brenda. Nancy would inquire about what they had done and seen whenever Brenda and either one or the other grandparent returned from a trip, addressing the group—

but never directly to Brenda. Brenda gave up hoping that her mum would treat her like a person, ever.

Gran was kind, gave her lots of hugs, and encouraged her to talk about D2, Sandra, and Sam. However, Brenda was reluctant to really get into talking about her feelings. It was noted that Brenda kept well away from Dexter, though. Gran tried to give all sort of excuses as to why Dexter had killed the dog, saying that he was under a lot of stress. Brenda just listened to it all, and thought, *Well, what about me?* And she would scream inside herself. She started to worry about returning to the station and what life would be like there and how bad it would be having to pretend all was okay.

All too soon, it was time to head back to the station. Gran gave Brenda some cookbooks to help her, as she was the women of the house now. Brenda was sad to be leaving, as she had enjoyed Gran's hugs and chatter. As they got into the car in preparation to leave, Nancy bent down and smiled at Brenda, waving. *Bit late for that, Mum,* Brenda thought.

They went as far as Miles, where Dexter booked into a motel, and they walked across to a roadhouse for dinner. Brenda watched the big rigs come and go, wondering where they were headed. After dinner, Dexter went to the pub for a few drinks. Brenda walked slowly back to their room, a plan forming. She had no desire to return to Bemerside to be ignored by her dad, and it was so obvious her mum didn't care. *So I think I'll just go where the wind blows me,* she thought.

She got the make-up out of the bottom of her bag, inexpertly applying it to her face. She checked herself out in the long mirror, pushing her chest out and sucking in her stomach, turning this way and that, practising smiles. *Yep,* she thought. *I could pass for sixteen.* Redressing, leaving her blouse open to reveal the rise of her breasts, and packing only the necessary items into her bag plus the money she had found before coming to the city, she headed back to the roadhouse. She had tucked the spare pillows into her bed, thinking, *Dad will be drunk when he gets back and will not miss me till morning—and, with a bit of luck, I'll long gone by then.* She waited in the truck parking lot till a driver emerged from the roadhouse and started to climb into his cab before approaching, smiling, and standing in a provocative manner. Taking a deep breath, she asked, "Catch a lift, mate?"

The driver jerked his head around and looked her up and down slowly. "Love to. But why do you want a ride, girl?" His voice was rough, but he had kind eyes. *He is not all that old, I think,* Brenda thought. "How old are you, girl?"

Brenda grinned back at him. "Sixteen, and my step dad has been abusing me." She hardened her eyes. "I'm over the bugger. My name is Lu." Softening her look again and cocking her head to the side, she said, "Please, mate. If I stay here, I'll kill the bugger. And I can be nice to you."

The driver thought briefly. "Oh, I see, girl. Come on, then. I'm Cliff." He held his hand down for her bag before catching her hand, pulling her up into the cab. His took in the quick rise and fall of her chest. Brenda gave him what she thought might be a seductive glance as she slid over him to the passenger seat.

"Let's get out of here before I'm missed. Where we going, Cliffy?" Brenda whispered close to his ear. Cliff took in a sharp breath before lifting her over onto the seat and engaging the gears to drive out of the roadhouse parking lot. As they drove slowly out of the parking area, another driver yelled out, "Thought you were coming over for the game, Cliff!"

Brenda sank low in her seat, but as the cab of the rig was pretty dark, she went unseen. "Think I'll get a start on the next leg 'ole mate." And he gave the chap a wave, receiving one in return. Cliff gave her a glance. "Headed south en route to the Melbourne markets,

Lu. That good for you?" Brenda nodded. "We'll stop up the road a bit so we can get to know each other better."

Goodness me, thought Brenda as she settled herself in the seat and wondered what he really meant by that. Her heart beat painfully in her chest, and her breath came in swift little gasps. Gradually, she felt herself relax and drifted off to sleep. The events of the past months and week finally caught up with her, and she fell into a deep, deep sleep. Cliff eased the rig to a stop, and, as he turned to wake her, he sat for several moments looking at the small, pretty girl as she slept. *She's only a baby, and she's lucky she got me, not one of the other truckles,* he thought as he got a blanket from the bed behind the driver's seat and flicked it over her. She never felt Cliff stop or felt him cover her with the rug. He gently lifted her head and slipped a pillow under her head.

When she awoke, the truck was rumbling down the highway, and Cliff was whistling though his teeth to a Slim Dusty tune on his cassette player. She watched him though her eyelashes for a time and realised he was quite young and had a strong jawline. His exposed arms were sinewy and brown. As he glanced over at her, she felt a fluttering inside her. His eyes were a bright, penetrating green. She had never seen eyes so green, and she liked the way his lips curved up at the corners as though he must smile a lot. *Those are smile lines at the corners of his eyes, I'm sure,* she thought before squeezing her eyes closed and sitting up with a huge yawn.

"Morning, Lu." Cliff smiled at her. "You must have been buggered out, love. You have slept for ten hours." He added, "You look cute when you're asleep." He gave her a small grin, but there was a question at the back of his eyes.

"Humm," said Brenda, her voice very husky and low. She suddenly again wondered what she had got herself into and glanced sideways at him. "I need to pee."

"Not to fret, Lu. We're stopping at a fuel stop shortly. You hungry? I have waited breaky till you woke up." Cliff turned the tape down, and Brenda found he had a really deep voice. "We are in New

South Wales now," he added. While they travelled to the fuel stop, Brenda sat up and stretched, looking about the cab of the truck. *No sign of smokes, and no cigarette smell, either, so that's good.* The smell of smoke reminded her of Sam, and she shuddered a little. The cab was meticulously clean, with only a fine dust over the dash. There was a photo of a little puppy that looked a bit like D2 stuck to the top of the cap, and that made her give a little smile to herself. She snuck a look at his hands and noted that, like her dad's, they were a little callused on the side of his palms and fingers. *No smokes, clean, hardworking and good looking,* she noted to herself. *So maybe I'll be okay.* However, she felt herself go hot inside as she remembered what she had done when he'd lifted her into the truck. Her mum had told her once that it is always the woman who controlled how far to go before marriage. *Hells bells*, she thought. *I certainly gave a shocking impression last night.*

Cliff observed her out of the corner of his eyes as she furtively gave that cab of the rig the once over. *Maybe she is regretting her brazen move last night,* he wondered. *Time will tell, and there are a few issues to be dealt with first before this goes any further. She is definitely not sixteen, I bet. And the way she flinched, even in her sleep, when I touched her could indicate she's been abused.* Cliff gave his head a little shake. There was such sadness in that pretty face when she was asleep. Bugger. *In a way, could have done with the distraction of sex on the trip.* He shrugged and sighed. *Hope I can help her with whatever is bothering her.*

Brenda turned fully towards Cliff and indicated the photo of the puppy. "Your dog?"

Cliff felt his heart give a jump at the softness of her voice and realised that she was extremely beautiful with the morning sun behind her giving a halo effect to her face. He took several glances before answering. "Yep, that was Rebel when he was little. He and I went everywhere together for a few years. But he was a half dingo, and some farmer shot him last year while he was off to the side of the road doing his business. He apologised after, but did help much."

Cliff's mouth took on a firm appearance, and his eyes hardened before he sighed and went on. "The farmer offered me one of his Border collie pups, and I may do that one day. At least they don't look like the dingo."

Brenda's eyes filled with tears as she quickly looked away out the window. *So he's known what it's like to lose something you love in a senseless act.* Her heart warmed a little more towards him. The stop was only a small fuel stop, but there was a small cafe across the street that Cliff said made excellent burgers and great coffee. Cliff's hand was strong as he held her hand while she alighted from the cab. Brenda used the facilities at the fuel stop while the truck was filled. As she returned from the toilets, she got her first real look at the decoration on the truck door. It was a decal of a striking cobra. She gave a small cry. *Not another snake man! And just as I was thinking he was okay,* she thought.

Cliff came over to her to take her for breakfast. He looked from her white face to the snake on the door. "It's okay, Lu. It's just a picture."

Brenda slapped his hand away as he went to put his arm round her shoulders and swung angrily towards him, tears filling her eyes "Did you put that there, and why?" Her voice trembled from all her inner turmoil.

Cliff was confused at her reactions and a little disappointed and sad for her at the same time. *She most surely has some major bad stuff in her history.* He stepped back from her and spoke slowly. "No, I didn't put that there, Lu. This is my uncle's truck. See? His name is on the door too—Peter Chaffey—and he liked the picture for no particular reason that I know of." He touched his chest. "I'm Cliff, and I'm doing this run for him, as he's on an oversees holiday for several months." He waved his hand at the café. "Come on, Lu. Let's go and eat, and I'll tell you all about my family."

Brenda followed, keeping out of his reach. Over breakfast, which was excellent, although he did show surprise that she didn't drink coffee, he told her about his family, finding that he really wanted her to know. He was twenty-two, and his mum had died last year, round the same time as his dog. Brenda nodded at this, as she knew about multiple losses. His dad had had a dairy farm before his mum had died, and they had made cheeses and yoghurt for most of the local cafes and restaurants, feeding their pigs on the rest of the milk. They sold the pigs to an abattoir in Rockhampton. His dad, Bill Wallace, named after a famous Scottish freedom fighter, found that too hard after that, and so sold all his milking cows except some for his own use and most of the breeding pigs before he went into buying young steers from stations and growing them up for the local butcher's shops. The property because of the recent dairy was set up with small paddocks and improved pastures. The transition to growing cattle was a simple one. Most of the dairy bales had to be pulled down, with only a single one left for their own milking cows.

His dad's place was called Lochlea, meaning lakes and meadows, taken from his Scottish heritage. The closest small town being Wilted. Cliff, who had left home after he'd finished school, had gone to work as a stock man in the top end, in a rough place called Iron Range, and then Mt. Norman in western Queensland. Then, he'd finally come home to help out. Cliff never took his eyes off Brenda's face and noted that she did seem to understand the concept of cattle work, as she gave small nods when she found a parallel to her life in his tale. Cliff told of Uncle Pete, his mum's brother, who has always had long-haul trucks, carting anything from peas to cow. Pete was a single man, so being on the road was no drawback for him. Cliff had driven for him a couple of times when needed, and that money he'd gotten for doing that came in handy. Besides, he was single too, so it was easy for him to get away. His dad was not a trucking man and refused to drive them.

Brenda's altitude softened towards Cliff as he talked. His voice was easy to listen to as well. She asked if had heard of Bemerside or High Low, which he had, but he'd never got close to that part of Queensland where Bemerside was. He had been to High Low with one his bosses to buy bulls and had met her granddad. He had worked in country very different to Bemerside which was mostly open, flat country, whereas where he had worked before had been rough, hilly, and heavily timbered country.

Her heart lifted when he said he was single, so she decided to go on with him and just wait and see. So far in, he'd been a gentleman, except when he'd lifted her into the truck. She was taken aback when he leaned towards her slightly, his eyes boring into hers, asking, "You're not sixteen, are you?" Her first reaction gave her away as her head gave an involuntary shake. He sighed and looked down at the table. "I guessed not." He reached over and touch her lightly on the arm. "Plenty of road ahead, so let's go. And you tell me about yourself when you're ready. We're restricted to daylight travel only for the next bit, so it will be an early night." And he left it at that.

Brenda made him open the door so she couldn't see the snake as she climbed up into the cab, and over the next few hours, with a little persuasion, she told Cliff everything, including her real name— except the bits about Sandra and the boys. It became easier to tell as he cut in with probing questions during the telling, though he was quiet when she told about Sam and how she and Jewel had trapped him into exposing himself. He asked why she'd not go back to Brisbane and be with her Mum, at which she showed some fire, saying that if her mum didn't want to acknowledge her, then she wouldn't acknowledge her mum. And before he could suggest she go back to her dad, she growled though gritted teeth that he had killed her dog in his fit of rage, and she couldn't forgive him, ever.

They made good time, arriving at the next stop, a small-but-tidy (and very popular) roadhouse surrounded by trucks and campers. It was way before dark, so they showered before getting their meal, and they ate at the outside tables, watching the sun go down. After they had finished, Cliff leaned across the table, looking straight into her eyes. "You're safe, Lu. We can both sleep in the bed at the back of the cab. It's pretty wide, so we'll fit okay. I'll not hurt you."

And so it was.

Brenda fell asleep in the soft bed, waking in the morning finding that she had moved over to Cliff's side, and he had his arms wrapped over her waist, his breath blowing softly on her ear. She felt safe, really safe.

NANCY AND DEXTER

Dexter

Brenda had been wrong with her thought that Dexter wouldn't care if she disappeared. She was right in thinking that Dexter wouldn't notice till morning though. He had returned to the room after midnight, very drunk, and fallen onto his bed before passing out. He was feeling sad and sorry for himself in the morning, and he showered and shaved before going over to Brenda's bed to give her a shake, flipping the top cover back so he could give her a tap on her head. He stood for a minute looking at the empty pillow, hardly breathing. A vice-like feeling gripped his heart. *Bloody hell,* he thought. *Not her, too. Maybe she has got up early and gone for a walk like she used to do with the dog.* He closed his eyes as the memory of how he had killed the dog filtered through his mind. *I really shouldn't have done that, but I was so angry, and possibly a little insane, at the time. How was I to know that Steve knew D2 was half dingo? I thought he would have insisted that the dog be destroyed, knowing how he felt about dingos.* All this ran through his head as he stood holding the bed cover, starting at the empty pillow.

Yep, that's it. She's gone for a walk. I've never given much thought to how all these events have effected Brenda, he thought has he dropped the bed cover and strode out of the room. *She cannot have gone too far.* His mind was racing as to where she might have gone. He rushed over to the roadhouse, but no luck there. He almost ran to the hotel end of town, but no one reported having seen her. Dexter sat on the seat outside the pub for a while, catching his thoughts as a truck revved up to head out in to the early morning road. A light-bulb moment hit Dexter as he sat there and stared at the trucks rumpling past on their way to goodness knows where. He rushed back to the roadhouse to find out if any trucks had left in the night, but he was disappointed as the night shift had gone home and pretty much all last night's trucks had left.

One driver volunteered that he had heard that many of the truckies had had a game of poker last night, and as these games were much enjoyed, he felt that only old fogies like him would have missed the game. He had gone to bed early so did not know if any truck had left during the night "We are close to NSW, where we can only drive 6:00 am. to 6:00 pm., and so I doubt if a truck heading south would have left, mate," he said. "It would have meant sitting at the border till 6:00 am. Most of us heading south prefer to stay here so we can get a decent breakfast," he concluded and shrugged. "The guys heading north would be your best bet, I reckon."

Dexter went back to his room and packed up, noting that Brenda must have just taken the small backpack. He was unsure if any or what of her clothes were missing. It did filter through his head that the new dress Gran Hay had made was missing. He drove to the police station and had to wait two long, agonising hours till it opened, seeing as the local policeman was away and the fill-in chap had to come from Ipswich. Dexter was right behind him as he unlocked the front door, almost yelling frantically in his ear, "My little girl has been abducted by a truck driver!" He was shaking in his distress. "Or someone has done her a mischief."

The copper, who was a man in his mid-fifties, sighed and wondered, *Why me?* as he unlocked the door and went about opening windows before sitting at his desk, indicating the chair opposite to Dexter, picking up his pen, and pulling his notebook out of the drawer—all before looking fully at Dexter. "Sir, please slow down. I can see you're upset, but take a breath, and tell me slowly about the situation. My name is Brian Newton." He held out his hand, which Dexter automatically took as he sat down.

Dexter rested his elbows on the desk and held his head for a moment, his thumbs rubbing his temples as he gathered his thoughts. He took a deep breath, trying to tell how he was sure Brenda had been taken away from him. He went slowly at first, describing Brenda as a little girl with bright, pale-blue eyes, longish fair hair, about five feet tall. "She is a good and sensible girl." His voice hardly kept up with his train of thought. Inside himself, he started feel the panic rise as it suddenly dawned on him that, over the past months, he hadn't given Brenda much thought or credit as to how she had coped with the events. He started to feel ashamed of his behaviour, and to his dismay, burst into tears.

Brian got up and let Dexter cry himself out while he made them a cup of coffee, thinking, *There is a bit of a story here, I think. That poor bugger looks and is acting guilty.* He returned to the desk, placing the coffee cups down gently so as not to spill any liquid on to the pristine desk top. Dexter shakily picked his cup up, causing some to spill onto the desk. Brian made a sound of annoyance and went and got a dishcloth to mop up the coffee and got a coaster for Dexter to place his cup on so it didn't make a ring on the desk. "Come on now, mate, get a hold of yourself. Let's hear your story." He felt within himself that this fella was acting very guilty, which in a way was true, as Dexter had only just realised how badly he had treated Brenda.

Dexter took a long, deep breath and related why they—he and Brenda—had been in the settlement, on their way back to Bemerside, where he worked. Dexter told most of the whole story since Sandra had died, leaving out the fact he'd killed the dog. He continued to hesitate often in the telling. Brian started to take notes at the start and stopped as the silent spaces in the retelling came more often. Brian felt sure that a lot of the story was a made-up yarn to cover for the guilty feelings Dexter had. When Dexter got to this morning and how he was sure she must have been taken because she was such a sensible and reliable girl, he went to say why. Brian realised he was going over stuff already said, and he raised his hand and stopped Dexter. Dexter sat, transfixed, his cheeks still wet with tears, his eyes red and his lips trembling.

Brian stood and indicated for Dexter to follow, which he did, and not until he found himself being directed into a cell did he come out of the shock he had gone into during the telling and the realisation of his guilt over being mean and uncaring to Brenda. He swung round to the policeman and resisted, who pushed him back inside the cell. Brian gripped his arm up behind his back, pushing him into the cell and quickly closing the door. "Take it easy, pal. I'll ring Bemerside and check on that bit of your yarn. Must say, though, it's not looking good right now." Dexter tried to ask about Brenda, who was possibly getting further and further away. It fell on deaf ears. *Shit,* he thought. *This bloke thinks I've hurt Brenda, and even worse.*

Brian had a few folks coming into the office, including a lad for a driving test, which he dealt with before he got round to contacting Bemerside. His call was answered by a cook, who said she and husband were minding the place, and said she was very new and didn't know many details about the events that Dexter had described, but had heard rumours. All the regular workers were away as well, attending a rodeo. She didn't know Dexter and said that the boss and family were away on a holiday too and had no contact number for them. But she was happy to pass on any message, as they called every couple of days. Did he have a number they could call? Brain relayed the number, saying to ring any time.

Brian left his number, then he told Dexter he would be spending the night in jail most likely, unless Steve Hasting called beforehand. Dexter was beside himself with guilt and worry, plus his hangover had given him a splitting headache and a thirst. Although he kept asking for water, it took Brian a while to get round to it. Every time he heard the phone ring, he would get up and stand hopefully at the barred gate of the cell. He agonised over whether to tell the Hays or Nancy, deciding against that, as Nancy was still very fragile. He felt he had got through to her that Sandra was really gone but was sure she couldn't take another hit.

Brain toddled off to the pub after the office closed and got them both a meal. Dexter ate hungrily and wondered if Brenda had eaten. Where was she? So many desperate thoughts twirled round in his head. He was surprised to wake as sunlight filtered into the cell. He sat up and rubbed his eyes before getting stiffly to his feet to call for the copper to escort him to the toilet. He found the cell unlocked and open. He almost ran into Brian returning from the dunny as he stepped out of his cell. "Go and wash up, mate," Brian said. "Then, come through to the office."

Dexter's head was spinning. *Steve must have rung. Has he found Brenda?* His muddled mind made him feel numb. Brian had a bacon-and-egg burger on the desk, which he had covered with a large towel, and a large cup of fresh coffee. Between mouthfuls of food and coffee, Brian told him Steve had confirmed his story, and he had contacted as many trucking companies that used the road as he could. However, some offices had been closed, plus there were a couple of independent truckers that were hard to contact. His advice to Dexter was to go back to Bemerside so he'd be contactable when any news came through. Brian assured Dexter that the grapevine would spread the word up and down the highway in no time. Meanwhile, Brian would further investigate strangers that had passed through. He had advised all the police stations north and south and they would keep an eye out for a young lass. He was sorry he couldn't offer any better news.

Dexter sat slumped in his chair, listening. He guessed that all was being done that could be done, and he should go home to Bemerside, as advised. He asked to ring Brisbane to tell the Hays, who could then work out if it was safe to tell Nancy. Brian apologised, offering his hand as Dexter left. Dexter left wondering what else he could have done. It was a long drive home.

Nancy

Every morning since coming to be at her parents' house, Nancy had sat at the sewing table with her mother, who took in mending and ironing to keep the home fires burning. Nancy was good at both, and, although her mind was very shattered, she was still able to help with these jobs. Her dad built wooden toys that he sold by word of mouth out of his garage attached to the side of the house, plus, he did timber repair work round the neighbourhood. The Hays were not well-off, but they had enough to get by. When the hens were laying well, they sold some eggs, and Gran Hay was renowned for her birthday cakes. The Hay house was always busy, but, in general, it was a happy house.

Before Dexter and Brenda's visit, Nancy had spent most of her time in her room. Gran (Anna) was extremely worried about her and was upset that they couldn't afford to get her into counselling. That was just too expensive. Their regular GP advised that they go on talking to her and telling her bits and pieces of news, and, fingers crossed, she would come back to herself soon. Nancy kept a very rigid schedule, showering early, wandering outside, calling for Sandra before sitting at the breakfast table, weeping silently as she ate her toast and jam, washing it down with really sweet tea.

Anna would then set her to ironing or mending, which she managed to stay at for no longer than two hours. She would accept a piece of cake for smoko before saying, "I'll wait for Sandra on the patio." There, she would sit till lunch, time after which Anna would suggest a lie down, as was their habit. Nancy would go to her room, but never lay down. Instead, she would unpack and repack all her drawers, muttering to herself. This went on till dinner time, when she would pick at her food and sometimes managed to help wash up. She was so inattentive, she broke a number of plate and cups. Sitting at a window, looking hopefully up and down the road, Nancy only spoke when address directly and never commented on any of the news Anna relayed to her.

During the visit from Dexter and Brenda, Dexter had yelled, and, taking hold of her shoulders, had shaken her gently in frustration over her lack of acceptance that Sandra was gone. That had shocked Nancy and had brought her back into some sort of focus. "Stop this, Bun! Stop this!" Dexter had his face close to hers, and the words had hissed through his teeth. Dexter had led her back to her room, and, taking her by her shoulder, had shaken her again—gently at first, and then quite hard. Nancy had tried to step back from him, looking wildly about the room, her eyes stopping on a photo of Sandra on the dresser. Her eyes had filled with tears. Dexter had noted what she was looking at and had reached out and put the photo face down. Nancy had given a tiny whimper as Dexter had pulled her in close, kissing her hair. "Sandra is gone, Bun." He'd pulled back so he could look into her sad eyes "Gone!" He spoke in a very rough voice.

Nancy had stood gazing at him with wide eyes for a full minute before lowering them to the floor. She'd given a huge sigh, then seemed to hold her breath. Dexter had stood still, holding her shoulder as she'd slowly released the air she'd had trapped in her lungs. In a trembling voice, she'd spoken quietly. "Truly gone? Truly?" Her eyes had questioned him, and when he'd nodded, she'd broken down into body-shaking sobs. Dexter had done nothing till she'd stopped sobbing, and then he'd taken her gently in his arms, swaying with her as if she were a child. He'd known she still had a long road back from her depression to full-functioning heath, but this was a start.

Dexter had become her whole world. She'd known Brenda was there, but it had been too hard somehow to acknowledge anyone other than Dexter. For the first time since Sandra's death, Dexter had held her and touched her. She'd fallen in love again, revelling in the smell of him and the pleasure of him touching her body with his rough, work-worn hands. Dexter had taken the lovemaking process slowly, letting her set the pace as they lay each night— sometimes silently, and other times talking about long-passed events. Eventually, the conversations came to the present time, where she wouldn't talk, but whispered, "I'm sorry to have been difficult." And, for the first time, she'd kissed him full on the mouth.

Dexter had held his breath as the kiss had become deeper and more passionate. He'd reached through the buttons on her nightgown and found her nipples erect. A moan had escaped his lips round the kiss. Nancy had twisted her body onto her back, taking his hands to her nipples before moving her hand to undo the string on his pyjama bottoms. A sense of urgency had overcome both of them as Nancy had frantically pulled Dexter on top of her, spreading her legs and raising her hips to meet him After a few frantic thrusts, it had been all over for Dexter, but as he could feel Nancy hadn't come, he'd continued the process as his penis had softened.

Following that event, the lovemaking continued every night and became more satisfying for both of them. Nancy had become like a young girl again, laughing and even offering to cook a couple of times. However, her whole focus was on Dexter. She knew who Brenda was, but to her, Brenda was a backdrop to her real world, which, at the time, was Dexter. As Dexter and Brenda were leaving, without thinking she'd leant down and given Brenda a wave and smile—the first time she had actually looked at her properly since they had arrived.

After they'd driven off, Nancy and Anna had headed inside to do some mending, where Nancy, with eyes downcast to the mending, spoke softy. "I'll miss him, Mum. I have two girls, don't I?" And then, a short break. "No, I only have one daughter now, don't I?" She'd raised her eyes to meet her mother's gaze across the table. Anna had nodded and hoped she would continue to talk about everything and anything. Not that day, but over the next few days, Nancy spoke more and more freely. Anna had let her talk and never asked questions about any past history unless asked.

When Dexter rung about Brenda being missing Anna told him that, in her opinion, Nancy shouldn't be told just now, in this crucial time in her recovery. She advised Dexter to stand to for a bit, in case Brenda was found or came back. Dexter agreed with her, as he felt he was very much to blame for Brenda getting abducted or running away.

LOVE

Cliff was surprised to find Lu—he now knew her name was Brenda, but he kind of liked Lu and had decided to keep calling her Lu—so close to him when he woke up, and to find her body so relaxed. She had been looking nervous about the sleeping arrangement, so he had put his back to her when they'd retired to the cab of the truck. She had flinched as he touched her, giving her a lift into the truck. She had curled herself up as far away from him as possible. He eased himself away from her and lay still, wondering how he was going to get out of the sleeping compartment, as he would need to climb over her, and he reckoned that that may alarm her. Fortunately, Brenda stretched, yawned, and sat up, glancing at him as she did so. He felt his heart do a flip at the flash of her eyes sliding over him. *Going to have to watch myself here*, he thought.

Cliff showed her where there was access to water on the side of the truck, so she could wash before they went over to have breakfast at the small roadhouse. Brenda was pleased she had had a wash first, as most of the people there, travellers and transport drivers and co-drivers, all looked like a very ragamuffin lot that hadn't had enough sleep. There did seem to be a number of women among the trucking people. *Must ask Cliffy about them when we get on the road,* she mused to herself, not realising she had already picked up on a bit of trucking jargon. She grinned at a couple of the women, which was not returned. She did feel as though she were being studied. Cliff didn't seem to be affected.

As they were cruising down the highway, Brenda asked Cliff about the women. He laughed and laughed, though she couldn't see anything funny and got quite cross and glared at him. Cliff caught the flash of her glare out of the corner of his eye and stopped laughing. "Well, Lu, guess you will be the cause for some gossip within the tight-knit trucking fraternity." He explained that some of them were drivers, some were wives, and some—he hesitated—were hitch-hikers who were often free with giving themselves over to paying for the trip with sex. Somehow, he didn't feel odd broaching the subject of sex with her, as she seems so much older her almost-fifteen years. Brenda blushed as she recalled her behaviour when she had first gotten into the truck and now realised what he must have been thinking about her. A brief flash of jealousy knifed through her, and she turned towards him with eyes open wide, asking how many such girls he had picked up along the road.

Cliff laughed again and explained that he had never got lucky enough to pick up a female hiker till her. He paused, flicking glances at her as she opened and closed her mouth several times but didn't find any words. He leaned over and patted her knee. "This truck may have seen some goings-on, as Pete is a bit of a ladies' man and seems to attract the ladies." He went on to talk about some of the odd bods he had picked up along the road, some obviously crooks, some very sad individuals, and some just getting around Australia in the cheapest way possible. One of the nicest, he said, had been a German chap hitching round Australia before returning to Germany to be conscripted into the army for two years. All young folk, male and female, were obliged to do so at the age of twenty-one in Germany. Once, on an outback Queensland run, he had found a chap almost dead from dehydration on the road, as he had run away from a rough employer. Another just into Victoria, where he had picked up a seemingly nice couple and took them all the way to Melbourne, later fining out that they were wanted for murder. The stories went on for the rest of the day, only interrupted by fuel and food stops.

When the stories had run out, Cliff handed her his collection of tapes so she could choose the music. She found it very comfortable listening to Cliff breaking in over to top of music humming, whistling, or singing some bits of the songs. Brenda marvelled the changing countryside. Granddad Willows's place, High Low, had been a mixture of black soil flats and lightly timbered country. Bemerside was mostly flat, open plains, the only trees along waterways or the ones planted near stock yards or the houses. This country seemed to be greener, and it had lots of tall trees where there was not obviously cleared ground. They went though some ranges where the trees towered way above them, almost obscuring the sun.

They stopped on the NSW/Victoria border so they could stand with a foot in each state holding hands and laughing. Brenda did a little dance. It had been so long since that she had felt so free. They stopped not long past the border crossing for the night, as Cliff said he wanted to get into Melbourne before dark the next day so as to be in the front of the queue to be unloaded. Brenda was far more relaxed going to bed the next day, and although they started off on separate sides of the bunk, they generally woke with their bodies close to each other. They both had similar thoughts— that they could get used to the situation. Brenda felt as though she had known him for a long time and slipped her hand into his as they went to breakfast. That surprised him, but he smiled to himself as he gave her fingers a slight squeeze, thinking, *Jeez, I wish she was older.*

They got in and out of the unloading dock with very little fuss. The whole exercise was a great fascination for Brenda, who had never been exposed to such goings-on. There was a lot of yelling and instruction being tossed about, forklifts zooming about, but somehow, everything got unloaded, and Cliff procured a return load to Brisbane. That meant that they had the rest of the day to themselves. Cliff locked up the truck, and they walked round the streets into the city. Brenda was totally amazed at the array of the outfits in the shop windows. Lots of colourful, flowery material and seemingly loose-fitting pants and blouses. Brenda dragged Cliff into one of shops and fingered the materials, marvelling at how soft they were. She checked their reflection out in the windows as they meandered along, and, seeing glimpses of them in the shop windows, didn't like her clothes, though Cliff looked tall and handsome. Brenda hardly came to his shoulder.

"I've a bit of money, and I'm going to get some new clothes," Brenda declared.

"How much money?" Cliff asked her. And when she got it out and counted out the few coins and notes, Cliff led her to a charity shop so she could get a lot more for her money. She got really excited and spent most of her mum's money. "Some of those outfits are totally inappropriate for wearing on the road," Cliff said laughingly, but quickly stopped after she glared at him.

He got pleasure watching her going through the racks, trying on some of the clothes. Brenda was on a real high. She was almost floating on air as she and Cliff continued on their walk. Brenda couldn't fathom why so many people where rushing about in the streets. They didn't look happy, either. *Who could be happy in the midst of all this rush,* she thought. When they got into the main part of the crowed city centre, she held Cliff's hand very tightly and was relieved when they passed through and made their way along the banks of the brown-looking water.

As they strolled, she noticed several groups of people sitting under trees or back against buildings across the road. Brenda asked what these people were waiting for, only to be told that they were homeless people and or drug addicts. The fact that there were people who lived on the street and had no real shelter shocked her to silence, but only for a short time. Words kept flooding out of her mouth almost faster than her mind could keep up with. She questioned Cliff about all the new sights she was seeing. Cliff answered the best that he could, although there were quite a few gaps in his knowledge in some things.

Brenda loved the last thing they did, which was catch a tram back close to where the truck was parked. They strolled back hand in hand, and, for the first time that day, Brenda was silent. She was wondering what was going to happen next. Would Cliff abandon her back along the road? He had kept saying he could take her to her mum if she wanted. She was adamant that she was not ready to get back to her old life just yet. She decided to say nothing and see how the next events panned out.

The next load was secured and paperwork filled out, and back on the road they went, settling into a steady routine. Cliff kept it to himself where they were going, just saying it was a bit out of the way. Sometimes they ate at roadhouses or cooked on an open fire as they stopped on the side of the road. Brenda impressed Cliff with her damper-making skill, and the fact that she seemed to enjoy the rustic adventure of camping. Most of the girls he had known preferred the finer methods of overnight stays. Even the girls he had met out on the stations wanted some sort of home comforts, even when camped out in the mustering team. Cliff eventually told her that the load was destined for Ironway, dangerously close to Bemerside, being the town closest to Bemerside. She had realised from the signs they'd passed that they were on the road to Ironway, so it was not a surprise. Brenda became more and more anxious as they got close to Ironway. *Be okay, so long as no one from the station is in town,* she thought. All went well as they got to the drop-off point and unloaded.

As Cliff disappeared into the office, the manager of the yard gave Brenda a local paper, saying, "It's a few days old, but it's all I have, love." Brenda sat with it on her knee for a time, her mind racing round and round in her head about where she was and how close she was to the one place, before the truck, which she now considered her home, that she had been happy. A lump stuck in her throat when she remembered D2 and how she had died.

At that thought, she straightened her shoulders and knew she was definitely not ready to face her dad just yet. Cliff would ask, she knew. Although he hadn't brought the subject up, he would have been waiting for the right time, she guessed. *There is no right time* she said angrily to herself. Cliff seemed to be taking a long time, so she picked up the paper. She sat very still, staring at the headline, "Local Girl Feared Abducted," and a photo of her taken last year. A lifetime ago from where she was now. She was wearing some of her new, bright colours, and paisley clothes with a bandanna tired round her head, and she had let her hair hang loose, and that morning had put on a little of her mum's lipstick and eye-shadow and really looked very little like the innocent girl in the photo. She stared at the word *abducted* and felt very afraid. Cliff could get into real trouble if they were discovered. She slid the paper under her bottom, vowing to get rid of it without Cliff seeing it.

Cliff walked very slowly back to the truck, wondering what Brenda was thinking. Would she want to go home or not? He found himself hoping she would stay with him. He climbed into the cab and settled himself in his seat before turning to look Brenda straight in the eye before speaking. "Well, Lu, what do you think?"

Brenda stared back at him, noting that his eyes and face looked a little sad. *He expects I'll want to go back to Bemerside.* She shook her head, and, taking a deep breath, said vehemently, "I'm not going back to that place, ever." She lifted her head defiantly. "Never, ever, and you cannot make me!"

Cliff felt a sense of relief run through his mind, and he grinned at the defiant girl in front of him. He felt his heart almost jump out of his chest. *Dear God, she is so beautiful. I love her. Please let me protect her from all the hurts that life is going to throw at her.* All these thoughts ran through his mind as he impulsively leaned over and kissed her lightly on the lips. That took all Brenda's defiance away, so she wriggled over and sat on his lap, burying her face in the front of his shirt. He smelled musty, she thought. She forgot the paper she had hidden under her bum. Cliff held her for a little while, his eyes taking in the headline and photo before taking a deep breath, untangling himself, and holding her away from him. "There is a tractor to be picked up at Bemerside to go to Brisbane."

It took a couple of moments before those words got through to Brenda. Her hands went to her white face. Her mouth opened and closed several times before one word squeaked out of her mouth. "Why?" She went back to her side of the cab and sat very quietly for what seemed like an age.

Cliff allowed her several minutes. "I saw the paper yesterday, Lu, and the chap back there told me about the girl being abducted. Apparently, all the trucks heading north were questioned last week. Now, they are looking at the trucks that were heading south from where you found me." He continued when there was no reply from Brenda. "I'm going to go to the police station here." Brenda swung round to look at him with wide eyes, but before she could say anything, he held up his hand and shook his head. "No, Lu, I'm not going to report you. Thought I might just tell him I never saw anyone, and that you're my girl coming back home for a visit. That okay with you?"

Brenda nodded. "I'm not going to get out of the truck." She repeated that again before adding, "I'll hide in the bed while you're at Bemerside." And she repeated that again as well.

Cliff nodded his agreement to that and wondered how he could get her to let her dad know she was okay. He reported to the police, who simply took down his details, got him to sign the statement, and that was that. The copper was not in the least interested in checking out Brenda and took Cliff's story at face value. Cliff doubted anyone would recognise Brenda with her new clothes and her hair out, unless they were very familiar with her. Cliff bought some comics, snacks, and drinks for Brenda to have while he loaded up at Bemerside.

Brenda was exhausted from all the tension, so she crawled into the bunk and slept all the way to Bemerside, waking only as she heard Dexter's voice telling Cliff where he could load up. She snuck a look out through the curtains and was shocked at her dad's appearance. He seemed to have aged ten years, and he hadn't shaved. His eyes were bloodshot and his clothes very dirty and rumpled. He had always been quite particular in keeping clean and tidy. She shut the curtains as Dexter gave the truck the once-over before asking Cliff if he had seen or heard of Brenda.

"No, sorry, mate," Cliff said over his shoulder as he climbed back into the truck. "Keep my ear open, though." He stuck his head into the bunk space and gave Brenda a hard look, to which she shook her head. Cliff sighed and started the truck.

Brenda peeked out as they drove to the loading ramp where Dexter was headed on the tractor. She saw Holly, as usual, sitting in front of her easel, and Albert over by the horse yard pushing a wheelbarrow of horse droppings towards the vegetable garden. Albert stopped, and Brenda felt his eyes touch her, even though he was at least a hundred yards away. Albert stood, with hands on his hips, watching the truck. Brenda was frozen, staring back at Albert. Eventually, Albert raised his hand and continued on towards the garden. Brenda heard the boys squabbling about who had won the race to the loading ramp. Everything was a competition to them. A woman came out of the store to watch the truck rumble past. *Must be the new Sam.* Brenda trembled as she remembered events not that long past. Steve came over and invited Cliff to have lunch with them, which he accepted.

He was hardly out of sight before, to Brenda's horror, the lads climbed into the cab of the truck. Brenda lay frozen, hardly breathing as they discussed the gears and switches in the cab. She knew it was only a matter of time before they would get to checking out the bunk area. As the lad's curiosity was almost done with all the gadgets in the cab, she heard Albert telling them to get down before the driver caught them, as they shouldn't be in there without permission. The lads climbed down, and Brenda heard Albert lightly tap the side of the truck. Brenda began to breathe again, still amazed that Albert had seen her from so far away. Deep down inside herself, she knew he wouldn't tell.

The lads were still circling the truck when Cliff returned, and they asked if they could ride to the front gate with him. Brenda was fuming when he said of course they could, and he went on to explain how everything worked and a lot of technical stuff about the truck's engine. One of them turned round to pull the curtain between the cab and the bunk. Cliff spoke sharply, saying for it to be left alone, and before that could be questioned, started to ask them about the stock that ran on Bemerside. He told them how his dad bought young steers to fatten for butcher shops. That kept their attention till they got to the gate, where they thanked Cliff and jumped down to let the truck through the gate, waving Cliff on his way. Brenda crawled back into the front, still trembling a little from the close encounter with Fred and Harry, and still a little cross with Cliff for allowing them to ride in the truck.

She was still angry. This was the first time Cliff had seen this side of her, and it surprised him. Cliff pulled over to the side of the road and turned towards her, meeting her anger front on. As he went to open his mouth, Brenda reached out to slap him. He just caught her hand in time, her strength also surprising him. "Well, well, Lu," he said with a slight grin on his face.

"Bugger you. My name is Brenda!" she yelled back at him, tears coming unbidden to her eyes. Her voice cracked. Suddenly, all her anger faded away, and she suddenly went limp. Cliff leaned over the console, and, sliding his arm round her shoulders, held her gently to his chest. She looked up at him, her bottom lip trembling. She looked so forlorn, it broke his heart, and he gently kissed her hair. He ran his thumb across her cheeks to clear the tears that had gathered there. Brenda looked up at him with wide eyes that were no longer angry, but full of questions. She turned her body so that she faced him and smiled weakly. *Steady lad*, he thought. *She is too young. Way, way too young to get involved with that way.* They both felt some reaction to the intimacy of their bodies pressing against each other. He so wanted to kiss her properly, and not stop. He noted her cheeks were very flushed. Cliff leaned down and kissed her hair very gently before sitting back and looking at her sadly. "Kissing is fine, but you're way too young."

"Don't you want to mate with me?" Brenda grinned at him, knowing that, full well, his body certainly did.

Cliff was both surprised and shocked by the question and took a while to answer, thinking of what his reply should be and how to put it into words. Eventually, he put his fingers under her chin so she couldn't look away and tried to explain that he most certainly did want to do that to her, however, she was way too young. And if she was still about when she turned sixteen, that activity could be talked about. He asked her bluntly if she had ever done such a thing, to which she shook her head, but she knew all about mating from watching animals.

That caused him to blink rapidly, and he felt relief. *She truly is innocent. Thank God for that, and it's a good thing it was me and not uncle Pete in the truck. Doubt he would have treated her decently.* He sat silence for a time. "Yes, Brenda." He was pleased with himself he had gotten her name right. "That happens, but you and I will give your cheeks and hair kisses until you're of age, and then only if you want to. Is that understood?"

Brenda pressed herself to him and said that was okay as she walked her fingers up his arm to his chin and across and up to the corner of his mouth, flicking her finger across his lips. Cliff caught hold of her hand, putting it back firmly on her lap before telling her she would need to talk to her mum about that, or some other woman. Brenda sighed and slid over to her side, not saying anything, as she doubted that her mum would tell her anything—or, in fact, even care, the way she was now. *Might be able to talk in Gran Hay, maybe.*

Before they set off again, Cliff said he had to check the load, which Brenda thought odd as they had only just loaded it. Brenda was quiet as they continued on their way to Brisbane. She considered all that had taken place that day, the sad sight of her dad, the close encounter with Harry and Fred, to the gentle lovemaking. That was the most confusing bit. It had all felt so good, so really good. She glanced at Cliff, who was concentrating on driving. His profile looked so strong and handsome. Better than Fred or Harry, that was for sure. *I love his eyes,* she thought, and then thought about what a real kiss might be like. She felt stirrings in her tummy, and her heart was fluttering strangely. Cliff noticed the shudder and assumed she was crying, so he reached over and gave her a pat on her back. The pat was like an electric current running through her body, as it coincided with the warmest feeling. It took her breath away briefly, and afterwards, a feeling of fulfilment engulfed her, and she slept for a while.

She woke as she felt the truck come to a stop. Looking out the window, she noticed they were at a truckies' overnight rest stop that had showers and toilets. A few trucks were already parked up for the night, and the drivers had a fire going, standing round swapping yarns and drinking beer cans or rum out of pannikins. She looked at Cliff, who sat staring ahead, gripping the steering wheel. He sighed, and, without looking at her, he flicked a wave towards the other drivers "Any of them would most likely take you on board if all you're looking for is sex," he said before looking at her. "I like and respect you too much to take advantage of you like that, baby." His face was very sad looking and serious.

Brenda blushed and stared back at him for a long time. Thoughts whirled round in her mind. *Maybe he doesn't like me and just wants me to get out of the truck for good. No, no, that is not right,* she said to herself. *He must like me to be so nice to me back there.* She sighed. *I think that this must be what love is like, and I feel so comfortable when I'm with him.* Finally, Brenda spoke strongly and clearly. "I want to stay with you! I think I l—"

Cliff put up his hand to stop her, as he was sure he knew what the next word was going to be, and it was not the time or place for that word yet, even though he felt the same way. They sat in the truck discussing who they would say she was and how she came to be in the truck. Brenda suggested that they stick to Lu as her name, so that they couldn't associate her with the missing-person story in the paper. Cliff came up with that she was his girl, so they wouldn't make passes at her. Besides, she looked older than she was with some make-up on. Brenda agreed to that, and, as they both slept in the truck, the drivers would accept that scenario. "Mind you," Cliff told her, "some of the comments may be a little crude, so stay close to my side."

They strolled over to the fire, hand in hand, being watched all the way by curious looks. The story of her being Cliff's girl was accepted, and Brenda was flattered that they kept their language fairly clean while she was there at the fire. Several of the drivers who knew Cliff expressed surprise that he had sprung his girl on them, as they didn't know he had a girl hidden away. Stopping on the road for one more night alone was the coincidence. One of them offered Cliff and Brenda a sausage sandwich that had been cooked on the fire. She was surprised to see quite a number of women in the group and found some were wives and girlfriends, some drove their own trucks, and a couple were hitch-hikers.

After they had eaten, a couple of the drivers pulled out a pack of cards, asking anyone for a game of poker. Cliff looked down questioningly at Brenda before he replied. He realised her eyes were drooping and her body, leaning into him, was going soft. He nodded yes to the game, and, putting his arm round Brenda's shoulders, led her back to the truck. Giving her a hug and light kiss on the top of her head, he lifted her into the truck before getting his bottle of rum from the truck's tool box behind the cab and returning to join the game. Brenda fell into a deep sleep. She was exhausted from the day's events. Cliff woke her as he crawled across her body to his side of the bed. He smelled strongly of rum. Brenda snapped at him to roll away from her so he didn't breathe the fumes onto her.

He ended up flat on his back, snoring loudly to be woken by a banging on the truck doors. "Mate, wake up! Your girl is screaming her head off out here! Come on!" Two drivers were yelling loudly through the open window. "We tried to talk to her, but she only screamed louder," they said.

He struggled out of the truck to the sound of Brenda screaming, "What is that? Who is it?" as she stared out into the night. Following her line of sight, Cliff could see the bobbing white light she was transfixed on. "It's a spirit, a lost spirit! Why is it coming for me? Is it Sandra?" The final comment was a wild screech as she sank to the ground, her head between her knees.

Cliff thanked the guys. "She has never seen the Min-Min before," he explained, and he ran over to her, lifting her in his arms, where she burrowed her face into his shoulder. She was shaking all over, and he could feel her heart beating a tattoo in her chest. When they got back to the truck, Brenda lifted her head for a peek over his shoulder as he opened the door, but the light was nowhere to be seen. "Albert told me that the light is a lost spirit. Maybe it's Sandra."

Cliff looked at her tea- streaked face, his heart breaking at the amount of terror shown there. He explained that, yes, that is what the black fellas might think. However, the lights were floating chemicals released from the earth, blown about by the movement of the air. She clung to him as that idea was processed. She nodded and leaned back from him and apologised for her behaviour. She had got out to go to the toilet, and when she had come out, *it* had been there and seemed to be following her when she was returning to the truck. "Sorry," she said again. Leaning back further, she said, "You stink." She wrinkled her nose at him.

Cliff left her on the seat of the truck, grabbing his toiletry bag and towel, and went off to have a shower, returning after cleaning his teeth to find her still sitting in the seat. She leaned towards him and sniffed. "Still sink of rum." She shook her finger at him as they crawled into the bunk. "You turn over so I cannot smell your breath, please," she whispered before rolling away from him.

Somehow in the night, they came together, waking close together, backs touching. *Guess rum is a no-go, then,* he mused as he awoke. *But that will be a small price to pay for this girl.* He gave her bum a pat, rousing her to face the next day. *Wonder what Dad will make of her and how much should he tell him.* Cliff sighed to himself. *Got to get a few things sorted out before we get there.* He liked the thought of the *we* bit and felt happy.

DEXTER AND NANCY

Dexter had tried really hard to get back to some sort of normality when he returned to work. He still felt very resentful about his treatment at the police station. Steve didn't ask about Brenda. He assumed she had stayed behind with her mum, and Dexter left it at that. He was very pleased that he didn't have to say where she was or that he had lost her. Steve did question him as to why the police had wanted to confirmation that he was who he said he was. Dexter made up a story which seemed to satisfy Steve. This all worked till some journalist from the local paper heard about truckies being questioned about Brenda going missing. He came out and interviewed Dexter, getting permission to print the story, advising it may assist in helping find her. Dexter let the Hays know so they could keep the paper away from Nancy.

The new store person was a very straight-laced woman, Laura Le. She would only allow him one bottle of rum a week. She would sniff and look down her nose very disapprovingly when she gave it to him. "Drink is nectar of the devil," she would say. It made Dexter quite angry inside, so he stopped going to the store for it at all. He would get a lift into town most weekends, drink till he fell down, and bring a few bottles back with him. He spent most of his money on rum, so had little left over to send to Nancy. The odd weekends he couldn't get into town he found very difficult, as he couldn't settle into anything like reading or fishing, things he had usually found easy and relaxing.

As the mustering team were in full swing, and they had a cook, Dexter was allowed to eat with them. He was pleased with that, as he found it difficult to be in the unit—besides, Laura had been moved in next to him. She was very nosey. He had once found her in his unit poking about a couple of times, and she asked endless questions about his family—even some about Sandra and Sam. Her eyes would glisten with excitement when she broached that subject. Dexter request that he move over to beside Albert to get away from her, even though it was where Sam had lived and possibly had Sandra in there, as well. Holly and the boys had scrubbed the place and repainted it, so nothing of Sam was evident any more, so he could cope with it as long as he went to bed only when he was really tired. Not long after he had moved over to beside Albert, Albert surprised him by talking about Brenda as though he had seen her recently. Albert assured him she was not in danger.

Packing up the things in the other unit became a huge chore. He packed everyone's items separately and put the girls' things into the store and sent Nancy's things to her. He was surprised to receive a letter from Nancy requesting that he send Sandra's thing to her so she could go through them and work out which ones to keep for Brenda. The letter gave him some hope and despair at the same time, and he came to the conclusion that he must tell her about Brenda's disappearance. He decided to get her mum to tell her, when she could find the right moment, and sent both the girls' things to Nancy with a covering letter about how he was and left it at that. He knew it was not the right thing to do, but it was all he could manage at that time. Anyway, that is what he told himself. He would go to see Nancy when the muster had finished.

Nancy was surprised to get both the boxes, which gave Gran Hay the opportunity to tell her Brenda had gone missing. Nancy went very quiet for several days after that, and her mum and dad were afraid that she would slip back into her confused state. However, she announced at the table one morning that she thought that they should put a missing person advertisement in several papers and put flyers out on poles about town. She seemed to be quite motivated by the ideas and got very busy planning the adverts and flyers. She put the flyers on poles all over Brisbane. Eventually, they were washed off the posts and lay unread in gutters.

LOCHLEA

Cliff and Brenda stopped just a little way from Lochlea, as it was late, and they really were not expected by his dad, and they didn't want to wake him. Secretly, Cliff wanted to have Brenda to himself for one last day. He still had to decide how to explain her to his dad. Telling Bill that they had camped just up the road would tell him that they had been sleeping together, at least. Brenda took a long time to put some make-up on so she looked sixteen. Cliff knew that his dad would work out pretty quickly that she was younger.

Bill heard the truck coming up the road, and, after putting the kettle on the stove, went out to greet Cliff. He was stunned to see a slight young woman alight from the truck to open the gate into the yard. He waved a greeting as Cliff swung down, and, putting his arm round Brenda's shoulder, walked over to meet Bill. After the introductions and usual questions about how the trip had gone, they all moved inside to have bacon and eggs for breakfast. Brenda was very quiet and sat very close to Cliff. To Bill, it seemed she was afraid not to be touching him.

After several attempts at conversation with Brenda, Bill continued to tell Cliff about stuff that had happened about the place and events that were being organised in the district. It seemed as though busy times were ahead, both home and social. One event was the local show the next weekend, where Bill had some steers entered as well as his rooster. Brenda was fascinated that he also had made lime jam to put in the show as well.

After a time, Brenda left the men to it and wandered outside. The property was very tidy, though most of the old flower beds were weedy or bare. Some large shade trees grew towards the back of the house, with a couple near the chook house and in the yards situated behind a large shed. The vegetable patch was flourishing, though. It was enclosed by a high, wire-netting fence. Brenda guessed that was to keep out the hens she saw scratching round the house and sheds. Several cackles came from what appeared, at first glance, to be a cubby house. She found out later that it had indeed been a cubby house first, before being converted to house the laying boxes for the hens. She heard a rooster crowing close to the house and walked round the side to find a huge, speckled rooster in a small cage, close to what was the laundry, a small building away from the house. There was no evidence of dogs, but a cat darted out of laundry when she peeked inside. As she progressed round the yard, a flock of geese confronted her, hissing and running at her, their necks outstretched. When she stood her ground, they simply fluffed their feathers, but continued to graze as though nothing had ever bothered them.

Bill took the opportunity to question Cliff about Brenda when she left the room. "Who is she? How? When, son?" He looked squarely at Cliff, shrugged, and raised his hands, palms upwards, in a questioning manner.

Cliff decided that he may as well come somewhat clean and told the story she had first presented him with, that she had run away from an abusive step-dad and that she was not sixteen yet. He didn't add in all the problems she had had at Bemerside. Yes, he explained that they had slept together, but to this point, hadn't engaged in sex. Bill sat silently for a time before saying, "Well, you should sleep in mine and your mum's room with the big bed, and I trust you to do the right thing. I'll set up in the room your mum used to use as her sewing room, as there is a bed in there. Not keen to go into yours and Pete's room. Will sort the cupboards and clothes later."

Brenda returned to the room to hear the bit about the sleeping arrangements and sighed, assuming that Cliff hadn't dobbed her in.

Brenda started to clean up the breakfast things before Bill smilingly told her to get herself unpacked and make use of the laundry. Cliff informed her that he had indeed told some of her story to his dad, including her age, while they were getting their things from the truck. She became very cross with him and was just a little embarrassed that Bill knew some of her story, even if it was the fictitious one. Still, she was pleased she was still sleeping in the same bed with Cliff. She had gotten used to having him close to her at night.

Sorting out the room and washing took Brenda up to lunchtime. Bill and Cliff had gone off to look at the steers for the show, so she had the place to herself. The cat even allowed her to pet it while she was washing. It kind of made her remember Dinky, though this cat was very different in colouring. It was very ginger with white socks, whereas Dinky had been black. Still, Brenda was happy to hear the rumbling of purring while she petted it. *If you do not have a name yet, I'll call you D3,* she thought.

Over lunch, Brenda forgot she was cross with Cliff and not taking to him, and chatted away, asking the name of the cat and the rooster. She found out the rooster was a Plymouth Rock type of fowl, and indeed was called His Royal Duke. Bill said he like chickens that were speckled and had started with Barnevelder, Belgian d'Uccle, Sussex, Plymouth Rock, and Wyandotte hens, but kept rotated roosters of these different breeds same to keep the chicks to be sold interesting. He bought a new rooster every six or seven years and always took them to the local show. The crossbred chickens he sold to friends and neighbours. The hens were good layers, and he was considering taking some eggs into the show as well. Brenda was fascinated when she discovered that His Royal Duke needed to be groomed. Bill offered to teach her. Brenda tried some of Bill's lime jam as well, and found it sweet and just a little tart at the same time.

Cliff watched Brenda as she and Bill talked and loved the way her eyes shone with so much interest. Her eagerness to hear about new things was not lost on Bill, either, who thought, *This lass is an empty sponge, and I'll have to see where she is with her education.*

Brenda almost wriggled with delight when she found out the cat did not have a real name and was simply referred to as *the cat*. "Well," she said with glee, "I'm going to call him D3, or just Three for short." The men nodded agreement and didn't stop her when she cleared away the dishes and leftover food. Bill glanced at Cliff and felt a shock, as he had such a look of adoration on his face as he watched Brenda move about the kitchen. *So that's the way it is,* he thought.

Over the next week, Brenda filled her days with doing all the laundry, housework, gathering eggs, helping to milk the cows, learning the animal feeding routines, and getting to know His Royal Duke. She discovered one of the hens was sitting on eight eggs. Bill told her they should hatch out before the show, so they could take them in and sell them. "If you keep an eye on them, I'll let you keep the money," Bill told her. She was so excited about that. She checked the hen and egg at least three times a day, bolting out of bed early to check them. Sometimes, she even beat Bill out of bed. She helped hose the pen of steers off every day so their coats looked good.

Bill had brought them into the yards for the last couple of weeks' preparations. They would be judged on calmness, condition, and evenness of markings before being transported to the abattoir, where the carcasses would be judged for evenness of fat distribution. After that, steaks from each one would be cooked and judged for flavour and tenderness. All the scores were added together, and the winner declared at a formal dinner held on the last day of the show. This event was hotly contested between the surrounding properties. Bill had never won, but he was hopeful this year. He was a little different from most of his neighbours, as he didn't actually breed his steers, but still felt proud of the way they looked. If he won, several butcher shops may want to buy his steers for their shops. This was an easier and more profitable way to sell them.

Cliff was busy with the truck, carting local cattle for the show-cattle sale and some of the steers to be shown. He used a smaller truck for this. He asked Brenda if she wanted to go with him, but she declined, as she was on egg watch. This gave Bill the chance to talk to her about her education. It took quite a bit of prodding before she answered his questions. He discovered she was only a few months off finishing her year ten-school year, as she had started formal school when she was only four years old. When he asked if she wanted to finish, she shrugged and didn't reply. She sat for a time with her eyes downcast before getting up and walking slowly outside.

Thinking about school brought back all her memories of Sandra and her mum's illness. She bit her lip and pushed her fists into the eyes to stop the tears erupting from them. She walked over to where the hen was sitting firmly on the eggs. The hen fluffed up her feathers and made cross sounds when Brenda bent down to pat her. Brenda sighed and leaned on the shed door post, letting her gaze take in the panoramic views without really seeing them for several minutes. She shook her head and thought, *It has been a while since someone has even cared what I do with myself.* And as disturbing as it was, it was still comforting, in a way.

Straightening herself, she went back to where Bill was preparing the lunch basket for the next day. She sat down heavily, saying, "Yes, it would be a good idea to finish the year off. I'll do something about getting the required papers. Be important too, as I want to become a nurse and look after babies."

Bill didn't push the issue, just nodded and got her to help with gathering to required items for the basket.

THE SHOW

Brenda thought the town, Wilted, a nice enough place. Bill took her for a tour. The streets were all tree-lined and tidy. The main shopping took up several blocks in a square, behind which were workshops and a place for curing hides from the local and other abattoirs situated just out of town. Another shed made shoes and other leather-related products. It had a school, hospital, and police station, plus three pubs and a motel. There was a swimming pool close to the school which had many people playing, swimming, and just lying about the edge of the water. A large building on the other side of the shops, Bill told her, was the council offices and workshop. "Hopefully, we'll get the railway here soon."

As he finished his tour, he stopped to look over the River Grey, which brought fishermen to town as well. He pointed out a group of demountable buildings on the edge of town, telling her they were a mining mob investigating a deposit of coal located near the town. He looked at Brenda, asking if she liked fishing, and as she nodded, he put his arm round her shoulders saying, 'This is a nice town, and folks are friendly. When you're a nurse, you can help set up a ward for the local ladies to have their babies closer to home and not have to go away to have them."

Off they went to the show grounds to watch the camp draft and horse sports, followed by a mini rodeo. "Today is for the cattle breeders and children," Bill told her. "Plus, the judging of the pens of steers, after which the pens will be sold off, but—and it's a bog—no one will know which pen of steers has been judged the best." After a pause, he went on to say, "Tomorrow is for the sheep breeders and dog show."

Brenda had never seen anything like it and was captivated by how brave the children were, wheeling their mounts through obstacles. *I could never do that in a million years,* she thought. Bill came and sat with her as the riders did battle, guiding a beast round the camp draft course, explaining how the animal had to be directed through a figure of eight, plus taken out and put through a gate. They were racing at such speed that Brenda had her heart in her mouth for most of the event. The rodeo commenced with smaller children aboard sheep, clinging tightly to the animal's woolly back. The crowd, including Brenda, cheering the young kids on. She clapped so hard her hands got sore. Bill watched the range of emotions sweep across her face and smiled at her absolute enjoyment as he came to check on her periodically.

As the adult section of the rodeo commenced, Brenda realised that the crowd had grown significantly, and she suddenly felt very out of place and just a little frightened. As the riders and horses, steers, and finally bulls did battle, Brenda sat quietly, wishing Bill would come back, as she found these events disturbing and somehow cruel. It was Cliff who came, after the final bull had been bucked, to find her sitting with her arms wrapped tightly round herself, eyes filled with unspilled tears. She stood up stiffly and silently and walked without saying a word to where Bill awaited them to go to the sale of the pens of steers.

No one had taken a lot of notice of Brenda and didn't connect her with Cliff, who was working in the yards She was darting about, checking out everything between the ring events so much that she was hardly beside Bill at all, either. Once, when she was looking at a different pen of steers, she heard two girls talking about Cliff. How handsome he was, how they both wanted to get to dance with him at dance following the final dinner. Brenda felt a stab of jealousy go through her and wanted to yell at them that they had no chance any more, as he was hers now. Cliff had asked her to go with him and Bill to the presentation dinner and dance. She had been a little reluctant to go with them, but after hearing the girls, decided she just had to go, if only to show those girls they were too late. Brenda and Cliff had discussed his girlfriends, of course, while on the road, and he had told her he had never had what he called a *real* girlfriend.

The weather that day had been prefect, sunny with a slight breeze, and just cool enough at night to require a light jacket when the trio headed into the show sale with the pen of steers. Bill had held off taking the steers in till the last minute so their coats wouldn't be very dusty. Brenda thought they looked very nice, all an even red colour and even height. Not a scrap of white on them anywhere. There were all types of breeds being presented to be judged. Brenda looked them over, and, feeling herself relax again, leaned over and whispered to Bill, "Yours are the best."

The judging had been done, but any announcements and prizes were to be revealed at the dinner. The cattle sale took up the evening, and it was a very tired girl who watched on. A local butcher bought Bill's steers, declaring he would be able to promote that he would have the winning beef in his shop the next week, as he was sure the steers would win. Bill bought some of the younger cattle on offer, so Cliff loaded them onto the truck, and he and Brenda took them home. Brenda was anxious to get back, as the chicks hadn't yet hatched. This would be the first time they had really been alone since they had arrived at Lochlea, as Bill was staying in town.

When Cliff and Brenda got back to Lochlea with the pen of steers Bill had bought, Brenda raced over to what she called *her* eggs, while Cliff was settling the steers into their pen and giving them some hay. He had told Brenda they would be kept in the yard till after the show, when they would bring in some other stock before taking them out to the paddock. Brenda hadn't emerged from the shed where the eggs were, so he wandered quietly over and stood watching Brenda, her bottom lip tucked in behind her top teeth, painstakingly peeling shell off the chicks. She left the bit round the chick's bum to come off on its own. He felt as though his heart were going to burst with the immense feelings going through him. She was so intent on her task, she didn't see him. A slight groan escaped him, causing Brenda to look up from her task and gave him the most beautiful smile "Look, got all of them out okay. And only just in time too. I think the egg shells must be very hard, as they were all having trouble."

She came over to stand beside him to watch the hen tucking the chicks under her. Brenda wrapped her arms round Cliff's waist and looked up into his face. Without thinking, he bent down and kissed her, a brief brush of lips, as he wrapped his arms round her and hugged her, resting his head on top of hers. Eventually, Cliff lifted his head, and, cradling her head into his shoulder, said to himself over and over, *Hell, she is only fifteen.* They stood like that for some time as their emotions subsided. He realised she was shaking. It took a while to realise she was laughing. He stepped back, holding her at arm's length as she looked up at him, eyebrows raised and eyes twinkling.

"Very nice, that hug?" She grinned, and he had to nod and join in her laughing as they walked back the house. She glanced up at him. "I'll come to the dinner thing, I think, but will need to get a new outfit." She dug him in the ribs. "Can we go in a bit early tomorrow, so I'll have time to look for something?" After a hesitation, she said, "I'll pay you back." And she stepped back from him, looking him square in the eyes, raised eyebrows.

He gathered her back into his arms, giving her a tight squeeze, and, sighing, said, "What am I to do with you, you little minx? Come on, girl, let's eat. We'll have an early get up and a big day tomorrow."

They both bounded out of bed before sun up, breakfasting on toast and jam. They fed up the animals and got Duke into his travelling box. He looked magnificent as he crowed loudly and gave his wings a little flap. Brenda went off with a carton to gather up her chicks while Cliff secured Duke in the back of the truck, covering his box with a light sheet to keep out any dust. He heard a sharp scream coming from the shed and raced towards the sound. He found Brenda backing slowly out of the shed, her face deathly white and her wide eyes staring into the shed. He looked over her head and saw the huge snake laying near the nest, the hen on her side, kicking feebly, beside it. It had a chick halfway down its throat. Several lumps along its body indicated that it had had quite a feast. Grabbing a shovel from the tools leaning against the wall, he strode past Brenda and bashed the snake several times on its head, then, gathering it up, came back past Brenda, who was still backing away, and tossed it into the pit they used as an incinerator.

By the time he had gotten back to Brenda, she had reached the truck, and she was just standing there, silent tears running down her cheeks. He gave her a tight hug and helped her into the truck. He could not find words of comfort for her, and he felt so sorry for her. He reached over and gave her hand a squeeze several times on the short trip to the show ground. Bill was waiting for them at the gate to take Duke in for his judging. Cliff jumped out, quickly whispering to Brenda to stay put. He told Bill what had happened to the chicks, and Bill shook his head and expressed how terrible that must have been for her. Cliff said they were going into get her an outfit for the dinner and dance and would catch up with him later at the dog trials. Brenda refused to go shopping, so they went up to the local lookout and generally known lover's lane. He knew it would be quiet there. They sat close together. Cliff had his arm round her, holding her gently, and he felt the stiffness slowly go out of her. He kissed the top of her head, and, without having said any words, they returned to the show.

Brenda found all the noise of sideshow alley a little daunting and shuddered at the thought of the rides. Cliff had a go at the shooting galley and won a huge teddy bear that brought a smile to her face at last. She had a try at the knock 'em downs and managed to win a tiny silver horse. Try as he might, Cliff couldn't get her to go on any of the spinning rides, but did get her into the Ferris wheel, and, after a few circuits, she relaxed and enjoyed the views even though she never let go of his hand. After that, they still had some time before the dog trials, so they walked through the pavilion with the flowers and conserves. Bill had won first prize for his jam. Brenda spent some time looking at the flowers and asked lots of questions about how hard they were to grow and could she grow some at home. Cliff was happy that she hadn't been completely turned off by the snake incident.

They watched some wood chopping events before making their way to where Bill was sitting in a small stand, watching the dogs being put through their paces. The first event was a high jump for the dogs, where they had to leap over a structure to the back of a ute. Brenda even managed a laugh at some of the failed attempts. This was followed by a dog race across the ring. Brenda was amazed that some really little dogs were very competitive against the bigger breeds. The dogs held Brenda's attention, so she didn't notice Bill and Cliff climb down and have a short conversation before Bill left. Cliff bought Brenda her first ever soft drink and was amused as she wrinkled her nose, saying it was way too sweet. There was a break in the trials while the obstacles were cleared away and other equipment brought in. This was an array of jumps, tubes, and sticks that the dogs had to negotiate with minimal encouragement from their owners. She turned to Cliff, her eyes shining. "My D2 would have been good at that stuff."

She sighed and put her head on his shoulder. As she did so, she saw the girls who she had heard at the sale yards looking at them, so she reached up and gave Cliff a kiss on his cheek, and he, in turn, kissed the top of her head. The girls turned away. The next dog event was dogs working several sheep through a course and eventually putting them in a small yard. Brenda was amazed at how the dogs responded to whistles not words. She was amused as some of the sheep would stamp their feet at the dogs, and some would simply go in different directions. When there was a break in the proceedings, she went to check out the pens of sheep being judged, and she was not impressed with them and didn't like the smell of them. *Cows are much nicer,* she thought.

She had almost forgotten the early morning event till they went back to meet Bill at the poultry pavilion. Duke had won his section and been named reserve champion of the show, beaten of all breeds by a tiny little bantam rooster. *Very colourful,* Brenda thought, *but nowhere as handsome as Duke.* Brenda sat quietly on the way home. The events of the day had left her very tired, and she leaned into Cliff, who held her to his side. She went straight into the house, not waiting to see Duke get let out back to his hens. Bill took the travel box back to the shed and discovered one chick had survived and was sitting beside its dead mother's body. He took the dead body of the hen to the incinerator, gathered the chick up, and took it up to Brenda. The sight of the chick brought tears to her eyes. She reached out, taking the small creature in her hands, and looked up fearfully. "Do I have to sell it?"

Bill shook his head. "No, girlie. Well. if it is a rooster, maybe then. But let's hope this is a little hen. Come on. Let's make the little mite a false mother hen, as they must be kept warm."

He showed her how to cut up old clothes into strips and hang them through the lid of a shoebox for the chick to use as its night bed. They lined the bottom of the shoebox with old newspaper and gave it some water and Uncle Toby's Oats to peck at. Brenda sat watching it for several minutes, then, rousing herself, asked what Bill wanted her to do for dinner. "Only us tonight, girl, as Cliff is carting cattle for the rodeo and camp draft tomorrow. Should take him most of the night, so he will sleep in the truck in town. So we'll just have a sandwich." And he added, "We can take the chick with us tomorrow in Duke's travel box, which we'll be able to put in the poultry pavilion."

Brenda smiled her thanks and sat watching the chick as Bill got on and made the sandwiches, looking up only as Cliff came in to get his dinner before heading off. He was carrying a shopping bag that he handed to Brenda, telling her it was for her. She pulled out a long, black skirt and colourful blouse made of the softest material, and at the bottom of the bag was a pair of sparkling sandals that had high heels. She was overwhelmed and jumped up, throwing her arms round Cliff's neck. She planted a kiss on his mouth before running off to try on the clothes. Bill watched the kiss and suddenly wished he had given her the clothes, almost. He sighed and grinned as Cliff looked at him, blushing from the show of emotion. Brenda floated back to the kitchen to show off her finery. Both the men said, "Just beautiful" at the same time. They all laughed. "Might need help walking till I get the hang of these shoes," Brenda said laughingly.

Brenda felt a bit lonely in bed by herself that night and was sure that she wouldn't sleep a wink. However, Bill had to bang on her door to get her up the next morning. The chick, D4, cheeped at her as she let it out onto the grass near the laundry before scooping her (it just had to be a hen) and putting her in the prepared carry box, where the chick pecked happily at the dish of food. Brenda raced off to feed the rest of the animals while Bill milked the cow and fed the new steers. They packed a lunch and put all their clothes and Cliff's suit into a suitcase, got D4, and headed into town.

Brenda said hi to Cliff, depositing D4 in the poultry pavilion before finding a seat in a stand to watch the ring events. There was so much going on, jumps being set up on the far side, so she went over there, as it looked pretty exciting. Jumps had been set up, and Brenda watched them for some time, admiring the horses as they went round leaping over the different types of jumps. She saw Bill obviously looking for her, so she went to have breakfast with the two men. Lots of people stopped to speak to them as they ate in the big catering hall. Brenda knew she would never remember all their names. Her face ached from smiling. After breakfast, there where hacking events where ladies and gentleman got their horses to hack, a slow canter, walking slowly in circles this way and that. It was almost like a dance with the horse changing lead legs often. Brenda sighed, thinking, *I could never do that, but it could be nice to try.*

The rest of the day she spent watching the ring events as the guys were working in the backyard, getting ready for the rodeo. She laughed so hard she nearly fell off her seat when the young children, under eight years old, came out clinging to the backs of the sheep. She simply had a fantastic day. Cliff collected her late afternoon, and, after seeing to D4, took her to a friend's place to shower and get ready for the presentation dinner dance. Brenda was horrified to find it was also the home of the girls she had heard talking about Cliff. The girls showed her where to go, and other than that, left her alone to get ready. *They are older than me*, she thought. *But they better keep away from Cliff.* The girls were talking to Cliff when she came into the lounge where everyone had gathered for a drink. The girls were gazing up at Cliff and saw how his face changed as Brenda came into the room. All his love for Brenda was plastered on his face for all to see, so they turned to look at Brenda. She looked beautiful and had let her hair out so it hung long and shiny over her shoulders.

"Quite an entrance," the girls hissed at her as they all trooped out of the room. Brenda tossed her head, taking hold of Cliff's arm, and smiled to herself, not bothering to reply.

Brenda clung to Cliff's arm as they were all seated and food served. Beef from the pens of steers featured in the first two courses, though no one knew which pen the meat was from. Presentations carried on throughout the three courses for champions of various age groups and classes, from children up to the wood choppers. The final announcement was for the pen of steers, and Bill had won the first prize. Brenda felt so happy for him as folks slapped him on the back in congratulations. Music started up, and, against her protests, Cliff led her to the dance floor, and took her in his arms. Holding her close, he grinned down at her whispering, "Just let me guide you." She found it a very exhilarating experience as they moved as one to the tunes.

It was a very tired girl who was hardly awake enough to open the home gate for Bill. Cliff had stayed in to deliver animals back to their homes the next day. She put D4 into her mother hen box and thought, *I'll just lie on the bed for a bit.* She woke the next morning still in her finery. Bill had taken her shoes off only, and had murmured to himself as he'd watched her fall into a deep sleep, thinking, *You're alright, girl.*

EDUCATION

Cliff was away carting the show cattle to their various properties so Bill took advantage of the situation to sit Brenda down and try to see if he could help her get the required papers to finish her education. The opportunity came as they were having the mid-morning cuppa, sitting on the front patio, watching the chick peck about. "Have you noticed that chickens always scratch and then step back, peck, step forward, and scratch again? Scratch, back, peck, forward, over and over," Brenda mused "And why do the older chooks scratch holes in softer ground and almost bury themselves?" She swivelled round to look straight at Bill, eyes questioning.

Bill almost gasped as he turned away from gazing at the chick, wondering how he should bring up the subject of her schooling. The sun shone directly onto her face, showing her face in all its perfection, light-blue eyes shining. *No wonder Cliff fell for her*, he thought. *She sure is a beautiful lass.* "Oh, they use the dust to give themselves a bath." He stopped briefly as a tiny frown came onto Brenda's face and she started to speak. He held up his hand to stop her from speaking, and, nodding, said, "Sounds odd, I know, but it's what they do. Remember, we didn't actually bathe Duke much and used olive oil to help give his feathers a better shine. I find that they are not fond of water washes and can catch cold easily. Duke is a professional and has been through the process several times, so accepts it okay." He paused "As D4 gets proper feathers, you can introduce the occasional wash. They do have a mixed breed section at the show."

Brenda looked away from him to bend down to pick up the chick, as it had come over and was pecking at her feet. She held it gently in her cupped hands, where it settled down, and, after a few little chirps, closed its eyes. "Oh, I have decided that all this D stuff is a little silly, so as this little one is of royal blood, she is a duchess, so will call her Duchess, I think." With a tone that sounded just a little cross, she looked back at Bill. "And she is a *she*, you know."

Bill smiled back at her show of defiance and nodded his agreement, thinking, *Good grief, if it isn't a hen, this girl will not be happy.* Looking away, he asked, "How did you do your schooling?"

Brenda sighed, and, putting the chick back into her shoebox, thought, *Looking at the box this is a bit like when I got D2 and kept her in her first box in my room.* Sitting back up, she sat staring out over the landscape, not really seeing anything. She replied, "We, my sister and I"—she took a deep breath before continuing—"got papers sent to us, and my mum"—another long pause—"taught us, well, supervised us. All our textbooks were sent as required." Brenda gave her head a hard shake, causing her soft, fine hair to whip round her face. "I was good at most of it really, particularly writing stories, and always got better marks then Sandra, who really had to work harder than I did. It annoyed her a lot. After Sandra died and my Mum went away, I found it hard to keep going at it. Couldn't really see the sense in it." She drew herself up a little taller in her chair. "I was up to date when I stopped, and that was about four months ago, so I guess I'm still registered to get papers and suppose they will still be sending them to Bemerside, unless Mum or Dad have stopped them."

Bill noticed the subtle changes that swept across her face as she spoke and the fact that her eyes were moist. *She has been through a bit, and none of that tallies with the story Cliff told me when they first arrived*, he thought, but he decided not to question anything about that at this time. *It will all come out in time. Fact is, she has certainly had it tough.* "You really want to do nursing?" Bill thought this might be a better way to ensure she got back into her schooling, if she could see a reason for it.

"Oh, had thought of being a nurse or maybe something with caring for animals." She leaned down and picked up Duchess, who had woken up and was cheeping, but settled down once she got into Brenda's hands. "Mum had trouble when I was born and said that the nurses helped her get through it, and I've helped a cow that had the calf stuck halfway out." She shuddered. "Albert had to shove the calf back in and try to get it right, but we still had strife getting it out. The calf was dead before we got it out, and the next day, the poor cow had a prolapsed uterus hanging out of her vagina and had to be shot. Very sad day that, as she was a really good milker too." Brenda went on to say how she had read a few anatomy books and had bits and pieces of the inner workings pointed out on killing days, so she could understand the differences between animal types. She shot a sideways glance at Bill. "Guess humans are not that much different, really."

Bill tried not show any expression at the graphic tale of woe. It surprised him a bit that she used the correct terminology. "Nursing is a great idea, and you can get into that with good marks in your junior years. For the animal stuff, you may need to do the two senior years and go to study at university." He paused. "My wife was a teacher at one time, and I still have most of her books packed away. Maybe I could advise the correspondence school, and you could finish your junior years here. I can contact the place that has your missing papers and get them to forward them to you."

Bill stopped, as Brenda had gone quite white as he'd said the last few words. He wondered if he had lost her at that point, however, she didn't move away, but seemed to withdraw back into herself. She surprised him by replying that she would contact the school herself and get any books and the remaining papers sent to Lochlea. She asked for some writing paper and pen so she could write the letter before he went into town that afternoon.

Bill got the materials and watched as she sat at the table, Duchess in her lap, occasionally tapping the pen as she considered her next sentence. Brenda told the school a whole lot of waffle about family strife with her dad changing jobs, and could they forward her what she needed to carry on from the last paper she had submitted? She indicated that they should get the books from Bemerside returned to them and forward them and the papers to her as soon as possible. Fingers crossed, she sealed the letter in its envelope and propped it against the vase on the table, and, feeling washed out, decided to go for a long walk. Bill's questions had shaken her up a lot, bringing up a lot of things she had kept suppressed. Bill watched go and noted the tired slump in her shoulders. *She is carrying a lot of hurt, that girl,* he thought.

Brenda nearly always rose in time to start feeding before Bill and continued to do that most days after Cliff returned home. Bill had had a conversation with Cliff about Brenda's schooling and the information she had revealed about herself. Cliff refused to enlighten him about Brenda's life, saying, "She will tell you when she is ready." Bill had to admire his resolve in keeping true to Brenda, realizing that, from now on, she would be Cliff's first priority—and it hurt a little. Brenda was quiet at dinner and excused herself as soon as the dishes were done, taking one of the textbooks Bill had brought out from his wife's belongings and retiring to bed.

Bill had received a letter from Pete, who had informed them he was not coming home for a few more months, if they could manage without him. Bill thought they could now that he had Brenda to help him while Cliff was off in the truck doing the long hauls, taking produce south and bringing back whatever where possible. Bill was sure he could manage the small cattle moves with the small truck locality. For once, Cliff really didn't want to be away as much, but knew that that was the way it was going to be till Pete came back. Brenda was still reading when he flopped down on the bed, giving her a hug, telling her he was happy she was going to get back into her schoolwork. As he lay beside her, cradling her head on his shoulder, he felt such an overwhelming feeling of affection for her. He hoped she would be okay.

Cliff need not have concerned himself, as Brenda threw herself into the papers as soon as they arrived, plowing through them quickly and easily, catching herself up to where she had left off. Bill was amazed how easily she did it. After she caught up, she worked on the papers in the morning and tagged along after Bill in the afternoons. He showed her how to drive the tractor, and she slashed some of the paddocks he used to make hay. He could hear her singing over the top of the motor often. He came along behind her, racking the hay into rows, and, after a few days, they baled it, and Brenda drove the tractor with trailer to pick up the bales and bring the bales back to the shed. It was very hard work, but they managed. Her biggest effort was learning how to back the trailer into the shed. Bill had to smile to himself as she struggled with the trailer not going where she wanted it to, but she crossly told him she would get it, and, eventually, she did. After that, she would hook up the trailer and practice till she got the method correct. "Make a truckie out of you yet," Bill told her as he patted her tousled hair.

Working the steers came with another hard lesson for Brenda. She had never really had much to do with horses after they'd left High Low and Casey, her granddad's horse. The memories of the people and young folk she had seen at the show kept coming into her head as she prepared herself to confront this new fear to conquer. She had, of course, fed the stallion at Bemerside, and liked petting him, and that was about it. Bill had several horses and got her to ride the one he had chosen for her round the yard for several days before they had to go out and move some of the steers onto the paddocks that had been slashed for the hay, so they could pick on the stubble and lick up the loose bits the baler had left behind. "Could do it by myself, maybe," Bill told her. "But the new ones are in this mob and might need a bit of backup."

He made her ride bareback round and round in the yard, and, only after she could trot and canter, gave her a saddle. Brenda didn't feel at all comfortable either way. The horse was very tall—sixteen hands, Bill had said, but he was quiet and knew his job. He was a plain brown with a bit of white on his nose and one white sock on the near side front leg. He didn't really have a name. Bill simply referred to him as *the brown horse.* Brenda was having none of that and decided to call him Ace. She even named the other three horse as well—Diamond because he had a star on his forehead a bit like a diamond, Rabbit because she had extra-long ears, and Ruby because she was a dark chestnut and almost red.

Brenda would stand at Ace's head, talking to him for ages before she got on him to ride around the yard. Bill had asked her how she knew when to get on, and she told him that he would give her a gentle push with his nose, which meant he understood that he needed to look after her. Bill shook his head, as he didn't believe that horses were that smart. However, he found after the first day of moving the steers about that perhaps they were smarter than he had thought. The new steers were a little bit frisky and balked at the paddock gates, turning to face the riders and look for avenues of escape. Ace knew his job, and if he moved too quickly for Brenda and she got unbalanced, he would do a little movement to put her back in the saddle. He did it more than once, and Bill realized he was looking after his rider as well as doing his job. After a bit of a stand-off, all the steers were moved onto the cut grass. Bill watched Ace's ears as they trotted back home, as they flicked back every time Brenda spoke. *I'll be blowed,* he thought. *The old bugger is listening to her.*

Lochlea, having been a dairy farm before Bill's wife had died, had many smallish paddocks, and most had been planted with different grasses. There was a large dam to one side of the property from which water was pumped to a large tank on a hill and fed various paddocks with water. And on the other end of the run, there was a bore with a pump to draw the water up and transfer it into smaller tanks that fed several troughs. The house water came from the tank on the hill. Brenda found it all very confusing, but quickly worked out which pipe to have switched on for each trough, depending on where the cattle were paddocked.

Cliff came and went at regular intervals. When he was home, Brenda would be stuck to his side like a limpet mine, Bill said. She helped him service the truck and give it a polish. "Pete may be a bit rough, but he insists that the truck is kept spotless," Cliff told her as they lay under the truck, greasing the nipples and changing oils, basically checking every nut and hose on the vehicle. Brenda would wash the bedding in the cab and always left him a little memento when she made it before he hit the road again, like a cookie or pretty flower she had found. He never said anything but looked forward to finding the new item every time he headed out again, watching her wave him off whenever he left in daylight in his rear view mirror. Duchess, who they now knew was a cockerel, and whose name had been shortened to Dutchy, was either in her arms or sitting on her shoulder.

Dutchy didn't spend time with the other chooks, as they pecked at him, so he followed Brenda about as she went about her chores. While she was working on her studies, he at first was allowed to be with her inside, but as he grew, Bill built some barriers across the doors, and he would then march up and down making little noises. Most of the time, Brenda was so wrapped up in her work she didn't hear him till she stopped to give her mind a rest. If she spoke to him, then he would make sort of musical sounds in response. *I swear, that bird thinks he is a human,* Bill thought often. *It will be hard when he has to go.* Dutchy was slowly evolving into a miniature version of Duke, so it would seem he was a pure bred.

Bill had retrieved the cages to go over the flower garden beds from the shed. His wife had always loved to have flowers, and the domed cages kept the chooks from scratching up the plants and kept them out of the dust baths they had in the middle of the garden beds. Brenda poured over some gardening magazines and picked out the flowers she wanted to grow, so Bill took her into a local nursery to get the little plants. Brenda asked the chap at the nursery so many questions about what and when to plant that Bill was almost embarrassed, but Allan at the nursey didn't seem to mind and told her how to prepare the beds. Brenda followed his instructions to the letter, bulking up the beds with soil from the cattle yards and chook house. Dutchy would hang round her as she dug everything into the beds. She would toss him a worm when she found one. He would gulp this down quickly before any of the other birds could get to it. If it was a big one, he would need to race round and round the bed, with hens close behind, with the worm hanging out of his beak. Most of the time, Brenda would pick him up so he could devour the tasty morsel, but sometimes, the hens beat her to Dutchy and stole his meal. The little plants thrived.

Cliff arrived home after one of his long hauls with a surprise for Brenda—a cute little black and white Border collie pup. Brenda was beside herself with delight, but nearly had her one and only argument with Bill, who insisted that the pup was not to be allowed into the house. Brenda made up a bed just outside the back door and sat outside with Prince, and Dutchy refused to come in and have dinner. Cliff found her asleep, leaning against the wall, and then carried her to bed.

The next morning, Bill, indicating for Cliff to be quiet, took him round the house to show him bird and pup cuddled up together on the makeshift bed. That was odd, as Dutchy usually spent the night near the front door. Brenda came racing round the corner as they stood looking at the two creatures. She had a worried look on her face from when she had found that Dutchy not in his usual place. The three of them watched as the puppy and bird woke and ran over to Brenda, who sank to the ground, allowing them to crawl into her lap.

"Think you have a rival for her affections there, mate." Bill smiled at Cliff as Brenda collected the milk bucket and headed off to milk the cow, puppy and chick at her heels. Cliff nodded.

DEXTER

Dexter wasn't doing very well, drinking himself to sleep most nights and making silly mistakes. Steve had a chat to him about his behavior, indicating he must pull himself together or it could mean his job. Steve found him sitting outside his unit, hung over and feeling very tired and sick, trying to get up the strength to pull on his boots and get to work. Dexter could see Steve walking purposefully toward him. He was late and was sure Steve had come to sack him. He was surprised as Steve handed him a letter without saying anything, Steve's facial expression sympathetic. The letter was from the correspondence school the girls had been enrolled in, asking if he could forward the schoolbooks and papers back to them as Brenda had made contact with them and wished to continue her studies. so they could send them on to Brenda. The letter didn't say where she was, so after he'd let Steve read it as well, Dexter asked if he could ring the school to see if they'd say where she was. For the first time, he felt hopeful.

Steve agreed to the request, and they walked slowly back to the big house. For a little while, Dexter forgot that he didn't feel well and had a definite spring in his step. Steve saw him to the phone and gave him a pat on the back, saying, "Good luck." The school wouldn't disclose any details of where Brenda was, so Dexter lost his temper and yelled furiously at them before forcefully slamming the phone down as Steve returned with two mugs of tea. Steve pushed him down onto a chair, telling him that he really needed to pull himself together, asking if he'd like Brenda to see him like he was right now. Dexter lowered his head, shaking it. He had tears of frustration in his eyes.

"I'm going to let you go,' Steve said. "There's a truck coming today to take the old grader and plough to a wrecker's in Brisbane. I am sure the driver will give you a lift. You need to shake yourself out of the mess you're in."

Steve didn't reply or ring to let Nancy know he was coming. He simply walked out and went to pack up his few things. He'd known this day was coming, but it was still a shock to realize he no longer had a job. He was ready when the truck arrived. He recognized the truck as one that had been to Bemerside before—he recognized the snake painted onto the doors of the cab. After getting the equipment on the truck, they headed off. Cliff had been surprised to find out it was Dexter who required a lift, and he wondered how he could let him know in a roundabout way that Brenda was doing well and okay.

He needn't have worried, as Dexter, still a little angry from the phone call to the school, informed him he was going to Brisbane to have it out with the school, who knew where his lost daughter was. Cliff could still hear the anger in his voice and thought that now wouldn't be a good time to bring up he knew Brenda. Then he went on to explain how she'd disappeared a couple of months ago and he had a feeling she'd gone off with a truck driver. He asked if he had heard of anyone who had picked up a young lass. The last statement was delivered with a questioning glance. Cliff told him that drivers do pick up girls now and then, but he'd not heard of a really young lass, and it took all his resolve to not tell this sad, tired-looking man his daughter was well and happy.

They didn't get to Brisbane till nearly midnight so Nancy and the Hays were stunned to see him. They sat at the table drinking tea as Dexter informed them of the school letter and that he intended to take the papers up to the school and make them tell him where she was. All this news of Brenda going missing was surprising news to Nancy, who had never been told Brenda was missing. However, Nancy was very excited to hear the news that Brenda was at least getting back to her schooling. It surprised Dexter and everyone else how well Nancy handled the news.

He didn't tell her he'd been sacked but that he'd quit so when he found out where Brenda was so he could go and bring her home. Granddad Hay, Fred, said there was plenty of work going, so he'd be able to get a job easy enough. They talked on till the sun rose, and Nancy realized how thin and tired Dexter looked. Because it was Saturday and he couldn't go to the school till Monday, she gave Dexter some toast to eat and he went to bed, sleeping most of the day. Nancy found the box with the schoolbooks and papers. She sat looking at them for ages, her mind wandering back to happier times along with a definite sadness as they also brought memories of Sandra. She thought how she and Dexter had let Brenda down by just expecting her to cope with it all, and to think Sandra was letting them down for so long with Sam. Nancy eventually took the books out to the lounge, ready for Monday.

Dexter and Nancy got a taxi to the school on Monday since the box was too heavy to carry to the bus stop. The school refused to tell them any information about Brenda's whereabouts. Nancy had to physically take hold of his arm and drag Dexter out of the school when he started to get angry and banging his hand on the desk.

"Come on, love," Nancy enticed him. "If she's doing her schoolwork, she must be in a safe place." Dexter fumed all the way home and wished he had some rum. They picked up a paper, and Dexter poured over available jobs and picked out a couple to apply for. He got work within a week but still felt very angry.

RESPONSIBITY

Bill was impressed as to how Brenda took the responsibility of caring for and training the little puppy. She was kind but firm with Prince. To give Prince his due, he was from a breed considered to be very intelligent, and responded to the training with enthusiasm. Bill took her into the town library to get some books on the obedience training for the course that had been at the show. The next time Cliff was home, they built a full course for Brenda to work Prince with. Bill enjoy watching her in the evenings as she, dog, and rooster ran round the course. They made a delightful sight.

Bill realized that he was becoming very fond of this wisp of a lass. The sight of the little flowers growing brought back many memories of how the place had been before his wife passed. She impressed him how she applied herself to helping with the chores, her study, and the pets. She'd taken to the everyday running of the property well, not worrying about getting her hands dirty when mending fences or servicing machinery. He'd taught her how to drive the ute as well as the tractor and how to change the pipes to keep the water up to the stock. The only thing she struggled with was riding, though she was gaining in confidence. *Cliff could do so much worse than her*, he thought, *but she's so young*. He felt there were still secrets she kept to herself, and sometimes she showed a maturity older than her years.

Cliff had a break of a week off before heading to Western Australia with a consignment of machinery. He'd be away for close to a month and wasn't pleased with this job as he would be out of contact for most of the trip. He'd only been home for a day or two here and there before this West Australian trip. He and Brenda laughed their way through the servicing and cleaning the truck. Bill watched them playing at squirting grease on each other to a full-on water fight while hosing down the rig.

Cliff finally had time to see the changes in Brenda, how tanned and alive she looked. He, along with Bill, found watching the unusual trio in the evenings amusing, and he was impressed at the progress in the flower gardens. He could see Brenda was making Bill more relaxed than he'd been since his mum had passed. Brenda showed Cliff how good she was at backing the trailer with either the ute or tractor. He confided in Bill that it was possibly a good thing he was away a lot, as his affection for Brenda was growing, and he was finding it increasingly difficult not to want a more physical relationship with her.

"Five months, mate," was all Bill said, "and it will be worth the wait. Perhaps you should bring back an engagement ring after this trip, hey." Bill dug Cliff in the ribs.

The day Cliff drove off, Bill told Brenda he was off to check the back fence line and he was taking a crib lunch and may be late getting back. Brenda nodded as she got stuck into the last lot of papers, as she wanted to be finished with the school stuff before Cliff got back from West Australia. She lost herself in her work, losing all track of time, only to be roused by Prince giving a few little woofs from the front door. It was getting dark, so she raced about doing the evening feedings and getting the milking cow's calf in. She realized that Bill hadn't got back, but at this point, she wasn't too concerned as he sometimes would stay out after dark to finish whatever he was working on at the time. So Brenda ate some cold soup and took a book to bed, leaving the light on for Bill.

She became really worried when she discovered Bill hadn't come home during the night, so after all the morning chores were finished, she hopped onto the tractor and went to see if she could find Bill.

She made quite a sight with dog and chook sharing the seat as they bounced across the paddocks. On her way across the paddocks, she noted that one of the watering points was dry, and she made a mental note that it would need to be seen to as soon as she found Bill. She drove for quite some time along the boundary fence line before she saw the ute laying on its side almost obscured by bushes and a high bank in a gully. Her blood ran cold at the sight. The animals felt her fear and sat very still but alert beside her.

Brenda parked, jumped down and told Prince to stay. He whined but obeyed the command. She called out to Bill as she climbed down to the ute, but didn't receive any reply. Skirting carefully round the ute, she found Bill lying half under the cab; he was unconscious. She stood frozen to the spot for what seemed an age before kneeling beside his head and tapping his cheeks gently. Bill moaned and half opened his eyes before he made some sounds like he was trying to talk. Brenda could only see one arm, so she squeezed his hand, saying, "I will get help." She received a slight bit of pressure, so she knew he'd understood. She whistled for Prince to come to her, and dog and rooster arrived quickly. Telling them to stay, she bolted back to the tractor and headed back to the house as fast as the terrain allowed, her heart beating wildly.

The next few hours all happened in a bit of a blur. The local police and fireman arrived first, and Brenda showed them her tractor tracks to follow to find Bill while she waited for the ambulance. It wasn't far behind them, and Brenda went with them, so she could take them a more defined route, so Bill wouldn't be too badly shaken on the return trip. When they arrived, they found that the others couldn't do anything to rescue Bill as Prince and Dutchy wouldn't let them near him.

"Would have shot them, but we could hear you coming." the policemen said. "Even that goddamn chook was having a go at us."

One word from Brenda and the animals came to sit beside her while the others worked out how to get Bill out from under the ute. It appeared that Bill had parked on top of the bank and had boiled his billy in the shade of the bank, and the bank had simply caved in under the weight of the vehicle. They got a strong rope attached to the side of the ute and hooked it up to the tractor pulling it up so they could gently pull Bill out from under the cab. He was drifting in and out of consciousness and appeared to have a broken arm at the very least. After he'd been strapped onto the gurney and the ambulance dispatched to the hospital, the others checked the ute over and decided that if they pulled it away from the bank, it could be put back on its wheels. This worked, and it started straight away, even though there was a fair bit of external damage here and there. Brenda drove the battered up ute back to the house with one of the firemen for company. She assured them she'd be okay at the house beside someone had to look after the animals as she waved the men off, saying, "I will be in later to check on Bill." Not one of them questioned that she wasn't old enough to drive.

Brenda didn't really have time to think about how she was going to manage, just acted purely on instinct over the next few days and weeks as it turned out. She drove the beat-up ute into the hospital that arvo, telling herself that she wouldn't try to contact Cliff to come back just yet. Bill had apparently been trapped under the ute for a long time, the accident happening as he was sitting beside the bank in the shade having his morning smoko, not realising that the recent rain had weakened the structure of the bank. He hadn't been quick enough to get right away before the ute hit him. The doctor expected that Brenda—he'd met her at the show as it was his house where they'd gotten dressed for the dinner dance—was Cliff's partner and therefore could be informed of Bill's condition.

Bill had a broken arm and collarbone and a serious concussion, so he was being kept sedated to give the brain a chance to get more back to normal. On top of that, the doctor suspected crush injury to his hips that required an urgent specialist attention, so Bill was being transferred to Brisbane that same day. Brenda looked in on Bill, thinking how he seemed to have shrunk a little. She kissed his cheek, murmuring that she'd look after things till he got back. She thanked the doctor and went to the store, fuel supplier, and feed barn to inform them that she'd be looking after Lochlea till Cliff or Bill got home. They'd all heard of the accident, so they were very understanding, agreeing to keep her supplied with any goods she may require.

Brenda had her first win when she was able to fix the broken pipe she'd noted at the dry water point while going to find Bill, the next day. It took several knocked knuckles and quite a few rude words before she figured out which tools to use to cut the broken bit of pipe out and add in a new piece to get it all working again. She simply went about the day-to-day activities in a methodical manner, to the point of getting up the courage to move the steers about, this being made easier with the assistance of Prince, who instinctively knew what to do, even though he was still a puppy. Ace also knew his job herding cattle, so Brenda had to do very little once the steers were heading in the right direction. She even managed to collect some steers from one of Bill's neighbors in the small truck. She'd never driven it before but found the gears weren't much different to the ute, although the steers moving round on the back made keeping it straight a bit difficult.

Brenda made a call to the hospital where Bill had been taken every evening. She was told he was progressing well. She was disappointed she hadn't heard from Cliff, but he'd said he'd be on the road and away from phones. Still, it disappointed her. A week after Bill had been taken away, he was brought to the phone when she made her regular call. It was great to hear his voice, and she assured him all was well. He was still feeling very weak, so he didn't chat for long and advised her to call on neighbors if she needed help. Brenda didn't answer this. She just said going okay now and would if she needed to. Cliff eventually phoned, and so as not to worry him, Brenda assured him all was hunky-dory. She didn't tell him about Bill because she knew he'd worry and possibly rush back.

Dutchy and Duke were becoming mortal enemies, so she had to build Dutchy a separate pen of his own. She had to wrestle with the post-hole digger and learn how to use the chainsaw to cut the posts. She used the fence round the garden as a guide, and when it came to stapling the wire netting up, her fingers suffered terribly. Duchy was ever so pleased when the run was finished, as he'd been cooped up in Duke's carry box while the run was under construction. He flapped his wings and crowed loudly when let loose. Brenda gave him a couple of hens for company, but Duke spent all the time strutting round the pen, and they fought fiercely through the wire, so she gave up on giving him hens, telling Dutchy his time was limited. She knew that when Bill came back, he'd insist Dutchy be moved on. She locked Duke and his hens away in the evening so Dutchy could run about with her and Prince in the dog-training area.

Brenda had settled into her new role and had become very comfortable in her own company, so it was a huge shock three weeks after Bill had gone to Brisbane when someone appeared. She was humming to herself as she prepared to dinner, occasionally breaking out in song. Her singing voice was pleasant, and she could hold a tune.

"Well, well, what do I have here?" a deep voice cut through her dreaming.

She swung round, large knife in hand, forcing the large figure to step back as he raised his hands.

"Whoa there girlie! I am Pete, Bill's brother-in-law. Bill contacted me from Brisbane as he couldn't get onto Cliff, and I came straight home."

Prince came shooting through the door standing between Brenda and Pete, growling deep down in his throat, baring his rows of sharp teeth, hackles standing up on his back. As she hadn't locked Dutchy up yet, Prince was closely followed by Dutchy, neck feathers spayed out and wings outspread in his attack mode. Brenda grabbed Dutchy before he flew at Pete and partially settled Prince with a soft instruction. Brenda wondered how this bloke had got in without Prince hearing him, and it made her feel very uneasy. They stood eying each other. Brenda saw a large solid man, very hairy arms, a snake tattoo on each arm, with chest hair showing out of his half-unbuttoned shirt. He had a long mustache that hung down to below his chin, longish dark hair, and almost yellow eyes. She supposed he could be good looking. However she did feel comfortable with the expression in his eyes. Even though he had a surprised look on his face, it didn't reach his eyes.

Pete, during this stand-off, observed the small, almost childlike girl. He let his eyes look her up and down, taking in her pretty—no, beautiful—face, long hair, tiny frame. He thought that she'd be a tight and fiery root. Bill hadn't told him much about her, just that he was concerned at her being by herself. He was amused by the do-not-touch-me defiant expression in her light-blue eyes. *Yep, a real firecracker, I'd say*, he thought. *Be interesting to tame this one.*

He smiled at her, and Brenda noted that the smile didn't quite reach his eyes, showing strong-looking nicotine stained teeth. At that time, Brenda got a whiff of rum on his breath. She only just stopped herself from stepping back, knowing instinctively that she had a feeling she shouldn't give this person an inch or show any weakness.

They both went to speak at the same time, but Brenda held up her hand, knife still in her hand, and said, "I will deal with these two please," and sidled past him, taking Dutchy to his pen and telling Prince to stay outside.

Prince did so, but kept some of his fore legs on the mat just inside the door his hackles still up a little.

"Sorry about that. I didn't know you were coming or hear you arrive. My name is Brenda," she said as she held out her hand. Pete didn't really shake her hand, just caressed it till Brenda extracted it from him, feeling it had been touched by something slimy. *Slimy like a snake* flitted through her head, and she felt an urge to immediately to wash her hand, so she turned and managed that, pretending to rinse off the knife.

Pete addressed her back. "Got a lift from town." As she turned back to Pete, she found he'd moved closer to her. Still with knife in hand, she indicated the table and chairs saying, "I have almost finished cooking dinner and have enough for you as well." After a moment's hesitation, she continued. "The beds in your room are made up with clean sheets."

Pete nodded his acceptance of her offer of food and smiled his thanks to the bed information. For the first time, that night, Brenda snuck Prince into her room, and, even though he wasn't normally allowed inside, Prince showed no indication of being in a strange place. He simply curled up on his mat between her bed and the door. A couple of times during the night, he jumped to his feet hackles up as he heard Pete walk past the door. Once, when Pete hesitated outside Brenda's door, Prince moved to wake Brenda by placing his wet nose on her leg and growling softly. Brenda was pleased she'd brought him inside.

She was up before Pete and had all the feedings and chores done and was straining the milk in the laundry when Prince brushed past her, growling, to meet Pete just as he was about to come into the laundry. As Brenda had a full day planned, she told him to get his own breakfast and left to do a water point and fence run. He wasn't home when she returned, so she just carried on with the rest of her day. He came home quite late, which annoyed her, as she'd put his dinner aside. That became the routine over the time till Cliff got home.

Heavens know why Bill called him home, if he isn't not going to even try to help, she thought. Also, he'd dumped his dirty clothes in the laundry, obviously expecting her to wash them. Brenda had left them for several days before finally doing them just to get them out of the way. One evening, Pete came home with a lady friend, and they made a huge racket most of the night. The lady, Sharon, spoke to Brenda like she was a servant, demanding breakfast for her and Pete, even though it was mid-morning. Brenda disappeared quickly after that that and was pleased the lady was gone when she came back, though she did reappear every other night. Brenda simply stopped leaving meals out for Pete at all, thinking that bloody Sharon could look after Pete. Sharon and Pete made such a mess in the kitchen, Brenda wondered if she'd won that battle at all. Brenda continued to leave their dishes in the sink, knowing they'd run out of plates eventually

Cliff rang to say he'd be back in a couple of days, and the day before he was due back, Pete hung around the place and actually cleaned up his and Sharon's mess in the kitchen—Sharon had packed up her things and left—before following Brenda as she did her chores. Although Prince had got used to him and tolerated Pete patting him, he kept very close to Brenda. As Brenda instructed him to his mat after his training, she went to have a shower, and as she was washing her hair, it took a bit longer than usual. She was feeling happy that Cliff would be back soon and went to her room, singing softly, wrapped only in a large towel. As she kicked the door closed and threw her towel onto the bed, she felt rather than heard movement behind her. Smells wafted over her, and she swung round to find a naked Pete grinning at her, the smell of alcohol very strong mixed with cigar smoke that hung in the room as well.

"Had the boy. Now you can have the man!"

He moved very fast for such a big man and had her pinned against the foot of the bed in an instant. Brenda tried to hold her breath against the stenches that assailed her nostrils and push him off her. She made no sound, but as he had her hands held tight in one of his huge hands, her only defense was to sink her teeth into his shoulder. As her teeth drew blood, Pete shook her mouth off his chest as blood trickled down over his chest hair. Brenda realized he was so much bigger and stronger than she that she just relaxed and let him do what he wanted. It was truly horrible. Surely, this wasn't all there was to the joining together of a man and a woman. After a time, Pete shuddered and, heaving a huge sigh, momentary relaxed his hold on her, so she flipped herself out from under him and ran.

She came to life and, with a twist and using all her strength, landed on the floor and was out the door before he could catch hold of her. She ran to the laundry, where she had some clothes, to find a distraught Prince chewing and scratching at the door.

B L Wilson

She gathered some clothes and bolted into the hayloft in the shed, where she got dressed and armed with a hay fork. A dull ache came from between her legs and, when she rubbed at the area, hoping to ease the discomfort, she found her fingers came away with blood on them. Her monthlies had been a bit over a week ago, so she knew Pete had hurt her.

She watched to see if Pete would come after her vowing to kill him if he did. He didn't. She was grateful when he drove off in the ute towards town. She went back to the house, taking Prince and fork with her. She discovered that her sheets had blood on them, so after cleaning herself, she took the sheets to the laundry to wash them. She felt dirty somehow. She wondered what she'd done to make Pete think he could do what he he'd done to her. She'd been dreaming of having a sexual relationship with Cliff and now wondered if all sexual encounters were like that. She sat on the side of the bed for most of the night. Every creak and rattle of leaves against the house brought both dog and girl to attention. Just as she drifted off to sleep, the throaty rumble of the big rig coming down the road had her out of bed and racing to the gate.

CONSEQUENCES

It had been a long—no, very long—journey for Cliff. One side of the country to the other with plenty of lonely miles traveled, so it was with a glad heart he found himself on the home stretch. He'd tried to phone home several times but had never been able to get through to either his dad or Brenda. His heart was skipping round in his chest, and he'd had a strange feeling in his tummy ever since he'd turned down the road leading to Lochlea. False dawn was lightening the eastern sky as he rounded the final curve to home. His air-brakes gave out a rattle as he geared down in preparation to stopping for the home gate. The sight of Brenda racing to the gate took his breath away. For sure, if breathing wasn't an involuntary action, he'd have passed out through lack of oxygen. A huge smile plastered itself to his face when he saw his Brenda get to the gate, closely followed by young dog and rooster.

Brenda swung the gate open, at the same time noting that the ute was back, indicating that Pete must be home. She shuddered as Cliff passed by her through the gateway. He didn't drive to the regular parking bay for the rig but slammed on his brakes as soon as he cleared the gate, bringing the rig to a sudden stop. He flew out of the cap and swept Brenda up in his arms and hugged her to his body, placing a solid kiss in her mouth. The kiss hurt as Brenda's mouth was still bruised from Pete's assault, so she broke the kiss off rather quickly burying her face in his shoulder. He smelt wonderful, dusty, sweaty with a tiny hint of diesel fuel and grease. Cliff took her breaking off the kiss to the fact he hadn't shaved for a couple of days. He placed her back on the ground, still with his arms round her, and they gazed into each others eyes for several minutes, neither wanting to be the first to break the moment. Prince and Dutchy circled them, not knowing what to make of the situation.

The spell was broken by Pete's voice as he walked round the cab. "Made good time, I see, lad." He came up to them and thumped Cliff on his back.

Prince growled, hackles, up and would have gone for him if Brenda hadn't spoken sharply to him as she bent down to pick Dutchy up before he could fly at Pete.

Cliff thought their reactions a bit odd. Brenda kept Cliff's body between Pete and her, her eyes downcast. She held Cliff's tightly to Cliff's hand, Dutchy tucked under her other arm, as the two men shook hands and greeted each other with familiarity of long association. Brenda deduced from Pete's comment that he'd known Cliff was getting home this day, which would be why he'd made his move on her when he did. Cliff had been a little surprised at the animals' reaction as Pete had arrived. Brenda was undecided as to how to deal with the situation. It was obvious that the men liked each other and now wasn't the time.

Pete offered to park up the truck so Cliff could go and get some breakfast and a strong cuppa into him. Pete, with eyes narrowed, watched the pair walk back to the house, arms round each other, and wondered whether Brenda would squeal on him. He rubbed his hand against his cock as it came awake at the memory of Brenda's tight fanny. *Lucky bugger, that Cliff,* he thought. *No wonder he is so pleased to see her, best I give them a bit of time to get reacquainted.*

Cliff smiled to himself as he watched Brenda move about the kitchen making his breakfast. *I do so love her,* he thought, *and sure wish this sixteenth birthday would hurry up and come. Time is ticking away but not quick enough.* The small box in his pocket seemed to be burning his skin. He wondered when he should propose to her and if she would like it. So many thoughts whirled round in his mind that he failed to notice that she wasn't as talkative as usual. He simply enjoyed the sight of her, drinking in all her beauty.

He had his head down as Pete entered the kitchen, so he missed the unguarded expression that came onto Brenda's face before she got herself under control, mumbling that she'd go and feed up and after that she needed to do a water run but would be back in time to get lunch. Cliff was a little surprised that she left quickly and didn't touch him before she left.

Cliff was asleep when Brenda returned, so she made Pete a sandwich and left it on the table for him and went to lie down beside Cliff. She felt so washed out, never had she ever been so buggered. She was still unsure how she'd be able to move forward after the events of the last day's events. Cliff was pleased to find her there beside him when he woke and gazed at her while she slept. She looked so young and defenseless. He carefully slid off the bed without waking her. Picking up the small box, he checked out the contents and nodded to himself—it was time.

Prince greeted him happily but looked past his body, searching for Brenda. *You love her so much, as I do*, Cliff thought, giving the dog a pat. He was surprised to find Dutchy was in a reasonably but amateurishly constructed pen and not running loose, so he let him out sure it was some mistake. Prince watched and gave a little whine as Dutchy flapped his wings and crowed loudly. Prince stayed with the rooster as Cliff went to check out the vegetable garden then round the front to look at the flowers. He was amazed as to how much they'd grown, plants standing tall, covered in lots of buds.

He was jarred out of his dreamy state by a sharp bark of alarm from Prince followed by loud squawking. He rushed toward the sound at the side of the house to find Dutchy and Duke locked in a serious battle. He stood transfixed for several moments and was almost bowled over by a furious Brenda, who yelled at him to not just stand there and to help her separate the birds. She raced over and grabbed the first bird she could, holding it high, with the other bird jumping up and racking her legs with claws and spur. The sight of her bleeding legs jolted Cliff into action, and he grabbed the other bird. He felt the full angry stare from Brenda.

"Dutchy is locked up for a reason." She almost spat the words at Cliff.

He was taken aback, as he'd never seen her so angry before. As it turned out, he had Dutchy in his hands, so he broke the spell by putting him back into his pen as Brenda strode off toward the laying house and locked Duke inside so he couldn't return to continue the battle through the wire. Cliff came to meet her and was surprised to find her sobbing uncontrollably, tears streaming down her cheeks.

He gathered her up in his arms and carried her back to the house, sitting her on a chair, got a basin of warm water to sponge the blood off her legs. Thankfully, none of the scratches were very deep and would only need some antiseptic cream to assist them mend. Brenda's sobbing had reduced to an occasional gulp. As he knelt at her feet and rubbed the cream over her legs, he thought, *Why not now?* and reached into his pocket and drew out the little box.

Taking a deep breath, he looked up at Brenda's sad face, and holding the box up to her, flicking it open, he whispered, "I love you, girl, and will you marry me?"

The silence seemed to drag on for ages as he held his breath waiting for a reaction or answer from Brenda. Brenda took the box with trembling hands, gazing at the exquisite ring inside. A bright white stone surrounded by tiny red stones that extended out from the center a quarter of the way down the ring. Brenda glanced up at Cliff and quickly back to the ring, terrible thoughts racing through her mind.

If he knows what has happened to me, will he still want me? Is he going to hurt me like Pete did? She remembered that Alvin had stopped giving her pleasure too. *Is that what happens between girls and boys, with the man only wanting to please himself?* She was so confused. Cliff watched the range of emotion cross her face and sighed. He went to close his fist round the box, but Brenda snatched it back from him, whispering, "I want to see my mum."

"Well, well what have we here?" Pete's voice boomed from the doorway, startling them both as they turned to see Pete wheel Bill into the room in a wheelchair. Brenda stiffened her body and almost pushed Cliff over as he was getting to his feet by reaching out to hold his arm. Cliff extracted his arm and held her gently to his body. He could feel her trembling and assumed it was the suddenness of his proposal. Brenda wanted to rush over to give Bill a hug, but he was to close to Pete. Instead, she gasped out, "Bill," and taking a deep breath, she said, "Bill, how, when … I didn't know you were coming home."

Bill smiled at the sight of the young couple. "I had arranged with Pete days ago." He glanced at Pete. "You should have told her, man." His tone of voice was accusing, but it changed as Pete wheeled him round the table, and he saw Brenda's scratched legs, and it was his turn to ask, "What on earth, girl? How did that happen?" He stopped when Brenda started to weep again.

Brenda extracted herself from Cliff and walked over to the doorway where Prince was whining and giving out menacing growls, keeping the table between her and Pete. "Let's have a cuppa, and I'll explain." She still had the little box in her hand. She glanced back at Cliff. "Don't you and Pete need to see to the truck?"

Cliff went to say he didn't but saw the beseeching expression on Brenda's face, so he slapped Pete on the back "Let's go do it, hey!" and both Cliff and Pete left the room. Brenda could hear Pete asking Cliff what had been going on when he and Bill arrived.

Brenda busied herself getting the kettle on and setting up the table with biscuits> She asked Bill if he wanted breakfast or toast. Bill said biscuits would be fine as he'd had breakfast before he left the hospital. To fill the silence, he said, "Must have good to have Pete here to help out. I contacted him as soon as I got to Brisbane, and he told me he'd come home straight away." He stopped when Brenda swung round, an angry expression on her face.

"He has only been here ten days, and he has not bloody helped me at all!" The last word spat out through gritted teeth. "Plus, he has had that ... woman here most of time as well."

Nothing else was spoken till the kettle had boiled and tea placed on the table. Bill was shocked that Pete had been so slow to get home, and was quite disappointed with him. He'd known he was a bit of a loose cannon from time to time but had felt he'd have come home as he'd said he would. Bill let Brenda take her time to start her story, and once started, all that had happened since Bill had been injured came out in a rush, ending with the roosters that morning. She didn't tell him what Pete had done to her, could not. She did add in that Pete had brought a lady home with him and how rude she'd been. She ended with the statement that she wanted to go to see her mum and she'd take Dutchy with her for her Grans hens.

"And then there is this," she said with a tremble in her voice as she held out the box containing the ring.

Bill took her hands in his and smiled kindly at her, saying that of course, she should go to see her family and he was happy to let her take the rooster with her. He asked her to wheel him onto his room, which was a bit of a mess as Pete had been using it as well, and it smelled of cigarettes too. Bill thought that he was going to have a long talk to Pete as he certainly had taken advantage of Brenda and lied to him. Bill asked Brenda to reach into the top shelf toward the back where a flat cigar box was hidden. She handed it to Bill who lay it in his lap as she wheeled him back to the kitchen. Bill looked kindly at her as he handed her the box.

"This is for you, love."

Brenda opened the box to find one hundred pounds in notes and coins. She looked at it, her mouth open in shock at all that money, and before she could speak, Bill cut in with the explanation that he'd been salted it away for the day she decided to go to see her family. Brenda threw herself onto Bill's lap and hugged him.

"Well. Well, what now?" Pete tossed the words into the room as he entered the kitchen. Brenda again wondered how such a big man could move so silently.

Pete went to pick up the money, but Brenda flew off Bill's knee, grabbing the money box and her ring up in one swift movement before retreating to stand behind Bill's chair. Cliff looked at Bill, eyebrows raised, eyes looking from the money to Brenda and back to Bill. Bill explained that he'd been putting the money away for when Brenda decided to go to see her family. Besides, she'd worked hard at keeping the place going while he'd been in hospital and Cliff off driving, pretty much on her own, and she deserved the money.

This last bit was said as he looked directly at Pete, who averted his eyes from Bill's direct stare. Bill knew then that Brenda had been correct that he hadn't been any help to her during this time. Brenda noticed Pete's shift in gaze and saw the first expression show in his eyes and knew then that she had some power as he was unsure if she'd told of what he did to her. She looked at Cliff who had just arrived over Bill's head and spoke defiantly and strongly.

"Yes, I will, but first, I want to go see my mum." She strode past Pete to take Cliff's arm and felt Pete move away from her feeling the power her body was radiating. "Come and I will show you Prince's commands and what I need you to do to keep up with his training."

BRENDA LOUISE

AVOIDING ENCOUNTERS

HOME AND THE FUTURE BEGINS

Before she left Brenda and Cliff spent a day going over Prince's training routines. Cliff asked her how long she intend to visit with her mum. She shook her head, saying she didn't know and would just see how things went. Actually, Brenda was a little afraid of saying she wanted to go see her mum because of memories of what her mum had been like the last time she'd seen her. Brenda's emotions were very rattled by Pete's assault, and she'd uttered the words before she'd even known she said them and she was having regrets about the impending visit. She was pleased Cliff was going to be there with her. She wondered if her grandparents and mum would say when she wanted to share his bed. Or if in fact she even wanted to continue to do share his bed. *Bugger Pete*, she kept thinking. *He has ruined everything. Bugger, bugger!* She vowed to herself that she'd make him pay one day.

Cliff was confused that Brenda didn't want to lie with her head on his chest for a chat as usual before they went to sleep, saying she was tired before turning on her side with her back to him. She'd even flinched a little as he patted her back while saying, "Night." The next day, they got in the horses to take the new steers to their paddock before lunch. Cliff and Bill were amazed how intelligent Prince was with the steers and how much Brenda's riding had improved. Over lunch Brenda apologised to Bill as the gardens all needed weeding and the vegetable garden needed quite a bit of work. Bill smiled a little secret smile and told it was all good and to enjoy her visit. She didn't want to let her mum know she was coming as she thought I will get the real feel for how things are that way.

Bill smiled at Brenda when she asked if she could buy Dutchy, saying, "He is yours, love, and I think that he'll be happy at your Grandparents place."

It was a tight squeeze to fit Brenda and Prince into the front of the ute. Dutchy protested loudly being placed in the back in Duke's show travel box as they drove away. Brenda had tried to convince Bill that he'd be okay to be in the cab with them as that is where he sat when she drove the ute. She absolutely refused to have Prince put in the back. Cliff spoke up for her as well, but Bill wouldn't allow the rooster in the front. However, as soon as they were well away from Lochlea, and at Brenda's tearful insistence, Dutchy was put in his usual spot on the shelf behind the seats, where he settled down to preen his ruffled feathers back into order. Prince sat calmly between Cliff and Brenda or lie down with his head on Brenda's lap. The dog had been a little confused to not have Brenda driving.

Cliff was happy to see his ring on Brenda's finger, but found the unwillingness to chat a little disconcerting. She'd always been a bit of a chatterbox. He tried to get her talking by asking about her experiences at Lochlea. Had she been lonely? Had she had any real trouble and had to call neighbours in? He received only one word responses, so he gave up and handed her his music collection so she could choose something to play. For the best part of the trip, she spent half turned away from him, gazing out the window at the changing countryside. They drew some odd glances when they stopped to let the bird and dog out for a run at a couple of roadside parks. At one of them, a small dog ran at Dutchy, yapping, and got the shock of its life when Dutchy didn't run away but fluffed out his feathers and went to attack the dog. Brenda and the dog's owners arrived to the duo at the same time, each picking up their respective pets, Brenda receiving a glare from the dog's owner. Cliff's heart flipped when he watched Brenda return to him laughing so hard she could hardly hold Dutchy. "Bet that dog won't do that again." she managed to gasp.

Brenda resumed gazing quietly out the window, lost in her own world of confusion. After a time, she drifted off to sleep. Cliff had to shake her awake when he pulled up outside her grandparents' house. They sat in the ute for a while as Brenda brushed her hair. She questioned Cliff how he'd found the house and was shocked to find that he'd dropped her dad here previously. She wasn't sure how she'd react to him, remembering how her mum and dad had ignored her the last time they'd all been together. Cliff was sure Dexter would be cross with him as he'd known Dexter was upset over Brenda being missing. The young couple both took several deep breaths, leaving the dog and bird in the ute, and holding hands walked toward the front door.

The Hays and Willows were sitting down to their dinner when the knock came on the door. Dexter went to see who it was, and stood open mouthed when he saw who was there. He looked from one to the other several times before whispering "You knew where she was, you bugger." He raised his closed fist and shook it at Cliff.

Brenda's heart sank as Dexter seemed to be ignoring her again. She was ashamed to find tears forming behind her eyes. Gran Hay came to check what was taking Dexter so long. When she saw Brenda, she pushed past Dexter and wrapped Brenda in a huge hug, dragging her into the house. Brenda burst into tears, sobbing uncontrollably. That surprised Brenda as she hadn't cried very much except when her legs got scratched, not even when Dexter had bashed D2 to death. Gran held her till the sob reduced to the occasional gulps before she put her arms round Brenda's shoulders and walked her into the kitchen. Nancy jumped up, causing her chair to crash over with a loud bang. Brenda was squashed between her gran and mum and started to sob again.

Granddad left them to it and went to the door where he could hear loud voices. Dexter was raging at Cliff for not telling him that he knew where Brenda was and asking if he had taken Brenda's innocence. He wasn't giving Cliff a chance to get any words of explanation into the one-sided conversation. Fred stepped in front of Dexter as he went to punch Cliff. Dexter swung away and pushed past Cliff, striding angrily away, pausing only to kick at the tyres on the ute. Cliff held out his hand to Fred thanking him for stepping in, but admitting that he possibly deserved a belting for not making Brenda get in touch sooner. Fred invited him in so he could hear what Cliff had to say for himself.

The women had taken Brenda into her mother's room to try and get her to calm down, so Bill poured Cliff a cuppa and sat down to hear his story. It took a while for Cliff to get all of the events out as to why he'd done as Brenda wanted. He explained that he'd encouraged her to let her parents know she was alright, but Brenda had stubbornly refused as she'd been so badly hurt by them. He finished by saying that he loved her and that they were engaged to be married. This last bit of information alarmed Fred, and he asked bluntly if they'd had sex. He was relieved when Cliff assured him that he hadn't for several reasons, the most important being Brenda's age. Cliff went on to tell how wonderful Brenda was and how she'd taken responsibility on the farm when Bill had been injured.

Then Cliff remembered the animals still in the ute, so they went out to fetch them. Fred was very impressed with the rooster, saying he'd be happy to keep him. Cliff carried Dutchy in his cage to Fred's chook pen where they caught the resident rooster before releasing Dutchy into the yard. The way Dutchy shook himself and flapped his wing before crowing loudly made both of them smile. Fred recognised he was a fine-looking bird. Prince was busy lifting his leg on lots of bushes and shrubs, stopping only to growl as Dexter stumped back into the yard, meeting Fred and Cliff as they returned from the fowl run. Cliff used one of the commands that Brenda had told him to use, and the dog stopped growling but still had his hackles up a little. Dexter had calmed down a little and apologised to Cliff but reiterated that he should have told him about Brenda.

No one got much sleep that night except Brenda, who had cried herself into exhaustion on Nancy and Dexter's bed. After much talk, with Dexter not allowing Cliff to get away with not telling him where Brenda was previously, at the end of it all, as daylight beckoned, Dexter, still angry, took himself off to work. Cliff was bedded down on the lounge that opened out into a bed while Nancy crawled in with Brenda. Nancy, Gran, and Anna were shocked when they got up to find Brenda snuggled up beside Cliff, her head on his shoulder and Cliff's arm holding her to him. The two ladies talked quietly over their morning cuppa how they should approach this unexpected, for them, situation. They were pleased Dexter hadn't seen the couple.

Fred, returning from feeding his chooks, sat down heavily with a huge sigh, saying, "That is just not right. What is happening in there?" He indicated the lounge area.

At this point, Brenda strolled into the kitchen, murmuring, "Morning," to them all. She didn't notice the odd looks or feel any tension, as she greeted Prince, until she'd got her cuppa and sat down. Elsie reached over and put her hand on Brenda's arm, saying with tears in her eyes, "Why, why love?"

Brenda was ever so confused as to what she meant till Fred growled at her. "You are bring shame to the family by sleeping with a man before marriage." He finished with the word "Shame!" slapping the table and striding out of the house, jamming his hat on his head. Prince jumped up at the loud voice, growling softly in his chest, not sure what to make of the situation. Brenda snapped her fingers and commanded him to lie down.

Brenda was so confused as she'd been sharing the bed with Cliff for so long that she thought nothing of it now. After all, Bill had understood. Nancy picked up Brenda's hand with the tiny engagement ring, saying that she'd talk to Dexter and give permission for the couple of marry as soon as it could be arranged before any babies were on the way. Brenda started to laugh at this, telling these poor worried ladies that she and Cliff hadn't done anything to have babies, finishing with the fact that she just liked sleeping in the same bed as Cliff and had been doing that forever.

Brenda looked from one woman to the other and declared that they hadn't had sex, though they'd wanted to, Cliff had said not till she was sixteen. At that point, Cliff entered the kitchen, which brought the conversation to an end, and the ladies put on the hats and went to pick some fresh flowers for the house. Glancing over their shoulder as they left, they saw Cliff give Brenda a kiss on the top of her head and a brief hug. Brenda was laughing, but Cliff was looking very serious. Prince followed Nancy and Elsie to sniff his way round the garden.

During the course of that day, Nancy and Anna became aware that the young couple were in love and that Cliff was a very respectable young man. Nancy went to meet Dexter to explain the bedding situation. Dexter was tired and simply shrugged his shoulders, thinking, *So be it*. It was most likely too late to stop anything, but he agreed the couple should get married as soon as possible to stop any untoward mistakes that would bring shame to him and Nancy. Cliff and Brenda refused to rush their marriage, both wanting to wait till Brenda turned sixteen. The time apart now would see if they truly loved each other. It took Dexter several days to be able to bring himself to have any sort of a conversation with Cliff, though. He found himself bending slightly toward Cliff when he drove the ladies up to the correspondence college to get Brenda's results and junior certificate. She'd passed with flying colours. Brenda's teacher there sat Brenda down to ask what she wanted to do with herself going forward. Brenda said, "Maybe a nurse," so she could look after mums and babies. She was given some enrolment forms for nursing and the name of training hospitals. Cliff gave her encouragement saying that the local hospital often struggled to get nurses to stay on there because of the isolation. She agreed to give it a go.

There was a party atmosphere in the house that night. Fred, Dexter, and Cliff had a beer each, Nancy and Anna a light shandy, and Brenda some cordial. She still found fizzy soft drink too sweet. Dexter brought out a bottle of rum, and enduring the frowns from the ladies, Fred and Dexter had a snort each. Cliff refused, saying Brenda didn't like the smell and would refuse to go to bed with him if he did. This statement brought a moment of silence before Dexter laughingly said that women rule our lives as he put the rum away.

The rest of Cliff's stay went smoothly enough, with beach picnics and Prince running on the sand and snapping at the waves and drives in the surrounding countryside. They went and looked at where Dexter had been while he was in the army, and to marvel at the construction of yet another bridge being built over the Brisbane River. They rode on the trams from almost one side of the city to the other. Cliff and Dexter were glued to newspaper reports and gazing at televisions set up in shop windows of the Olympic games being held in Tokyo, Japan. It annoyed Fred and Dexter as they'd both been haunted by the fact that Japan had come so close to invading Australia not that long ago. They were delighted that America and Russia won more medals than Japan. Plus, Australian athletes did well. Nancy would sigh as the men went off to watch the TVs, saying wouldn't it be great if everyone could have a TV at home. She was sure that it would never happen.

Cliff put off going back to Lochlea till after the games were done and dusted, declaring he'd come back for Christmas if he could but would definitely drop in from time to time if he was doing any driving for Pete. Brenda shuddered inwardly at the mention of Pete's name. She'd nearly put that episode of Pete's assault out of her mind. She mentally shook herself and buried her head in Cliff's chest, wrapping her arms round him, as he made to go. Just as suddenly she dropped her arms and ran back into the house. Nancy offered to make up the bed in the sewing room, but Brenda wanted to continue to sleep on the lounge, sleeping each night hugging Cliff's pillow. Long, newsy letters passed between them. Cliff sent photos Bill had taken of Prince and him working in the training area and of the flourishing flower garden, which Brenda displayed behind the lounge. Bill and Cliff both worked at keeping the garden going till she returned.

She missed all the activity at Lochlea, particularly the interaction with the animals. Nancy and Brenda meticulously went over the requirements for the nursing application and were excited to find that one of the Brisbane hospitals took in trainees. There were verbal and written test to get through, which had to meet very strict criteria. Brenda felt sure she'd be fine owing to her reading of the encyclopaedia Holly had let her study at Bemerside. Dexter was nappy with the plan of nursing as it would keep her away from Cliff. He still felt resentment towards him. When Nancy escorted Brenda to the hospital for her interview, they were surprised to find Albert and his "niece," Cindy, in the waiting room. The encounter made both Nancy and Brenda feel a range of different feelings. Brenda was glad for the distraction of meeting Albert again, as she was feeling rather nervous. She prattled on about Prince and Lochlea till she was called in for her verbal interview. She felt that Cindy should have gone first and told the lady who called her name that Cindy was here before her. Brenda got a sharp rebuke that it was her turn now! Albert shrugged his shoulders and gave her a small nod and smile as if to say it was okay.

The matron conducting the interview asked Brenda questions like why she wanted to be a nurse, whether she could handle the sight of blood, of she'd she be able to deal with the work and study required, and mostly if she could follow instruction. The matron was very astute and looked quite severe, peering over the top of her glasses at Brenda with a piecing gaze. Once the first question was asked, Brenda relaxed and answered with growing confidence, even bringing an expression of surprise into the matron's eyes a couple of times. They farewelled Albert and Cindy with hugs when the interview was over, bringing a look of surprise to the lady who had come to call Cindy into the interview as she'd never seen an expression of affection between blacks and whites before. Brenda wished Cindy well. Dexter was surprised that they'd met up with

Albert, and remembered that Albert had told him once that Brenda was okay. He went back and asked him how he'd known Brenda was alright previously to which Albert touched his chest saying my heart just knew.

Brenda eventually got a call to attend written test and was pleasantly surprised to find Cindy there as well. Most of the other young ladies were giving Cindy suspicious side glances and whispering behind their hands. Brenda felt a ripple of oohs go around the room as she greeted Cindy with a smile and a hug. They sat beside each other, with the other girls putting a bit of space between themselves and Cindy. Brenda found that strange, but when she mentioned it to Cindy, Cindy just shrugged her shoulders and murmured it didn't matter as lots of people didn't know how to relate to "us black fellas," and it was their problem really.

They were the first to finish the written test, which was mainly based on anatomy of the body, and they were allowed to leave the room. As Brenda glanced over her shoulder as they walked out, she saw several of the others glaring after them. Cindy said her uncle Albert had talked to her often how the insides of animals all fitted together, and she guessed people were pretty much the same. Brenda told her how Albert had shown her the insides of the animals slaughtered on Bemerside. They confided to each other what their future dreams were. Cindy wanted to go back to Dubbo and help set up clinics to treat, what she called "her mob" as they were sometimes too afraid to go to the "white fella" clinics or doctors. She wasn't sure yet whether she'd go on to become a doctor, but she'd need to work for a bit to get the money to see her through the years of study, though Albert would help as well. Brenda wanted to get into looking after babies and helping women get through the birthing process, because of her own difficult birth and the horror of the cow that'd had the prolapse on Bemerside. They chatted happily, wandering through the gardens in the extensive grounds, watching the wind moving the leaves on the trees gently and listening to the traffic zoom past on the road beyond the garden walls.

The other lasses eventually came out, and although they kept their distance, Brenda and Cindy heard comments like "That was ridiculous" and "How would anyone know that sort of stuff." One of the girls who had glared at Brenda and Cindy came over to them, asking in a condescending tone, "Find it all too much, did you? So you just up and left?"

They shook their heads and smilingly replied that they'd found the test quite reasonable and had finished. At that, the lass, whose name was Diana, turned on her heel and flounced off. Cindy and Brenda looked at each other and said at the same time, "Hope we don't have to work with her."

They need not have worried as Diana failed the test, being told she could try again in six months. All the others passed with Cindy gaining the top marks, closely followed by Brenda. The head of the organisation reminded all of them that they all needed to continue to put every effort onto their study as well as perform well in all the practical tasks on the wards. As they left the building and ground Cindy was given a note to tell her that Albert had had to leave and she'd need to catch a bus to his aunties. They found that the last bus had already left, so Brenda invited her back to her gran's for the night. Dexter had arrived in Cliff's ute along with Cliff to take Brenda home. Brenda flung herself at Cliff for a long hug before remembering Cindy who was standing beside Dexter with a huge smile on her face. Cliff and Dexter agreed that Cindy could indeed come home with them so long as they went and told her aunty first.

Cliff was amused and a little put out that for the first time since he and Brenda had met Brenda didn't sleep in the same bed as him but spent the night giggling and talking with Cindy. He was happy for her even though he was just a little bit jealous. He found that it was hard to get a word in between the girls telling about the exam and how well they'd done. Also, what their plans were in the future. Cliff found it hard to see where he seemed to fit into Brenda's future. Dexter who really had very little to say took him aside and reminded him that she was still a very young girl. He also added that Brenda had never really had a real girlfriend till she'd met Jewel and Cindy at Bemerside. No one at the Hay house was bothered by Cindy's dark skin. Besides, she had very excellent manners, a lovely, soft voice, and laughing eyes. Nancy was pleased Brenda would have a friend to go with her into this next adventure.

Brenda had enjoyed showing off how well trained Prince was to Cindy and introducing her to Dutchy, who despite having all his hens now, he'd follow Brenda around when the chooks were let out for a run in the afternoons. Cindy was both impressed and amused as her family didn't have any pets, although some of her relatives had very disobedient dogs and the odd cat. It made Brenda realise how lucky she was. Cliff had come to see if Brenda about some dog trials that were happening soon. Brenda was excited and asked Cliff to nominate Prince, the whole family thought they'd all go up for the weekend, even Cindy. All that made Cliff happy and assuaged his jealousy a little. He managed to get a little time alone with Brenda before he headed home when they ran Cindy home to her aunty's. They drove up to a lookout and sat holding hands, admiring the view, Brenda's head on his shoulder.

Cliff turned to her and, placing his fingers under her chin, lifted her face up to his, giving her the long, soft kiss. Brenda sighed deeply as she accepted the kiss and returned in kind. After, they gazed into each other eyes with both expectation and sadness. Brenda broke the spell as she broke off the look and wrapped her arms round Cliff's waist in a tight cuddle. "Guess the wedding will have to wait now, hey. I really want to do this nursing thing, and it may help us later on."

"We will see, lass, hey," Cliff whispered "Just maybe we can still be married when you turn sixteen and with your parents' permission just maybe. I love and want you so much."

Cliff returned her cuddle and agreed that the nursing was a great idea. They chatted all the way home, and Cliff felt happy when he left, secure in the knowledge that he'd have her at Lochlea for the trials. It was only a week after the tests that the girls were called back in to be told they could start straight away, not after Christmas as they'd first been advised. This caused a flurry of shopping and discussion as to whether they'd stay in the nurses' quarters or not. Cindy made the decision easy as she had to stay at the hospital as her aunty was going away for a holiday, so Brenda agreed to go in and stay in the quarters with her. To Nancy, it was like losing her daughter again and she found it hard to come to the realisation that Brenda was ready to venture out into the world on her own terms. At least this time, she'd know where she was. It was with great disappointment that it meant that they couldn't attend the dog trails as a family, but Brenda insisted that they should still go so they could meet Bill and see her flowers. Behind her insistence was the fact it was one year since Sandra had died, and she felt that Mum and Dad needed the distraction. She was upset not to see Prince in his first trails though and thoughts of D2 came into her mind.

The girls moved into the nurses' quarters of the week to be ready to start duties the Monday after the trials. It was a flurry of packing and racing back to get forgotten items. They were excited to be able to hang their starched and pressed uniforms in the lockers. Everything became very real. They met some of the other new girls as well as second- and third-year nurses. None of them quite knew how to take Cindy with her dark skin and treated her with some suspicion, which Cindy just brushed off with a toss of her head. There was a notice board with their rosters along with a comment on how well they'd performed in the written test. Beside Cindy's was a *very, very well done* and Brenda's only a *very well done*. Most of the others had *well done* and *good work* beside their names. Lots of secretive glances from the other girls after the sheet went up with them, wondering if Cindy had cheated somehow. Brenda was pleased to see she'd been assigned to a birthing ward as that was where she wanted to be. Cindy got a male surgical ward. So it would be with great trepidation that they'd don their uniforms and present themselves on that Monday, not really sure what to expect.

BACK ON THE FARM

Bill told Cliff not to hurry back as he left to take Brenda and her pets to Brisbane. Bill made a great pretence of being very stiff and unable to more than hobble about with the use of crutches, but mostly the wheelchair, so Pete had to push him about. Bill hadn't broken his hip, as the doctors suspected, but had several badly bruised tendons and muscles. His shoulder and arm were mending well. He could walk and didn't really need the chair. However, he kept up the pretence to teach Pete somewhat of a lesson. Bill discovered that indeed Pete hadn't been helping Brenda as he knew nothing of the feeding routines or how to milk the cow. Bill knew he could have done the milking with his one hand quicker than Pete's awkward tugging at the teats. It was almost laughable, so Bill had strife keeping a straight face on many occasions.

One of Bill's buyers contacted him, asking if he could pick up some steers that week. Pete was devastated because he'd hardly ever been on a horse and didn't like them. When he protested, Bill just smiled and commented that Brenda had never been on a horse either and she'd managed to do it. This made Pete fume internally. It wasn't the first time Bill had brought up how wonderful Brenda was. He began to hate her more and more every time her name came up. Pete was hoping to be able to cart the steers, but Bill insisted that he couldn't manage without him and had asked the buyer to bring his own transport for them. Pete wasn't happy since he hadn't been to town for a week

The muster was almost a scene out of a bad Western. Pete was terrified of the horse. The horse was unsure of the strange signals it was receiving from him as well. With Bill on the tractor and Pete flopping round on the poor horse, they eventually got one paddock of steers into the yard. Although Pete had carted a lot of cattle, he'd never had to have anything to do with them or get up close and personal with them. In fact, he was terrified of them. When the buyer arrived and the inevitable cup of tea drunk, they went to load the cattle. The buyer, James Carter, a butcher from town, had been told by Bill that he shouldn't help Pete in the yard. He stood outside the yard with Bill, who was making a pretence of counting the steers and watching Pete in the yard.

Pete had protested to Bill that perhaps James could help, but Bill had replied that Brenda had loaded some by herself. Pete stamped away into the yards, vowing to himself he'd make Brenda pay for his embarrassment in front of James. Both Bill and James had had a time controlling their grins of amusement as Pete sidled round the steers, keeping very close to the fence and making weird noises and waving his drafting stick about in his effort to move the animals onto the truck. If any of them turned to look at him, Pete would jump back to the fence, climbing half up the fence. It was a regular circus, but eventually the steers wandered onto the truck, and James slammed the truck door closed, shook hands, and went on his way.

As Bill and Pete made their way back to the house, Bill, watching Pete out of the corner of his eyes, said, "Few ticks and flies on that lot, so best we get the rest in next week and spray them." The horrified look that passed over Pete's face caused Bill to avert his face to hide his smile, thinking that Pete wasn't as brash as he usually was and good job too. "Get the horses in tomorrow so we can get a start on that, hey."

Other than forcing cattle work on Pete, including riding, which he wasn't good at, Bill had him checking all the fences and re-staining where required. This was another first for Pete, which, seeing as he'd grown up on properties, it seemed he'd avoided any of the usual chores required to up keep the maintenance. Pete pinched his fingers a lot with the pliers doing the fences. Bill thought about how inept he was and remembered that although his wife, May, had loved her brother, she'd said he could be a bully at times and, being the one of the eldest, had generally got all the younger siblings to do his share of the chores. There had been eight siblings in the family.

Bill's last punishment, and that is what it was, for Pete came when he got him to weed and loosen the earth round the flowerbeds and dig over the fallow vegetable garden beds, replenishing the beds with topsoil from the gullies, fowl runs, and yards. He even got him to cart sand to resurface the fowls' runs. This brought out the worst of Pete as he swore fiercely while attending this job. His hands weren't used to the constant chaffing of the fork, racks, and shovels, so his hands became blistered and very painful. His back and arms ached with all the physical activity. His hatred of Brenda grew with every bit of pain being inflicted on him.

The only thing that stopped him from telling Bill to "get f—ed" was the fact that he was aware that Bill was physically unable to do it because of his accident. Bill had been good to him over the years, providing the start-up finance for his truck and giving him a solid home base. Bill never frowned at him when, after a long trip, he went on a bender or brought a woman home. Pete was looking forward to the day he could get back on the road. It had filtered through his mind why all these job were so urgent they couldn't wait till Cliff got back.

Towards the end of the fortnight, Pete took Bill for a check-up in town, using the light truck. Then as Bill told him he'd been permission to walk using canes or crutches, they went to a cattle sale for Bill to buy some replacement steers. Pete felt good to be round the roar of semis as they manoeuvred to unload or reload the stock to or from the yards. Pete made contact with several of his previous customers and pals. He drank excessively, so Bill had to load his purchases with the help of the yard stock man and manhandle Pete into the truck. After unloading the new steers and tossing them some hay, Bill left Pete to sleep it off in the cramped cab of the little truck. Pete came to as the sun beat through the windscreen. It took a few moments to untwist his body back into a seating position. His mouth was extremely dry, and he felt like throwing up, so he jerked open the door and spewed foul-tasting bile onto the ground. As he spat the last of the bile out, a sound filtered into his head, past the pounding of his head. He swung his legs out and jumped down, avoiding the spew puddle, and realized Bill was whistling as he went about the morning chores. It took a few moments for him to realise that Bill was walking smartly about without the use of any aids. It dawned on Pete that Bill had fooled him into thinking he was disabled, getting him to do all the past fortnight's work on his own. He became very angry.

Pete forgot he didn't feel very well as he strode towards Bill. Bill sensed him coming and put down the feed buckets he was carrying, turning to face the irate figure striding towards him. Bill couldn't help the slight grin that came to his lips. Pete saw the lopsided grin before he could get any words out, and he stood on front of Bill, opening and closing his mouth several times before he could get any words out, fists clenched at his side. When the words came, they were laced very strongly with expletives about his treatment over the last fortnight.

Bill let him get all his rage out before he simply replied quietly that he should have been more help to Brenda and admitted that he'd faked the severity of his disablement. Bill ended by saying, as he turned away, that a trucking job had come through, and he needed to contact the agents in town before lunch.

That comment took the wind out of Pete's sails, and he walked quickly to the house. He couldn't wait to get away, his mind swirling with how he could make the little bitch pay for his discomfort. When he rang the agents, he found the job had been sitting with them for a week or more. Again, he blamed Brenda, vowing if he never saw her again, it would be too soon.

FATE

Fred had borrowed a car from a mate so Anna, Fred, Nancy, and Dexter could come for the weekend as well. Anna and Fred were very excited, as it had been a long time since they'd gotten away from home. They gazed out the car windows at the ever-changing countryside. Bill made the Willows and Hay families feel very welcome at Lochlea, and as Pete was off driving, he put the Hay family in his room. Cliff opted to sleep on the couch in the lounge, giving up his bed to Dexter and Nancy. He was going to get to girls wouldn't have much rest time anyway,. They spent the first few hours looking at everything about the homestead. Everyone was impressed with how well it was all set up. Prince followed them about for most of the time, but he kept returning to the car, sniffing round to see if Brenda was there. The ladies were a little tired and offered to see for dinner while Bill squeezed the men into the ute and took them off to look at the rest of the property. Dexter was well impressed and voiced his sadness at no longer working out of town.

Nancy and Anna made a cuppa as they surveyed the well-appointed kitchen, both commenting how quiet and peaceful it was, the silence broken by the distant lowing of a cattle and the clucking of a hen as she announced the laying of an egg. After checking the food situation and deciding on cold meat and fresh salad picked straight out of the garden and boiled eggs, they picked some of Brenda's flowers for the table as well. They were relaxing on the chairs out the front when the men returned. Bill produced some beer, and they chatted animatedly for a good hour before doing the evening chores and devouring the prepared meal, with Dexter commenting that food always tastes better in the country. The visitors prepared for bed while Cliff ran Prince through his final run. Cliff thought that for a young dog, he should go well at the dog trials to be held that weekend if he didn't get distracted by the sights and sound of the crowd.

Cliff drove down and picked up Brenda and Cindy for the day of the trials only. Brenda was happy to see the garden in its full bloom. She gave Cindy a full tour while everyone else got ready for the day in at the trials. They washed and groomed Prince, who looked ever so handsome. Brenda compared him to the others in the competition and the other dogs all were so much more mature and decided that as Cliff had been working with him last, he should run Prince through the course.

Prince got very distracted by the crowd and all the other dogs, some of them yapping in excitement. The under-one-year-old dogs were first up before Prince had time to get used to all the hubbub. He executed the obstacles okay but kept stopping to look around between them, even peed on a post in the middle of the arena, much to the amusement of the crowd. However, that misbehavior got him disqualified. Cliff was surprised at the end of the day to have Prince awarded an encouragement award with the judges advising Cliff to keep at it and to take him to places where there were crowds to acclimatize Prince, adding that for such a young dog, he showed plenty of promise. Cliff took all the advice and decided he'd take Prince to some dog shows whenever he could. He discussed this with Brenda as he took her and Cindy back to their quarters at the hospital, where the girls tiredly dragged themselves out of the car, giving small waves as he drove off.

The visitors enjoyed the day reveling in how the dogs' performances got better and better as the events progressed to the senior dogs, the top honor going to a dog called, of all things, Fred, with the announcer advising the crowd that Fred was a champion in the show ring as well as the trials and his service fee was 500 pounds and his next litter of pups would sell for 500 pounds for the bitches and 600 pounds for the males. Fred dug Anna in the ribs, whispering that she best save up as the service fee was now 500 pounds. Anna glared at him before bursting into laughter, saying he best be more obedient as he had now show ring qualifications, still his offspring was exceptional as she glanced at Nancy.

The day ended with dinner at the pub, everyone talking animatedly of the day before heading home to feed up before crashing into bed. As they packed up the next day Dexter took Bill aside asking him if he ever needed a man for work to please keep him in mind. Bill shook his hand and agreed to do that. As they were all climbing into the car, Pete came rolling into the yard, looking with amazement at the visitors. Pete jumped down quickly, coming over to see what was going on. Bill introduced him—he smelled strongly of rum—where Pete admitted he'd gotten into town yesterday and joined in the after-trials party. Cliff, who had returned from taking the girls back, saw Nancy looking at the decal of the snake on the truck door. He commented that Brenda hated the picture and for a long time Cliff had had to open the door for her as she wouldn't bring herself to touch the door. Nancy nodded and said briefly that she'd had a couple of bad snake experiences. Cliff went to tell her about the chicks but Dexter announced that they'd better get going because he had to get the car back to his mate.

As they drove off, Nancy and Anna murmured to each other that they weren't impressed with Pete, as he talked too loud and didn't really listen to anyone, breaking into the conversations before the comments they were saying were finished. Besides, he didn't seem to even care how well Prince had done. In fact, Prince didn't move to greet him at all and never took his eyes off him, and he'd let out a little growl when he was approaching the group. They concluded that dogs usually can be good judges of character. They were pleased Brenda was no longer there with Pete at Lochlea. Dexter raved on for most of the journey home about how he so did miss the country lifestyle, how well run Lochlea was, how he'd like to learn more about the improved pastures that was there and most of all he was excited at the prospect of driving Pete's truck. It was bigger than the trucks during his army days. On and on came the army stories, most of which they'd all heard before, so they just settled back and let his words wash over them. They were tired but happy to finally get home. It had been a great weekend and Nancy was keen to relay of how she felt about Lochlea to Brenda as they hadn't had much of a chance at the trails.

Nancy had to wait several days to see Brenda since she'd been given some night shifts. Brenda looked tired but happy and was extremely proud of Prince and Cliff for having a go. Nancy had brought back his encouragement award for her to display on the walls of her and Cindy's room along with the photo of Cliff. Cindy had no photos of her family because the aboriginal folks thought photos took away some of their soul. She was good at drawing, though, and had hand drawn some likenesses of her "uncle" Albert and her mum. Her dad was a white fella and had left when Cindy was only a baby. She looked upon Albert as her father figure, even after her mum got remarried to a really nice bloke. She like her stepdad, though, and her two younger half siblings.

Nancy took Brenda and Cindy out for lunch and listened while they talked about the hospital and the other first-year girls. Most of the other girls were polite but kept their distance, not inviting Brenda and Cindy to their get togethers. Nancy was sad about that. Brenda bombarded her with questions about Lochlea, and she'd liked her flowers. How did she find Bill? Did Nancy get to see her horse Ace? After a slight hesitation, did she get to meet Pete? Nancy thought about her reservations about Pete and wondered if she could ask more about him, but this wasn't the time, she decided, so just replied that he'd arrived just as they were leaving and left it at that. Brenda was pleased to hear she approved of her flowers selection. How much she and everyone else had been impressed by Lochlea, and, no, she hadn't met Ace. Nancy went on to tell how much Dexter had wished he could get back to that sort of lifestyle. They talked way past the curfew for the girls to get back to their quarters, but Nancy stood up for them with the housemistress, who said they'd received a warning and it must never happen again.

Brenda and Cindy were very careful not to late back again after visit from Uncle Albert and Brenda's family. They learned to talk about things they experienced on their wards. Like how straight laced the sisters were and all, what seemed to them, silly rules. Like not sitting down during their shifts, how to walk, never run, quickly and silently. The sisters moved about silently, and they often found a sister standing behind them, not having heard her arrive. Most of the times, they were assigned to washing the pans and had very little interaction with the patients. Brenda longed to cuddle the newborn babies, but that was a no-no. The girls, when not washing pans, were sent scurrying here and there, doing what to them seemed silly errands. They did get to do the rounds with the doctors, but not encouraged to ask questions. It amazed them how the senior nurses and sisters would bow and scrape to the doctors. Brenda and Cindy both broke the no-question rule, receiving glares from the sister in charge. However, the doctors seemed willing enough to answer the questions, even seeming to be amused by the questions.

The girls weren't put on the same wards after it was discovered that they were room-mates and friends, so they had lots to pass on to each other as they talked after retiring to bed. Very short chats as the work was demanding and the sisters more demanding. The other trainees kept their distance as well. For all that, they were enjoying the work and the learning, reading and watching, soaking up as much as they could. They both aced their first little tests much to the annoyance of some of the other lasses who thought of them as country bumpkins. Cindy confessed that after her first year she'd try to get transferred to Dubbo as she was feeling a bit homesick for the open spaces.

Their lives became a routine of sleep, eat, and work, not having too much time for idle chats most days. Two months past very quickly, and finally, they managed to day off at the same time. They lay in bed chatting, neither wanting to get up besides the sleep in was heaven. They were going to have the afternoon having a picnic on the beach with Nancy and Gran Hay. Brenda stopped talking rolling onto her side, head propped up on her hand, and said very seriously, "Cindy ... um ... Cindy," and after a long pause, she started again, "Cindy, I'm late! I'm late."

Cindy looked across wide-eyed at her friend. "Cliff?" she mouthed, and when Brenda shook her head, she said, "Who then?"

Cindy was sure Brenda hadn't been with anyone since they started their nursing. They lay looking at each other for some time before Cindy swung her legs out of bed, declaring that they'd better get Brenda checked out since it may just have been her body reacting to the change of environment, throwing her body out of kilter. That had happened to one of her cousins when she'd moved away from home. Brenda shook her head sadly and told Cindy of the encounter with Pete and how he'd hurt her. Brenda grinned at the end, saying how Pete had planned it and shut Prince up, knowing the dog would have protected her. Cindy was sympathetic but insisted that they must find out for sure. Brenda swore her to silence.

Brenda agreed to go to a clinic away from the hospital, though. She was sure that it wasn't her body, as her breasts were tender and she'd heard some of the new mums on the ward talking about that as a way they knew they were having a baby. There was one down near the river that took in disadvantaged folks. They could go there on their way to the beach. As Brenda was standing outside the clinic, gaining courage to go in, she heard the familiar sound of a big rig, and out of the corner of her eye saw the snake decal flash past. Pete was silhouetted in the cab. Brenda turned away and ran into the clinic. The clinic allowed Brenda in because she looked run down and tired, so they assumed she was either a prostitute or a runaway. Brenda found the experience of the examination very embarrassing. The old, sad-looking doctor gazed at her with kind eyes for a little while before he confirmed that she was indeed with child. He went on to offer advice about what unmarried lasses could do, giving her pamphlets on how to go through the adoption process. Also, he explained it could be possible to get a termination in South Australia. Brenda had no reply and left to join Cindy, swearing her to silence about it all saying her mum and gran must not know, and they'd talk later.

This was simply the worst possible thing that had ever happened to her, worse than D2 or Dinky dying. Her hands shook so much she dropped the tram money, and it went under the tram. The conductor on the tram wouldn't let her on, so she walked slowly back up the long hill to the hospital. Things in her life had been going along so well—her impending birthday which was to be followed by a small, private wedding in a registry office, Dexter and Nancy insisting on the wedding before she and Cliff made a serious mistake. She couldn't go through with it all now. Her pregnancy would soon become obvious, and Cliff would know it wasn't his. All these disjointed thoughts whirled round in her brain as she walked. No real decision had formed by the time she got back to her room. Cindy just looked at her and shut her mouth as Brenda shook her head and crawled fully clothed into bed, facing the wall.

RUNNING

Brenda became very quiet over the next week, not talking and hardly sleeping as she redressed her situation within herself. Nancy sent her a message that Cliff was coming down a day early that next weekend for her birthday and wedding forced her to come to a very quick and painful plan. Cliff would suss her out, and she couldn't have him learning about the baby. It would be her decision what she would and could do about it. Leaving a note just begging Cindy to keep her secret and without telling Cindy, Brenda called in sick to the matron, almost ran into town arriving at the bank as it opened and got all her money out. She'd packed a few items into her small beauty case, including the money left over from Lochlea, intending to get more clothes when she got to where ever she got to her destination, wherever that may be.

All the notes and coins didn't seem to be much once she held them in her hand, but she put a determined air and strode into the train station. The next train was going to Sydney in several hours, so she got a one-way ticket on that. Not really thinking through how she was going to get to South Australia, just knowing that she really didn't want to give life to this bastard child of Pete's. While she waited for the train, she bought a sandwich which stuck in her throat, so she fed most of it to the birds. Sadness filled her mind and body. She shut her eyes and could almost feel D2's nose under her hand like she had done when she knew Brenda was really sad. Prince had never been round her when she'd been this sad, so he hadn't developed the sensitive touch. Plus, he was a boy dog. *Bugger boys, bugger 'em*, she thought.

The train traveled mostly at night. Brenda had sat with her forehead against the glass, peering at the lights of the passing towns and villages or nothing. Her mind was completely void of rational thought. What would Cliff do? How long would it take for him to forget her? And forget her he must for she was now damaged goods and so unworthy. She knew, with the unwanted pregnancy, she could never go back home to bring such shame to her family. Tears sat behind her eyes, burning them, and so it was that she alighted in Sydney dry eyed. She took a deep breath and whispered to herself, "You can do this."

To give herself thinking time, she bought a pie and milkshake and devoured them, suddenly finding herself very hungry. As she sat with her hands folded in her lap, she felt a tiny flutter in her tummy. She jerked her hands away and stared aghast at her now not so flat belly. She hadn't taken any notice of the change till then. *Bugger, it's alive*, raced through her mind. She looked wildly about for a while before taking a deep, deep breath. "That changes things, I guess. I don't think I'll be able get rid of it now. Besides, the organization to get to South Australia would take time, and by then, it would most likely be too late, and besides, I'm not sure I have enough money." She mumbled out loud.

A trio of young painted lasses came and sat near her as she said that, and they glanced at the tired lass before chatting among themselves. They sounded tired but excited, and started to discuss, just loud enough for her to hear, how much money they'd made that night. The numbers seemed staggering. That much money would certainly go some way to elevating some of her immediate worries, she thought. She walked very quietly over to the girls, smiling shyly, arriving at their table before they knew she was there. The trio swung round as one when she said hello. They took in her tired appearance, her delicate looks, the huge, dark circles of tiredness under her eyes, and instinctively saw she was quite lost and desperate.

Before they spoke, all the girls glanced at the stairs running down from the road. A shadowy figure had appeared at the top of the stairs briefly before retreating out of sight. The lass closest to Brenda took her arm and led her away to another table behind the scrubs. The table was dirty and covered with chewing gum and bits of bread stuck to the table by some mysterious spilled drink. A body lay on the seat beside the table. Brenda felt herself forced onto the seat opposite this body.

"Don't worry about him, luv," the girl whispered. "He's out to it. You wait here till we have done our business, and I'll come and fetch you. Not a sound now, you hear." The last bit delivered with authority and some force.

Brenda was shocked into submission and sat staring wide eyed at the unmoving body, but after a good stare, she could see the rise and fall of the chest, so she relaxed enough to tune an ear into what was transpiring at the other table. Someone else had arrived and seemed to be speaking angrily to the group, snippets of words like "You lot need to spread out a bit more" and "Though that group idea worked out this time, there isn't the money in that." Some other spoken words sounded very cross. The last sentence was "And stop feeding that old fool back there and listening to his drivel. Be packed up and ready round seven p.m. tonight and maid outfits as we have a function to attend."

Brenda listened to the sound of the boots as they strode away in a confident manner. The body across from her farted and rolled over into a seated position, his dark eyes peering at her though matted hair and beard. The eyes were very bright and clear. One hand was scratching round his groin area, but as he opened his mouth to speak, Brenda felt a firm hand on her arm and allowed herself to be led away. She could still feel the eyes following her as she left. She felt as though they could see right into her. She shivered.

Brenda was feeling so tired and thus allowed herself to be led by the girls who were now looking as tired as she felt. Searching their appearance out of the corners of her eyes, she noted that the outfits they wore were very tatty and only held together with safety pins in some places. The painted faces looked grotesque and the weak sunlight filtering through the trees beside the road. They trudged for what seemed like ages before entering the yard of an old cottage surrounded by a weedy garden. Some girls of similar age met them as they were going in, and some pleasantries were were exchanged. An older woman sat beside a garden bed, pulling at the weeds. She sat awkwardly. Her legs sitting at odd angles from her body were very thin and white.

"You need to be moved, luv?" one of the girls asked the woman, who nodded.

Brenda sucked in her breath as the woman lifted her head. The woman's face had many disfigurements. One eye was completely closed, and the other seemed to bulge from her head with hardly any eyelids, her mouth hang down slack on the same side of the drooping eye. Besides of all that, her perfectly formed teeth were crystal white, and the one eye did show some intelligence. Two of the girls gently lifted her placing her beside another weedy bed and, after a search, placed a bell beside the woman.

"There you go, Silvie. You're doing a great job. You want your toast out here too, luv?" Without waiting for a grunting answer, they all entered the cottage, Brenda following. Inside was a very different sight to the decay outside. Everything was neat and very orderly. Colorful rugs were scattered round the lounge room, a small TV sat humming in a corner, and a wood fire gave the room a homey feel. The smell of toast and other cooking smells came from the kitchen. A couple of huge men sat at the table, drinking coffee.

"These are our minders and Silvie's bodyguards," they told Brenda, dismissing the men with a wave of their hands.

Brenda was shown the shower room and where she could put her things without much conversation. "Just freshen up and come back to the kitchen," Brenda was told. The five introduced themselves using first names only; no second names were mentioned. Brenda suspected these were made up names. Over tea and toast, she got the story. This was Sylvie's house, and she allowed them to stay so long as they kept the place clean and cooked for her. They hesitated before informing her that Silvie was—well, had been—a prostitute who had made good by being taken off the street by her now dead husband, whose house this had been. Gary, her son, now "ran" the girls in the house, procuring bookings and telling the girls when and where to go. They showed her an ivy-covered path down to another well-kept building that had six large rooms behind a reception area. This was for when clients came to the house for private "treatments" as they called them. Because of the good working conditions, there were always girls waiting to come and work for Gary and Silvie. Silvie insisted that the girls all do some form of study to assist them later on.

"This isn't a great way to live, but it's what we do for now. Silvie is great and makes us study a bit, much to Gary's disapproval, so that later on we may get out of this merry-go-round." one of the girls said.

Although Brenda had suspected that they were prostitutes, it still came as some sort of a shock to her, and she wondered if she was safe.

As they drank the tea and coffee, Brenda told a little bit of why she was in Sydney. Nods of understanding passed between the girls. They told her that although sometimes the clients were rough and asked them to do disgusting things, they were far better off than lots of other "working girls." Some of them had come from the street and told of being bashed regularly by some of the organizers who ran the street girls. There were always some battles being fought over where the girls could "work" between rival organizers, all very silly and unnecessary really, but the worst bit was the street girls having to live in really grubby, cockroach-infested hostels or boarding houses. Most of the time, they had to serve their clients in cars or dingy alleyways. They'd all been through that life before being lucky enough to come to this place. Most of these working girls hardly ever got out of the business. They went on to explain that they were really lucky to be in this house, as they were fed and had proper beds to sleep in.

Brenda shook her head fiercely at the suggestion that she may want to do that sort of work.

One of them said, "I'll speak to Silvie about keeping you away from Gary till you work out where you go from here. Be easy enough as he lives in a flash house near the harbor. This place's not good enough for him." They all sneered. "Gary keeps us very busy, and you can help keep the back rooms clean for us. Silvie will be fine with it."

She went on to say that if Gary saw Brenda's pretty face he'd insist she go to work.

Gary had kept up good relations with the police, so they were left alone, besides Gary employed some huge homosexual minders who worked in pairs round the clock. Silvie wouldn't allow illicit drugs or alcohol be used by the girls at all, but they all smoked endless cigarettes while they talked. Brenda found it odd that they didn't ask her too many questions about her circumstances, which suited her just fine since she was unsure about exactly how she felt right then. Feeling the movement in her tummy had thrown a lot of her resolve out the window. They took her out to meet Silvie and showed her how to move her when she rang the bell. Whoever was nearest dealt with that chore. Silvie had had a stroke several years ago, as well as being bashed, and had little or no speech, but could walk with sticks once she was on her feet. The whole morning, in fact, the last few days, had absolutely worn Brenda out, and she slept very soundly.

Brenda sat beside Silvie and watched her ineffectual tugging at the straggling weeds growing round pathetic, wilting plants. She looked around the yard and saw potential for a proper garden. She noted a falling-down structure in the back of the yard, and when she pointed to it, one of the girls said she thought it was once a chook house. Brenda felt a stirring of interest of something other than her situation for a while. She turned to Silvie, her eyes shining, and started to babble about setting up a vegetable garden with some flowers and fix up the chook house so they could have fresh eggs.

Silvie's face contorted, but her good eye was showing amusement, and she nodded that she agreed. Conversations round the table changed to what they could grow and so on. Even a couple of the minders joined in, giving advice on companion planting between vegetable, herbs, and flowers. So it was that a design of sorts was drawn up. Brenda and the minders got stuck in with gusto and soon had the makings of a functioning garden showing for their efforts.

Brenda found the house a very pleasant place to be. All the girls were friendly, and Silvie, although she had little speech, managed to convey her needs with movement of the hands and expressive eye rolls. Brenda took over the cooking duties for most of the time and, every few days, gave the rooms outside a good clean. She just let time slide by without much thought of what or where next. She was kept out of sight of Gary, who rarely came into the house, and all the activity that went on back there. Her made-up story of why she'd run away from her abusive father, except for the pregnancy, was retold over the next few days round cups of tea and meals. Some of the stories the girls told horrified her. She knew about prostitutes of course but assumed they were different to everyone else, but these girls were so normal. Each had her own tale of misadventure of how she'd ended up where she was. Some were very, very sad stories. They told her there were lots of less fortunate girls working on the streets, though with far more aggressive managers than Gary, who never hit them or used them for his own pleasure. With the education that they encouraged by Silvie to pursue, they all hoped one day to move on with their lives. There would always be replacements to be found when anyone moved on. Brenda was amazed they a couple of the girls had "real" boyfriends; it mystified her that they could be interested in men after doing their so called job.

Silvie watched Brenda with a bright, knowing eye and surprised Brenda about a couple weeks after she'd arrived. Silvie indicated that Brenda should take her outside, and as Brenda put her arm round Silvie to assist her onto her sticks, Silvie turned and looked straight into her eyes, her eye soft, and placed a hand on her tummy nodding knowingly. Brenda sighed and nodded, and that was that. Silvie wrote a name on a piece of paper and told Brenda to go see the old chap that she'd seen on the seat when she first met the girls. He, Dr. Harold, or Doc H (no one really knew his full name), was a disgraced doctor, a good one who'd gotten addicted to drugs and dismissed from practice and had escaped from the truck taking him to jail, hiding out in the parks and dilapidated buildings round Sydney, offering his services to the working girls and other less savory folk. He treated the underworld figures for gunshot wounds and the like. For these services, he got the drugs to feed his habit. He looked after the girls, who kept him fed and clothed. He refused to live in a permanent place, choosing to move about for fear that he be found and thrown in jail.

To find him was to ask about and eventually someone would know where he was at that time. It took Brenda several days to track him down that first time. She didn't fully trust this untidy-looking chap. The day she found him he was fortunately both clean of drugs and sober. Brenda was surprised to find that, underneath the dirty, tatty clothes, he smelt clean. He grinned at her realization of this, saying it was all part of the disguise. His hands were quite rough and reminded Brenda of Cliff's hands. He asked endless questions about how far along she was and so on, poking and prodding her tummy before sitting back from her and told her it was far too late to attempt an abortion. He laid out a lot of options, keep it, adopt it (and he knew people who would pay money for the baby), and left the decision up to her.

Silvie had told the girls about the pregnancy, and they all agreed that somehow they'd allow her to stay on. Besides, they were happy to not have to cook and clean, allowing them some free time for themselves or study. They all vowed again that Gary need not know about her as he'd only complicate the issue. Gary was surprised to find the garden in progress and questioned the use of the minders, which Silvie shut him down saying that they were just sitting about during the daylight hours most of the time anyway, beside it made the house being a boarding house for students for the activities that occurred in the rooms out back anyway. Gary had no comeback for that at all and returned the next day with some hens and actually got in and helped fix up the chook house.

Over the next months, Doc H became a mentor and friend. He still had some medical books, and they'd pour over them when Doc H was straight, which wasn't all that often. The street girls allowed him to wash at their places and kept him fed and gave him some money in return for medical assistance because they needed it, particularly the new birth control pill to stop the unwanted pregnancies that had plagued working girls in the past. He'd been a very successful doctor who had got addicted to drugs and gambling, had got in too deep, so through not being able to pay his debts had been giving drugs to his debtors in lieu of money and been struck off. He'd been sentenced to ten years jail but had managed to escape so he hid out on the street and drank and took whatever drugs he could get his hands on to hide his self-loathing. He did promise to be straight, though, when her time came. Through him, she met other homeless or lost folks and found them to be more educated than she'd assumed people living on the street would be. She decided to let things slide and stay where she was for the time.

As the time passed, the girls gave Brenda a very comprehensive instruction on sex, ensuring her that it could be very nice not like the experience she'd told them about: how to give a head job, places to touch a man to get him going and sometimes this could take a while, though most of them were real horny and it was all over quickly. Younger men were the worst for this, and they all preferred the old chaps who seemed to appreciate the service more. Every now and then, they got asked to service a woman, and that was a whole new ballgame. They explained the difference places to touch a women or men and indeed how to kiss. Brenda shuddered at the thought of having a man get inside her again.

"Get the right fella and you'll be fine, luv," they assured her.

Silvie found out her sixtieth birthday had passed, and they all made quite a big deal out of a late-birthday/Christmas party combined with home-made streamers and cake. They'd all made her little gifts of soaps and trinkets. Brenda scrounged flowers from the garden and from some of her new friends and found a cute cuckoo clock in one of the op shops. Everyone said they loved it. Brenda was overwhelmed, as it had been a while since she had been shown any kindness and spent the night with images of good and bad times whirling round in her mind. She wished Cliff was there to snuggle up to, and she could hear her mum's calming voice singing, as she'd done before all the Sandra-dying stuff. Again, she really wished she could see her mum.

WHY WHY

After sending a message to Brenda that Cliff was coming to help with all the preparations for her birthday and the wedding, to be held the next day, they were planning for Brenda's sixteenth birthday only a few days away. She so wanted to make it a great day. Cliff was coming to try and get Nancy and Dexter to turn it into a double celebration with her birthday one day followed by their wedding the next day. She and Brenda had had many long conversations covering why Brenda wanted to get married straight away. On the subject of sex, for once in her life, Brenda refused to discuss it in any way. Nancy and Dexter had resigned to the fact that Brenda and Cliff would have a sexual relationship anyway, so marriage seemed to be the right avenue to follow.

Brenda had asked Cindy to be her bridesmaid, and they'd shopped excitedly in a lot of charity shops for dresses, till Gran Hay offered to buy the material and make the dress. Brenda, who had been looking a little peaky, got a real happy glow when they had fittings. Cliff told them he was going to use Prince as his "best" man, but had sworn everyone involved to secrecy. Gran Hay had even made Prince a bowtie the same color as Cliff's. All their neighbors had been canvassed for flowers for the day. They'd saved up to make a double-tier cake to be used for both birthday and wedding. Everything was coming together nicely, and this visit of Cliff's would be the last before the big weekend. Both Nancy and Dexter liked Cliff and after their visit to Lochlea recognized that he had a stable background and a solid future. They'd been impressed with the things that Brenda had achieved while she'd lived there. Dexter often sighed and expressed the wish that they could get back to the "bush" lifestyle. Dexter declared that after the upcoming event he'd start looking for out of town work again.

Cliff arrived mid-afternoon and dropped Prince off at Golda Avenue before heading up to the hospital to collect the girls who he knew had just done several night shifts and would have three days off. He announced himself to the office at the nurses' quarters. He'd had a haircut and shaved that morning and received several glances from the girls passing in and out of the building. Even the sad-looking woman at the desk thought he was divine and wished she were young again. Cliff wanted to go up to Brenda and Cindy's room to surprise Brenda, as he'd arrived early. This produced a shocked look from the woman at the desk—a man entering the female domain of the nurses' quarters was simply not done. After quite a wait, Cliff saw Cindy walking slowly down the stairs. She had her eyes downcast, stepping very carefully, each step very deliberate, one hand holding the banister firmly. Cliff kept looking past her, his heart beating fast at the expected appearance of his girl and soon-to-be wife. Cindy got all the way across the office floor before looking up at Cliff, her face and eyes puffy and red from weeping. Cliff felt a cold hand grasp his heart as he took Cindy's hand in his, a question in his eyes. Cindy tried to speak, but a sob stopped any words. The woman at the desk was staring at them, her eyes shining with the anticipation of some juicy gossip. She didn't approve of coloreds being treated as equals. Cliff saw the look and felt a flash of anger and sending a withering glance towards the woman, put his arm round Cindy, and led her outside.

Cindy managed to get out the information that Brenda had disappeared the night before, saying she was going shopping after the night shift, and when Cindy had woken, she wasn't in her bed. Very little of her things were gone, only her personal things like toothbrush and hair brush. Cindy stopped short, remembering that

Brenda had sworn her to secrecy about the pregnancy. Deep down inside herself, Cindy hoped Brenda would be able to get herself sorted out and be back real soon. She watched the disbelief, hurt, and worry cross Cliff's face as he took in what she'd said. He felt a mixture of confusion, sadness, and anger, not knowing how to deal with this unexpected situation. Keeping his arm round Cindy, he led her back to his car, and they returned to Golda Avenue. Nancy went out to greet the car as it arrived, and she too became confused at the absence of Brenda, taking in Cindy's tear-streaked face and Cliff's stony expression. She felt her heart sink but reached out, taking Cindy in her arms, her eyes begging Cliff for information. Gran Hay came out to see what the delay was and to inform the group that the tea was getting cold. Her words froze as she took in the trio exhibiting confusion and sadness. Her presence broke up the silent, and without any words, they followed Gran back into the house. Here, Cindy sobbed out the story again. Nancy called Dexter and Fred in from the wood heap, where they'd been cutting up a new load of firewood for the stove. The story was retold and received silently for several minutes, each person lost in their own thoughts of how to proceed next.

Dexter broke the silence by slapping his hand on the table, declaring in an angry tone that Brenda had again simply run away from something she didn't want to face. "It is this bloody wedding," he declared as swung round to Cliff his fists clenched. This stopped Cindy from crying, as she knew in some way this was true, but knew in other ways it wasn't true and Brenda was trying to protect her family from shame.

Dexter raged on, "First, the silly business at Bemerside and that bloody dog, sneaking away from me with some truckie dude." He forgot in his tirade that Cliff was the truckie dude. "And now this bloody wedding. You've been forcing her to marry you, Cliff." Spittle flew from his mouth as he stepped towards Cliff.

Cliff didn't flinch or back away as Fred placed his arm on Dexter's arm, telling him, "Whoa, back a bit. Let's please discuss this over a cuppa."

They did, and after several cups of tea, no resolution had been reached, and so with a heavy heart, Cliff and Prince left. Cindy had observed everything and wished she could have told Nancy the truth at least.

HARD WORK CURES SOME THINGS

Cliff arrived stony-faced back at Lochlea and threw himself into work. He convinced Bill to invest in another truck so they could do more local and long-haul cartage. Pete had wanted to put a snake decal on the new truck, which Cliff refused, putting instead a picture of a border collie dog. Bill felt that there had to be something very bad happened to make Brenda leave without notice. Still, as he was left alone with Prince (Cliff refused to have him in the truck with him), with Pete and Cliff off, Bill took it upon himself to school Prince in his obedience training and found the dog keen extra "man" when moving the stock. Having never had a working dog, he found Prince's natural instincts fascinating, if fact the dog worked the chooks, ducks, but the geese wouldn't allow themselves to be pushed around by hissing and standing their ground. Often getting very aggressive. Prince tried and tried to round them up and, more often than not, was sent racing for cover with several geese necks stretched out, beaks inches from his backside. Bill decided to allow the geese and dog to work things out together.

Christmas came and went. Cattle were moved out and more moved in. Prices were good, and the season rain seemed to come at exactly the right time. Both Cliff and Pete were busy, with Pete taking on the longer city runs and Cliff concentrating on the movement of local cattle as more and more folks took to using trucks to move stock about. Towards the end of February, all three men were stuck at the house with a deluge of rain. It had been raining hard, so they pulled out the cards and sat round drinking rum and playing pretend gambling games using matchsticks as money. At one point, Pete and Cliff were bickering over the cards when Pete declared that Cliff needed to get himself a woman. Cliff shook his head saying he only ever wanted one woman and wasn't into prostitutes like Pete, before he could say more Pete burst into hearty laughter.

"Not into whores, hey? Well, guess what. I'm sure I saw your lovely little lady at a brothel I went to in Sydney." Bill looked from one and the other and vacated his chair as he could see this wasn't going to end nicely.

Cliff roared an emphatic, *"No!* She wouldn't do that. Never."

Pete continued to laugh heartily, declaring almost to himself that he wouldn't have minded another go at Brenda again. Pete suddenly was brought back to earth as both Bill and Cliff yelled, "Again?" in unison.

Cliff's face had gone completely white as he slowly stood up, and he whispered "Where the hell is this place you bastard, and again!"

Unwisely, Pete commented, "Thought you didn't use whores." Cliff reached across and grabbed Pete by his shirt pulling him across the table, their faces inches apart. "Where is this place and what do you mean *again?"* Cliff's voice was shaking.

Pete had had a lot to drink, and so all good sense had left him, and so, still with a smile on his lips, he told Cliff Brenda had given herself to him while they were alone. He concluded, "Cliff must have a tiny dick, as he'd made her bleed."

This was too much for Cliff. He let go of Pete's shirt and pushed him at the same time, knocking the table over in the process, glasses and bottles smashing to the floor. Peter fell back, almost running backwards in an effort to regain his balance, finally falling onto his back, his head slamming onto the solid floor with a sickening thud. Cliff jumped over the fallen table and grabbed Pete's shirt, jerking him into a sitting position, pulling his fist back, and punching him hard in his mouth, breaking teeth. He let him go at the same time, and Pete's head hit the floor with a squishing sound. His eyes rolled back into his head. Bill tossed a bucket of water at Cliff, telling him to stop. Cliff spun on his heel and went outside, and Bill, after a glance at the prone body of Pete, followed him outside.

Cliff was sobbing and turned to Bill, gasping out that he hadn't ever had sex with Brenda and guessed that her encounter with Pete would be why she'd wanted to get away. He punched the veranda pole and stood silently for a time as tears of hurt and frustration rolled down his cheeks. Finally, he spoke in a somewhat normal voice.

He declared, "I'll get him to tell me where he thought he saw Brenda and her, and I'll have him thrown in jail for this." They returned to the house to find Pete still lying where he fell. Cliff refilled the bucket and tossed it into his face, which brought no reaction. He kicked him, not very softly, in his ribs, snarling at him to get up and stop being such a wuss. Bill held up his hand to stop him, with a worried glance at Cliff, before kneeling beside Pete, patting his cheeks and saying for him to wake up. Finally, he felt his wrist and neck, looking for a pulse and finding none. He declared that Pete was dead.

Bill tried to call the police, but the phone was dead. They dragged Pete into his room and heaved him onto the bed, covering him with his blanket. The effort of that left Bill breathless with pain centering in his chest. As Cliff said he'd get a horse and ride into report the situation, Bill said nothing of his discomfort. By this time, it was late in the day, and Cliff had a difficult trip as some of the gullies were quite high. It took a while for Cliff to get the constable out of bed and retold the story over a cup of coffee. He didn't try to hide the fact that he and Pete had fought, saying it had been a drunken augment over cards.

False dawn was showing through, and the rain had stopped. Together, they found that the ambulance was busy elsewhere, so the constable decided that as Cliff had said Peter was dead, it would be alright for him to return with the body in his truck. He alerted the morgue at the hospital that he'd be bringing in a body later, and they drove slowly out to Lochlea, neither saying very much. It was a slow trip. Some of the gullies still had quite a lot of water running through them. They'd expected to see Bill waiting for them but found him inside slumped over the table. Bill's face was gray and his breathing shallow, and he was unable to speak so he just pointed to his heart. While Cliff sat with Bill, the constable checked Pete, confirming to himself that Pete was dead. With little commutation, they loaded the body into the back and laid Bill on the back seat. Cliff knelt beside him on the floor for the ride back to the hospital, where the doctor confirmed a heart attack and admitted him, telling Cliff he'd need to go to Brisbane quickly for specialist treatment. Constable George Alwell told Cliff there would need to be an autopsy on Pete before he could be cleared for burial.

Cliff found a phone and, with his heart in his mouth, called Dexter, telling him he may be able to find Brenda and asking him to come and look after Lochlea while he went to find Brenda. Dexter really didn't hesitate. After a few words to Nancy, he said they could be there in a couple of days. Those was nearly the longest two days Cliff had lived through, so keen was he to start his search. Cliff told them very little of what information he had of Brenda's whereabouts, just that she'd been seen at a house in Sydney. Staying a day to show both Nancy and Dexter the ropes he departed to Sydney by bus to Brisbane and, after a brief visit to see Bill, caught the train to Sydney. He had no idea where or how he was going to conduct his search just a whole lot of hope in his heart.

After checking in on Bill, Cliff caught the train to Sydney, arriving at much the same time of day that Brenda had, with false dawn filtering through the fog that blanketed the city. He stood and rubbed the tiredness out of his red-rimmed eyes. A janitor moved slowly along the platform, pushing disinterestedly at some rubbish before collecting it and disappearing behind one of the many doors.

Cliff walked out into the moist air being left by the fog, wondering, *Where do I go to now?* He noticed three young ladies sitting at a table and decided to ask them about accommodation and where he should start his search. The girls looked up, and all smiled hopefully as it had been a slow night. Before Cliff could open his mouth, one of the girls waved her hand at the others and said, "All of us for the price of one, sir!"

It shocked Cliff a little as he hadn't given a thought to the girls being prostitutes, but he quickly recovered and, with hope in his heart, smiled broadly back to the girls, who sat up a little taller, straightening their attire and hair as Cliff pulled his wallet out and produced not the hoped for money but the photo of Brenda. "I'm looking for this girl," he said. "I think she's in Sydney."

The girls took the photo, and all bowed their heads so Cliff couldn't see the expressions on their faces or the glances that passed between them. The photo was handed back as they all shook their heads, sorry that he wasn't going to take up their offer. Somehow they wished they could tell him they knew where Brenda was, as he looked kind of nice and respectable. They advised him to check out areas like Kings Cross as a lot of girls worked there, and some cheap accommodations were there as well, knowing that it was well away from anywhere Brenda went for her walks. As he left with shoulders hunched and heads bowed, he didn't see them rush over to a scruffy chap who had been sitting just out of sight behind some shrubbery and talk animatedly to him.

Over the next few days, Cliff walked the streets of inner Sydney, an area he wasn't familiar with, and spoke to many of the girls plying their trade on street corners. At one time, one of the so-called managers came to tell him to bugger off as they thought he was trying to muscle in on their girls. After a month of drudging through everywhere he could think of, he got a tip from one of the young girls to try a place away from the city that took private bookings. He rang the number given and spoke to a cultured chap who took his booking for the next day. He caught a taxi to the place, the driver seemed to be familiar with the address and smirked at him as he paid for the ride. He saw a respectable-looking cottage with neat rows of gardens sprouting a mixture of old and young plants. The taxi driver pointed him to a gate at the side of the house, so Cliff thanked him and walked through to find an attractive, newer house. He knocked on the heavy door. A small door slid open, and the same cultured voice questioned who he was and what he wanted. Cliff pushed a scrap of paper with the booking number on it and his driver's license through and was told to wait. After a minute, the door was opened by a well-dressed gentleman who ushered him into a room where two girls stood clad only in nighties.

"Only have these for you to choose from because of the early hour. Both are very good." He flapped his hand towards the girls. They were two of girls he'd first spoken to.

The man was bending down behind a desk, so he didn't see the girls indicate for Cliff not to say anything before rushing over to him and wrapping their scantily bodies round his and whispering in his ear to ask for both of them. Cliff was just a little embarrassed as he tried to unwind them, shocked to find his body was reacting to the attention. Gary watched with a wry smile. He'd seen this scenario play out many times, and he wasn't surprised to hear Cliff stammer out the request for both of the girls.

After a figure had been agreed upon and paid, the giggling girls led him to a very ornate room. The centerpiece of the room was a huge bed. They put on some wavy sort of music and started to sway about, touching themselves and each other, inviting him to join in with beckoning fingers. They moved closer and ever closer to him, letting their nipples brush against his cheeks and arms, running fingernails down his back as they unbuttoned his shirt revealing his well-muscled chest and arms.

"Do you know where Brenda is?" Cliff asked, his voice thick with emotion.

They gave each other a look and sat down either side of him. "Yes, and she's safe." There was a pause.

"We can't say any more. Brenda has asked us to keep her whereabouts a secret. She thought someone recognized her a while back, and so she's moved away from here because she was sure someone would come looking for her. Right now, she just wants to be left alone." They both hugged him. "Now, I suggest we finish what we started. You just lay back and enjoy. You don't have to do anything to us."

Cliff did just that, and found that he didn't need to do anything. The girls started by gently rubbing his body as they removed his pants before getting him to roll over while one ran her hands up his legs and reached in to cup his testicles. That did him in as he came in an orgasmic rush. He went to roll back over when they said, "We get you there again, buddy." They walked up and down on his spine and sucked on his earlobes before letting him roll onto his back. He found himself ready again and again he felt the relief of ejaculation. The girls knew that they'd given him value for money as they all lay still for some time before, as if by a prearranged signal, they all dressed silently.

"We'll tell Brenda you came." An alarmed look came over his face. "But not about this," they quickly added. "If she wants to, she'll contact you, but she's dealing with a bit of trauma right now though. Give her time."

Cliff was leaving, and then he turned to them. "Tell her Pete's dead, please, and I know what he did to her."

They girls nodded, and he was ushered out by Gary, who noticed he was more relaxed. Gary assumed it was his "treatment' and was a little taken back when Cliff shook his hand and thanked him as he left. "Anytime, anytime," Gary said, sure he'd see this bloke again.

The girls sat and discussed what and how much they should tell Brenda about this chap and the information he'd given her. In the end, they decided, owing to the lateness of Brenda's pregnancy, that they'd just give her encouragement to contact her home and those closest to her. Other than the letter to the Dubbo hospital, Brenda steadfastly refused to consider writing to or contacting anyone else. She actually got cross with being asked when she was going to contact her family or what she was going to do after the babies' birth. She really had no idea herself and just left it at that.

NOTHING IS AS IT SEEMS

Brenda slipped into a routine of sorts, cooking and looking after Silvie, taking her evening strolls. She and Silvie found they could communicate with a few words and gestures. Silvie had a sharp mind and a good sense of humor. After a while, Brenda hardly noted Sylvie's disfigurements. They'd come about by a "client' bashing her, breaking almost every bone in her face and several ribs. The man, Joe, who later became her husband, had found her unconscious and gotten her medical care, giving her a place to recover in. She'd been well on the way to recovery when she suffered a stroke, ensuring she'd never be able to "work' again. Joe was much older than Silvie and had been one of her clients, so he understood the value in the business. Joe and Silvie built the rooms behind the cottage and they started to build their business from there.

They recruited girls Silvie had known who were some of the most lost. Joe was a very successful businessman and had "money," so he set up communication with a college so the girls could do evening study in a lot of basic subjects, ensuring that they'd be able to step away from the "game" in the future. Joe and Silvie never sent the girls out to the streets at night. Any night work happened in the rooms and was by appointment only, coming at a high price. Very soon, they had girls contacting them for work, not only because of the conditions but also because Joe and Silvie set up bank accounts for them, meaning they had some money when they moved on to the "outside" world. Now, because of the education aspect, there was a regular turnover in girls and a long waiting list. Some girls simply using the work to set themselves up to attend night schools or university.

Silvie insisted that Brenda took on some form of study, saying, "An empty mind is good to no one." Brenda told her that she'd started to become a nurse, so they found a tutor, Kevin, once a nurse and a colleague of Doc H and retired now, to instruct her in all the theory. They bribed her way into some nurses' exams. Brenda felt a bit guilty when she looked at the tired and stressed faces of the "real" nurses. She aced the exams and received certificates of the results. Along with that and her sessions with Doc H, she felt that she'd be well equipped to return to nursing after the birth. As the baby grew inside her, she felt no motherly feelings towards it. The squirming and snakelike movements annoyed her. She felt this unwanted thing was holding her back from her "real" life.

The girls were happy to have her relieving them of home duties so they could do more study when they weren't out "working" for Gary. Several of the girls had had no basic education before being sold into slavery at an early age. Brenda found their stories the worst. When they escaped their "manager" and came to the house, their managers would hassle Joe to get them back. Fortunately, Joe had an inside running with the police and the underground warlords, so after several of these managers were arrested or simply disappeared, the girls and Joe were left alone. The police appreciated what Joe and Silvie were doing for the girls, so they gave Joe and Silvie protection when required. So many street girls were introduced to drug dependency, ensuring they had to work to get money for drugs, just as a mouse does in a wheel, sinking deeper till most were bashed to death or died of an overdose.

After the brothel was set up, Silvie got pregnant quickly, and she and Joe streamlined the business so that Gary had a perfect home life. To him, the house filled with girls was normal. It was only as he got older and attended school, having been home schooled up to year nine, that he got into fights over people calling Silvie a whore.

After he'd come home with black eyes, Joe and Silvie sat him down and explained the business to him and how much money it made for them. Gary never fought again. He just turned his back and walked away if anything had been said. He knew he'd be richer than most of the small-minded people in his school. Besides, he knew that his parents were doing good things and caring for the girls.

When Gary was in last year of school, Joe simply fell off his chair, dead. Silvie was devastated and cried for days. Gary quickly became the man of the house, helping to organize the funeral and other legalities. He discovered they were, in fact, millionaires, and he made Silvie a vow he'd carry on Joe's good work with the girls. Gary sailed through his final exams and left to study business in Melbourne, where no one may guess his background. While he was in his first year, one of the so-called opposition tried to muscle in by getting rid of Silvie. The henchman assigned the task was very enthusiastic—he shattered the cheekbones round Silvie's eyes, ending by breaking her legs and strangling her. This damaged her voice box and was why she couldn't manage many words. He'd left her for dead, reckoning that her lifeless body would show the girls a severe warning of what was to come.

The first girl home called the policeman Silvie used as a contact. He came straight away and arranged medical care, saying, "This won't go unpunished." It was later reported in the papers that several persons had driven into a river and drowned. Gary came home and transferred his study to Sydney. Nothing like that ever occurred again as Gary canvassed the homosexual community for strong chaps to be security at the house and for the back rooms. He chose them so that they wouldn't want to interfere with the girls. It worked very well.

Gary continued to live at home for a time while he continued his business studies, telling his fellow students he had a scholarship, which was believable, as he did very well. Towards his last year, he purchased a large house close to the harbor. A triple story house with magnificent views of the city and ocean. He sublet some rooms to the wealthier of his fellow students, and for a time, it was very much a party house. Until one evening one of the friends brought a prostitute to the house. It was one of Gary's girls. Gary managed to keep himself out of sight as the others had their fun with the girl. As soon as the lass had departed, Gary stormed into the area where the lads were all laid back, laughing about the happenings of they'd been part of.

"You should have come in, Gaz. She was great!" they all said together and then stopped as they noted the angry look on Gary's face.

"I *will not* have one of those girls in this house. Ever!" His voice was shaking with anger. It shocked the lads, as they'd often brought girlfriends to the house. "Who knows if she is clean or not!"

"Hang on there, Gaz. We checked her out, and she isn't just a street girl. She comes from a well-run place that looks after the girls that work there. And she cost a packet," one lad protested.

Gary smiled to himself but continued to angrily tell them all that they must leave, and after lots of bluster and carrying on, they all removed themselves from the house over the next week. As soon as they'd all gone, Gary wandered through the huge and now quiet house. He thought about what the lads had said about the reputation of his girls. He felt very sad that so many of the street girls—and boys, for that matter—had little or no hope. Round the same time, one of his security men came to him and asked if Gary could help a lad who'd belonged to a fellow who had got him into drugs and now had turfed him back to the street so he could take up with a younger lads.

For all Gary's shortcomings, he was a good man. He turned his lower floor into a semi-soundproof unit so that the lads could come down off the drugs in safety. He contacted a group that worked with troubled children to see the lads through his trauma and try to get him back to an education or into a job. Gary insisted that this *must* be kept very quiet. Otherwise, he'd not go through with it. A number of children were assisted at the house. No neighbors suspected. Neither did any of his girlfriends. He told them that the lower floor was sealed off because it was damp, with moisture seeping in through the walls that abutted the side of the hill. He kept his business and how he made his money very close to his chest, telling anyone who asked that he'd inherited money and had some very profitable investments. He continued to mix with the elite crowd and belonged to the best golf clubs and many other such places. He gave generously to various charities so was very popular and accepted part of the upper society.

Not long after Brenda arrived, a skinny, scruffy lad came to the house with one of the girls. He was an extremely good-looking boy. She'd found him wandering the street, seeking clients to get money for drugs. He was addicted to heroin; his arms were a mass of bruises where he'd been injecting himself. Silvie called Gary in to see what they could do for the boy, Tommy. Brenda watched through a crack in door of the room she'd been banished to. Tommy tried to run away when Gary arrived with his driver. The driver blocked the door successfully. Tommy was sweating and shaking, unable to sit still while his fate was decided. In the end, Gary took the boy with him since he knew Tommy would be difficult to control as he went through the withdrawal symptoms. Brenda felt so sad as he was bundled out of the house, sobbing uncontrollably. Silvie was visibly upset, so Brenda and Silvie sat for a time, holding each other.

The girls explained to Brenda that it was common to find boys on the street who were usually taken in by benefactors who treated them well till they got too old for their owners. Very few were homosexual but it seemed at the time to be their only choice. They were then tossed out back to the street, and this was when they suffered, being used cruelly by not nice homosexuals. They generally got addicted to some sort of drugs. Not many made it off the street ever. Brenda hoped Tommy would be one of the lucky ones, and she hoped that Gary would treat Tommy well.

Brenda wasn't really sure what Gary was like as she was kept well out of his reach when he came to the house to collect the money.

She'd spied on him through cracks in doors and was impressed at how respectful he was to Silvie. He did comment once that the house was looking cleaner, and he assumed that Silvie had "cracked the whip" on the girls. He was pleased to see the garden was progressing and producing. He complained that some of the girls were seeming to be a bit uppity, saying that they didn't need this education they were getting, and he resented paying for the books and course. "The girls have all they need between their legs" was his catch phrase. Silvie would simply give him a lopsided smile and give him a pat on the back reminding him that everyone deserved to try and improve themselves.

LIFE

Brenda settled into a routine of housework and study with Kevin or Doc H or both. She was actually enjoying the life, and it was good to get to know the girls. She'd never really had close contact with a lot of girls. They occasionally went as a group to the beach. Brenda felt a little scared of the openness with the water and the wide expanse of the sand. After she heard someone mention sea snakes, she refused to go near the water. Her pregnancy progressed and round five months into it, Doc H gave her tummy a squeeze and a prod. This was part of every examination. Brenda was chattering away, not taking very much notice. Suddenly, she realized that the doc was very quiet. He was looking at her with a sad expression. She sat up, straightening her clothes, raising her eyebrows in a questioning way.

He was silent for a long while before asking her if she was still sure she wanted to go down the adoption route. When she nodded, he informed her that she was going to give birth to twins and that would make the adoption process harder if she wanted to keep them together or let them be adopted separately. Brenda said nothing just got up and left, panic overwhelming her. Damn and blast and bugger Pete. She'd have been married to Cliff now without his bloody interference. She punched her belly, thinking, *Get out! Get out!* For the first time since she'd arrived, she didn't cook the evening meal. She just went straight to her bed, turning her back to the other girls she shared the room with. None of them had seen her like this, but Silvie indicated that Brenda was to be left alone.

Brenda had a session with Kevin the next day, but she found it hard to get her head around the study. Eventually, Kevin put the study books and, sitting back, told her that Doc H had spoken to him about the impending arrival of the two babies. Kevin went on to tell her he'd been a sister, head nurse, at a private hospital and thought he could get the hospital to allow her to give birth there instead of the home birth she'd been planning. He told her she must make a decision about the adoption, whether to adopt as twins or separately.

Brenda shocked Kevin by jumping up and almost screaming, "I don't care what happens to these things inside my belly! Just get them out of me and away from me as soon as possible."

Kevin nodded, sighing to himself that she might change her mind as the babies grow. She never did.

Brenda ignored what was happening to her body and got on with her chores. Sometimes, activity in her belly woke her through the night. She'd slap at it, cursing Pete for interfering with her life. The movements felt like squirming snakes, she thought, and it made her shiver. The girls all got excited and liked to feel her tummy when the squirming occurred. They bombarded her with what she felt were silly questions, like what she would name them and what she hoped she had. Brenda exploded one day, yelling at them that she hated these things in her belly and couldn't wait to be rid of them. She added that she hated the man who had put them there and he'd ruined her life. As some of the girls had been raped and some of them had had abortions, they were sympathetic towards how she felt. They were now very grateful for the invention of the pill, as it stopped most of the unwanted pregnancies they all feared.

Brenda got into the habit of taking an early morning walk. Her usual get-up time had been early. Besides, she liked the sounds of the city waking up. Silvie's house was set in a quiet residential suburb, and though many of the local residents knew about the business being run there, they were happy to pretend it was simply a boarding house for the high school and university young ladies. Newer arrivals to the area had no idea. Since the advent of the garden, the neighbors were pleased to receive donations of the produce and eggs. There was a row of terrace houses along the route Brenda took. She liked looking at the pretty little front yard gardens of the older folk. They reminded her of her garden at Lochlea, though most of the plants and flowers were quite different.

One particular older lady was nearly always sitting on the tiny front porch and always gave a cheery greeting when Brenda took her regular walks. Her name turned out to be Brenda as well, but she'd always been called Baby. As Brenda's pregnancy became more obvious, Baby would have a cup of tea ready for Brenda, and they'd sit and chat for a while, comparing ideas and knowledge of garden design and the like. As they moved about to inspect various plants, Brenda was fascinated at how bandy her legs were, and when she asked why, Baby laughed heartily.

"Always been a rider girl, and a fair buck-jump rider too in my day. Held my own with the likes of that Gill lass and others too."

Brenda thought of her rather sedate style of riding, and while she enjoyed the stories, she wondered how Baby had been brave enough to try such a thing. Baby did tell her that the rodeo association was trying to get the girls out of the sport and guessed that it wouldn't be too long before there wouldn't be any girl rough riders.

"Mind you," she added, "it sure shakes the heck out your insides and suppose that's why I've never been able to have kids, and that's something I'm sorry for." Baby sighed. "It's a tough way, and lots of people cash their chips doing it like my husband, Grant, who got trampled to death."

Baby never spoke of that terrible incident again but continued to chat about her experiences on the days Brenda stopped by. She gave Brenda a tour of her house, which Brenda found fascinating, how one could live in such a small space. It felt as small as the truck cab almost. All the mementos made it feel cozy, though. Baby told such wild tales of drinking and partying all night. She was amazed that Brenda didn't like the smell of rum as most of the rodeo crowd almost swam in the stuff. One of the best yarns was about the boxing tent that followed the rodeo circuit, run by a Mr. Johnston, who also fought professionally. A big drum would be banged to gather in the crowd, and the public would put their hand up to have a go at one of the tents fighters. Brenda thought that idea barbaric.

She was on a living on a wave of denial but became a familiar figure having her morning juice at the small corner cafe and chatting ti the paper boys selling newspapers near the of bus stops. The other group of people she enjoyed talking to and that only happened by chance were the homeless. She'd been hurrying past the vagrants who inhabited some dilapidated buildings occupying an area down near the substantial river till the day she heard an "Oi" and turned to see Doc H motioning her to come in. He was trying to treat a severely cut leg on a young-looking chap, and Doc needed someone to keep the chap calm while he stitched the wound. The man was still drunk and smelled of piss and stale booze. Doc H indicated that she should sit on the chap's chest, hold his head, and talk to him while several others sat on his arms and legs. He wriggled and made weird sounds throughout the procedure but never really came out of his stupor. After it was over, the group stood looking down at the semi-conscious bloke while Doc H issued some instructions.

"For fuck sake, get him washed as soon as possible and keep him off the grog till the wound is closed up. Stuff sake, you lot, there's a whole river to bathe in." He paused. "I'll check on this tomorrow."

While Doc H was dishing out instructions, Brenda glanced about and noticed that in amongst the shell of the buildings were areas that had been constructed to allow some privacy for the person who called that area home. Drink bottles were strewn about in most areas; cigarette butts and food wrappings lay about. A couple of them smiled at her and thanked her for her help. Brenda noticed how the groups' faces showed respect, and looking round at them, she saw some of them stood proudly, and others had slumped shoulders and kept their gazes mostly on the ground. After the lecture, someone had made a cup of tea, and they all sat in a semi-circle and drank out of a mismatched collection of mugs and cups. A few still wore clothes that had come from high-end store and, though tatty and hung on their skinny frames, still had a strange look of opulence.

Brenda had walked round her area also but had avoided talking to them till after the incident with Doc H. She then got to talk to lots of the homeless folks, finding them to be a strange, eclectic group, mostly friendly, and those that weren't, she was told to just leave them be. Some of them begged, which was illegal, and if they were caught they'd spend some time in jails, which to them was okay as they got fed there and usually a bed. A couple of them were accomplished burglars who would share their food with the old and sick people. For the most part, they looked out for each other in a strange sense of comradeship. She enjoyed getting out of the house and looked forward to the conversations, poetry recitals, singing, and tall stories. In a funny way, these people had accepted their fates and seemed happy. One night, she found out that one of them had died, and she observed the dead man's things be distributed out to those who needed them the most. Somehow, alcohol had been procured, and they toasted the departed several times. The body had been taken to where it would be found, and if the deceased name was known, a note would be attached to the body. Someone mentioned that the deceased had been bitten by a black snake. These serpents inhabited the part of the park that bordered the water, seeking out the frogs that lived there. Brenda shuddered and never ventured to that type of area again.

She walked part of the way home with Doc H, who told her that though most of the people living at that house were harmless but lost souls who simply wanted to be left alone, new ones drifted through the settlement and could be dangerous. He advised her to avoid the area. Over the next few days, Brenda timed her walk to coincide with checks on the injured man and found most the chaps quite well educated. He showed her books on poetry and short stories by a Banjo Patterson and the game of chess. For these lost people, they lived hand to mouth by scrounging in food bins behind cafes, bakeries, and restaurants. Some of them were very good burglars whose stolen goods were sold off to provide money for grog or drugs or both. On those drinking days, she stayed away, but that was all they looked forward to, it seemed.

She became very comfortable dropping in till the day she found them all going through one of the tidier areas. One fellow said, "Old Tom got bit by a snake while cleaning himself down by the river last night and died, so we're dividing up his things now. He don't need them anymore."

She felt sad as he'd been the one to read the poetry, so she asked if she could have that book. Would she ever be rid of the blasted snakes? They seemed to attack a lot of people and caused grief. The men told her that the body had been left where it would be found, and as no one really knew his real name, no note was left with the body. Brenda walked home very slowly that day, remembering the conversations they'd had over the last couple of months. *If I wasn't giving these babies away, I could have called one Tom,* she thought and then yelled at herself internally for even thinking such a thought.

As her time got closer and her belly got huge, she became very restless and tired. She'd got into the habit of taking a snooze on the lounge room couch after lunch. This was where Gary found her when she was in the last trimester of her pregnancy. He stood looking at her for a time, taking in her swollen belly but otherwise healthy-looking, pretty face. He cleared his throat loudly and stamped his foot, causing Brenda to jerk into a sitting position, gazing at him with wide eyes.

Silvie came stamping down the hall as fast as she could to confront an angry Gary.

"Who the blazes is this?" he snapped at Silvie, never taking his eyes off Brenda.

He shot questions at Silvie so fast she wasn't able to get a word in edgeways. Finally, Gary paused long enough for Silvie to indicate that he should be quiet and sit at the kitchen table, motioning Brenda to join them. Gary hadn't taken his eyes off Brenda all through this, marveling at how pretty she was and what an asset she'd be to his business.

Silvie took hold of Brenda's hand indicating for her to tell her story, holding up her other hand, shushing Gary when he started in interrupt. Brenda stuck to the violent father story and the fact she'd raped, how she'd stolen money from her abusive dad, fleeing to Sydney from her home in western Queensland after she realized she was pregnant. She added how she'd met the girls outside the railway station, and they'd brought her to the house.

"I was so scared as all the hubbub of the city was difficult to deal with for a country girl," Brenda blurted out.

She went on to tell how she'd repaid everyone in the house for their kindness by taking over the cooking and cleaning to give the girls more study time, and she'd instigated the development of the garden.

Gary frowned at this statement and growled at Silvie that the girls all had it way too easy. "Dad was silly to start all this education palaver. I have lost a lot of good girls through that idea. Besides, the girls—"

Silvie slapped her hand on the table and said in a reasonably clear voice, "Well, you were educated, so why not the girls? Besides, they keep you in the manner to which you have become accustomed, don't they?"

Gary blushed at the rebuke and sighed before going on to admit that his girls were indeed popular for high-end customers and performed well. Silvie waved Brenda away so she could plead Brenda's case with Gary, who agreed she could stay till the baby arrive. He was pleased to hear that Brenda wasn't going to keep the infant. They reached an agreement that after the birth Brenda would go to work for him while she continued her nursing studies. Silvie lied to him that she was going to go and work in the private hospital so she would still be able to work for him on her days off. Gary wasn't happy but agreed to this idea. Silvie told Brenda later, whispering to her that somehow between them Brenda would be able to escape if she chose not to work for Gary.

Brenda chose to not think about it too much, but at the back of her mind, she wondered if she could go back to nursing in Dubbo, hoping that Cindy had managed to get transferred to her home-town hospital. She dismissed the thought of restarting in Brisbane for several reasons. One, she was unsure how she'd be received at home, and two, there was Cliff. Would he ever forgive her? This bothered her a lot. She wrote a letter to the Dubbo hospital, sent her recently acquired certificates and the few months of her work history, citing family problems for her sudden departure from the hospital. She hoped her good marks would help her. She still couldn't bring herself to write to anyone else.

All these thoughts were running through her head as she went to the back rooms to deliver fresh towels and sheets. As she knelt down to deposit the items into the correct shelves, a harsh voice from her past sliced through her jumbled head. It was Pete. He was trying to be funny with the girl he'd chosen. Brenda peeked through a crack in the back of the cupboard and saw him grabbing at the girl's breast roughly with one hand while rubbing his crotch with the other hand, saying, "This will the best you have ever had, baby."

Brenda shivered in disgust and felt so sorry for the girl that she had to cover her mouth to stop herself from screaming. The head girl came out and told Pete not to be rough, separating Pete and the girl, telling the lass to go and get the room ready while procuring payment from Pete, who protested at the cost. He blurted out that the girl should be paying him with what he had to offer. He continued to bluster about the cost, getting quite angry and loud, which brought the minders into the room. They escorted a protesting Pete out the door.

Brenda was shaking and needed to use the shelves to help her stand up. She stood few several minutes, getting her breath to calm down and getting feeling back into her legs. The minders walking slowly back and asked her if she was okay. She nodded and looked up to smile her thanks just as Pete came roaring through the door, yelling that his money was a good as the next man. He stopped short as he and Brenda locked eyes before the minders blocked their view of each other and turned to physically carry Pete out again. Before Brenda could move, she heard a yelp of pain and several dull thuds before a car drove off.

Hope they hurt him real bad, she thought before returning shakily to the house.

Silvie noticed her pale look and patted the couch for Brenda to sit beside her. Brenda put her head down on Silvie's lap and cried tears of frustration, eventually blurting out the fact that she'd been recognised and was worried someone would come looking for her. Silvie sighed and told her not to worry. "You are part of this odd family, and we are good at keeping secrets," she said, finishing that even Gary would protect her as he saw her a future asset to his business.

Brenda was like a cat on hot bricks for a time but slowly relaxed as time passed. Besides, she had other concerns to think about. Kevin and Doc H had found people to buy her babies. They were going to be separated and would go straight to their new parents as soon as they were born. Doc H said both people were well off and would pay a considerable amount for them as they desperately wanted the babies.

Brenda couldn't care less. She did think, however, that the money would be a help later on. Kevin sighed and told her they must go and see the matron at the hospital very soon to get everything organized. He also told her that most of the money for the sale of the babies would be required to pay the matron to allow the birth to take place at the hospital. She'd use a false name and be passed off as a wealthy lass who had made a mistake and sent away to have the babies to avoid shame to the family.

Yeah, well, thought Brenda, *that's exactly why I'm here.*

BRENDA LOUISE

EXPECTING ENCOUNTERS

HOMECOMING DRAMA

Cliff had never felt so relaxed as he waited for the train back to Brisbane. He'd had other lovers of course but never ones who only thought of him and not themselves, and he was grateful. It was with some trepidation that he was only taking news that Brenda was okay and that he really hadn't found her. He felt in his heart that the girls were truthful that she was okay and not in the "game." While the knowledge that Pete had definitely forced himself on her still made him clench his fist, wishing Pete back to life so he could whack him again, he slept most of the journey back to Brisbane and caught a taxi back to Golda Avenue where he'd left his car, wondering if Dexter had returned home yet or if he was still helping Bill at Lochlea. Fred and Elsie were happy to receive the news that Brenda was fine, but sad that she still remained elusive, and she hadn't contacted Cindy either.

After the inevitable cup of tea, he was informed that it seemed Dexter and Nancy had permanent jobs at Lochlea, which surprised him a little. Bill hadn't said much when he spoke to him last, just told him he must get home as soon as possible as the police had questions. Cliff drove slowly home, deep in thought. He was surprised at the activity that was going on at Lochlea as he arrived at the front gate. Hammering seemed to be radiating from all sides. Nancy welcomed him home as she rang the smoko bell calling everyone in for morning tea. Bill, leaning heavily on a cane and looking smaller and older, and an assortment of men appeared from various parts of the property, one of whom he noted was Albert whom he'd met at Bemerside. The men all took their cups and retired to the shade of the trees to yarn and smoke.

"Let me run you through the changes." Bill looked at him with twinkling eyes. "Elsie rang with the news about Brenda." He touched his knee. "Sorry you couldn't have brought her home." The emphasis was on the word *home*.

Cliff listened to what the activities were that were happening. Pete's old room had been turned into a self-contained place for Bill, as he had trouble sleeping, and with his own space, he could read or make himself a cuppa without disturbing the rest of the household. Albert was living in his caravan, which had been placed under the shade trees behind the laundry and a toilet and shower added to the laundry for him at the end of the awning built off his van. He'd built a trellis on two sides of the awning and had vines already climbing up them. A small, two-room, self-contained cottage was being installed near the vegetable garden. It was almost more than Cliff could take in, and stiffly, suddenly feeling very tired, he followed Bill towards the yard to see what improvements were being installed there. *Crumbs*, thought Cliff, *and I have only been away four weeks.* He started to wonder where he fitted in to all this new.

Bill got Cliff to sit on a hay bale and, taking a deep breath, told him that because Pete had died there had been an inquiry and possible charges would most likely laid against Cliff, who at this juncture burst out, saying, "I don't care, and I'd kill him again in a heartbeat. I'll simply plead guilty and get it all over with very quickly." Suddenly, all the fight went out of him. "I feel buggered and will go in tomorrow."

Bill went on to say, "Well, you have a clean record, so it should be okay."

Cliff sat in silence for a while before he whispered, "Actually, I possiblly have several unpaid speeding fines in the Northern Territory. Plus, I was supposed to go to court for being drunk and disorderly." He hesitated. "Sorry, Dad."

Bill gave a deep sigh and inadvertently crossed his fingers. They sat for a time silently, each lost in his own world of thought till Prince came racing round the corner of the shed, pulling up with a jerk beside the two men, sniffing round their legs and feet before demanding a pat.

"This dog is a bloody marvel," Bill said as he ruffled Prince's ears. "I've stopped putting him through the obedience course now, and he thinks he's the manager of the place. He follows us about as we do our chores, and if we are late to feed up and milk, he gives out little woofs."

Bill thought it best to leave it go at that and continued to the yards where he'd had five new cow bails reinstalled. Cliff looked at him with raised eyebrows and received the explanation that both Albert and Nancy could make butter and cheese, which could be sold at the now regular markets in town, now that the town was getting so busy because of the impending mine. Nancy had put the idea to him, and he'd discussed it with his bank, which gave him the go-ahead.

"Besides, once a dairy farmer, always a dairy farmer." He gave Cliff a sad smile, "Think your mum would be pleased about the return of milking cows."

LET THE BATTLE BEGIN

Cliff drove slowly into town, his hands gripping the steering wheel till his knuckles turned white. He wished Pete were there so he could whack him again. He wondered how and if his previous bad behaviors would go against him, but he still would plead guilty and just let it pan out in the courts. He suddenly noticed the building activity happening in the town as he didn't go directly to the police station, deciding to call in at the pub first for a rum and find out what was going on in town. Apparently, a mining company had started to investigate the possibility of starting up a mine on the outskirts of town. They'd taken over the caravan park and added round twenty prefabricated buildings there as well as the managers and engineers had booked into the pub. The town had a real buzz to it, particularly in the main street, where a number of new shops were being constructed to house a bank, general stores, and an addition to the local newsagent and supermarket. He was amazed that it had occurred so quickly. He'd only been gone a month, and now he understood more of what his dad's plan was.

Now, this filtered through Cliff's state of mine. He really hadn't taken in this news Nancy and Bill had tried to relay to him the previous night. It was a dejected man who presented himself, smelling of rum, to Constable George Alwell, declaring that he'd plead guilty. He almost yelled the words as he slapped his hands down on the desk. This brought the sergeant out of his office, telling Cliff to settle down. The sergeant directed Cliff to go to a small room beside his office, wrinkling his nose at the smell of rum, in a building connected to the original cop shop by two covered ramps.

As he moved through to the room indicated, Cliff started to take in the changes in the police station and some of what he'd been told began to take seep into his brain. The addition of a sergeant and another constable had come about because of the increase in jobs being provided by a copper mine proposal on the outskirts of Wilted. The population had increased by half and expected to increase by that much again over the next two years.

The sergeant came into the room with a folder bulging with documents. "Now young fella, I need to tell you some home truths." He hesitated. "Let run some things past you, and I'll give—may give—you an hour or two to consider your options." He sighed and added, "My name is Brenden Forrest."

He spoke clearly as he went through the documents one by one, the first being the written requests from Bill and several of the townsfolk, saying he was of good character and that he should be given some time to find his Brenda. He finished this by saying, "Had I been here, I would have got a warrant straight away. The more I look into your background, the more I think it should have happened that way."

Cliff let the words wash over him, staring at the desk and not looking at the sergeant till the last comment had been made. The sergeant went on. His investigation into Cliff had been thorough, and he'd dug up all the NT misdemeanors as well as some fights he'd had while he was at school. Cliff found a feeling of dread coming over him.

The sergeant went on to say, "You will do time for this. How much will depend on how good your solicitor is, You do have one?" He stopped talking when Cliff shook his head. "Perhaps you should get one," the sergeant said in a hard voice, and as Cliff went to stand, Sergeant Forrest went on in a monotone voice to arrest Cliff.

Brenden Forrest, although he'd only been in Wilted for a short time, wasn't well liked and tended to bulldoze anyone he figured had done something unlawful and couldn't be reasoned with at all. He hadn't been impressed with the fact that Cliff had been given so much time to look for this so-called girl and was rather surprised that Cliff had presented himself at all.

To Cliff, it seemed to happen in a blur that he found himself locked up. The sergeant simply slammed the door closed and left Cliff blinking at the bars as the sergeant strode back to the confines of his office. As the sergeant disappeared from Cliff's sight, George appeared with some forms that Cliff was required to fill out.

"He's a cranky bugger, that one," George said softly. "Don't think he's happy about being here. Plus, in his first week, he had to deal with the fact that a death had occurred and that you had seemingly absconded following what he preconceived as a deliberate attack on another person. You're most fortunate that Bill had insisted that we get your month away signed off by the magistrate officially, so Sarge had no choice but to allow you the month to look for Brenda." He paused. "No luck there?" He sighed. "And all this case was made so much worse as Sharon Walsh, Pete's woman, has been at him this past week to get you locked up, and she keeps saying Brenda was a lazy little tart and so on. If you hadn't shown up today, he'd have put out an arrest warrant for you."

George pulled up a stool to the outside of the cell, indicating that Cliff should come closer as he pulled out a series of forms. "Let's deal with these, and then we best contact someone who can find you a lawyer."

Cliff's head was spinning. "You think I need one?" he said. "Sure, I was a bit wild in the past, but nothing for the past four, five years." His voice cracked as he held back tears of frustration. His fists clenched, and he spoke through gritted teeth. "Pete was a bastard, and he hurt Brenda. Surely, this Sharon woman won't be believed."

George shook his head. "If the case was heard here, no. However, I have a feeling that this case will be heard in Ipswich or Brisbane." He glanced over his shoulder. "Sarge is in there making phone calls to get you transferred out today so you have your committal hearing away from here. He really has got himself worked up about this case. Yes, mate, you really do need to get a lawyer before that, and for pity's sake, don't plead guilty."

Cliff went to open his mouth, but George stopped him by raising his hands and went on to explain the papers he was holding. First, a blank page for Cliff to write a statement, then one detailing the belongings he had on him at the time, plus a form for his next of kin, and access to his medical history—his doctor, dentist, and so on. When Cliff asked why all the personal information, George told him it was in case he committed suicide or self-harmed. It all seemed bloody silly to him, but Cliff complied with George's requests. The statement took ages as George kept getting him to put in more information of how he met Brenda, what sort of relationship it was, how helpful she'd been at Lochlea when Bill was away, and so on. George told him this statement would make or break him and could get him a reduced sentence. It seemed ludicrous to Cliff that he seemed to be doomed to spend some time in jail for something that was a terrible event, as he didn't want to kill Pete, indeed, and he wished he could whack Pete again.

By the time all the paperwork was completed, Bill and Albert had arrived. George had let them know of course, so Bill got Albert to drive him into town with him so Cliff's car could be taken back to Lochlea. The sergeant wasn't happy that they'd been told at all, and he very reluctantly allowed them to talk with Cliff. Had no choice, as they arrived with Bill's solicitor, who while he wasn't a trial lawyer, he was legal enough not to be pushed about. They talked for the full hour that the sergeant told them they could have. Cliff's transfer to Brisbane had come through, and he'd be leaving straight away. Cliff's mind was whirling round, so he found it hard to concentrate on what the solicitor was saying about getting one of his colleagues to look into his case for him. One of the issues he felt was the way in which he'd been arrested and near railroaded straight to Brisbane.

The next few weeks were a complete blur to Cliff. He failed to see the drama being built round his assault on Pete. In his eyes, he'd been justified to punch Pete. In fact, he was sorry he'd died—he'd like to have had him alive so he could mete out more punishment than the two punches. Most likely, he'd never felt the second one anyway. He conveyed much of this to the solicitor who came to discuss his case. He was tiny little man with quite feminine facial features, and it was a real surprise when he spoke for the first time, as he had a very deep and strong-sounding voice that he seemed to be projecting into all corners of the cell.

Cliff took his offered hand shake as he introduced himself. Cliff was again surprised to find the small hand had a really firm grip. "I'm James Holcroft, I work for myself, and it's fortunate for you I have a window of opportunity to be able of service to you at this time." He smiled, showing rows of alarmingly white teeth. "I've looked over what my friend in Wilted has sent down, and it's my opinion that your case has some merit."

Cliff was to discover that James never used one word when there was an opportunity to use several. The constant flow of words sometimes put his head in such a spin trying to keep up that he'd have to tune out, and he'd sit looking at James with a patient poker face while he went on and on about how he'd get him acquitted. He didn't seem to think any of Cliff's past should effect this case, particularly as he'd found ten people prepared to give character references for Cliff and Brenda. But also he'd found some people ready to say how Pete wasn't of the best character, and he felt he could discredit Sharon Walsh if she insisted on getting onto the stand. It seemed that Brenden Forrest had been appointed as his prosecuting officer for his committal hearing.

Cliff, inside himself, didn't feel all that confident, as Brenden Forrest had sent a chill of fear down his spine. The committal hearing was set up a week after he arrived in Brisbane. James advised that he should simply let him do all the talking, something Cliff was happy to do. He actually was over the whole thing, and the day before the hearing, he suggested to James that he should plead guilty and get it over with. James, for once, was speechless at this suggestion for a good minute before taking a deep breath and leaning towards Cliff.

James spoke in his most authoritative voice while shaking his head. "No, lad, no! You do that, and you'll be up for at least ten years prison and a maximum security prison. By pleading not guilty and going through a trail with a jury, you should only get at the most on the manslaughter charge four to five years in minimum security prison and, with your background, a possible place in a prison farm."

For once, Cliff had to admit it might have been the correct course of action. The morning of the hearing, Bill arrived with the suit he'd bought to wear at his and Brenda's wedding. He sighed and ran his hands over the cloth and felt tears well up behind his eyes. Bill crushed him to his chest in an unfamiliar show of affection. As he was escorted into the court room, he noted many familiar faces among the group in the gallery, including Fred and Anna Hay, as well as Sharon Walsh seated beside a well-dressed gentleman, with small, darting eyes that never seemed to stay an anyone object for longer that a second. Sharon glared at him and mouthed what he presumed were several swear words. He sighed inwardly as he was led to his chair opposite Brenden Forrest, who had a smirk on his face. Cliff, not for the first time, felt a little afraid of what was to come. They were all ordered to stand for the judge, who seemed very young to hold that position.

Cliff sat in a dejected manner while Brenden and James presented their cases on the circumstances that had led to these proceedings. Not a lot of it made sense to Cliff. The words seemed to get bigger and, to him, more ludicrous. The whole thing suddenly became quite amusing to him, and against his better judgement, he smiled. He immediately felt regret as Brenden noticed the smile, and it led him to point it out to the judge that he, Cliff, wasn't remorseful for his actions. James was sad Sharon didn't get to give evidence. She sat right in front of the judge and kept dabbing at her eyes whipping away nonexistent tears. On and on, the evidence was delivered by both parties, at which time the judge retired to consider his verdict.

Bill came to stand behind Cliff, offering words of encouragement. When Cliff asked who the fella was with Sharon, Bill shook his head, saying he thought it may be a solicitor, but he wasn't sure.

It all came to a screeching halt when the judge returned and declared that there was enough evidence to send Cliff to trial for manslaughter, setting a trial date for only two weeks away. He rejected Brenden submission of murder, which didn't please Brenden at all. The judge frowned at Brenden, saying that it was only because there had been a death that required a trail be held and there the case was shaky at best.

As Cliff was being led out of the court, he glanced back and noted Brenden talking to Sharon and her man. Again, he felt a thrill of fear. Bill came to see him before he traveled back to Lochlea, telling him that Fred and Elsie had offered to get him anything she needed and to keep his chin up.

It was a very sad, forlorn figure that Cliff projected as he was led to what he hoped would only be his home for the next two weeks. He paced about for most of the first night, panic rising up inside his mind. *What if he had to go to jail?* The officer who had locked him away had smirked at him and called him a pretty boy, telling him that he'd be enjoyed in prison. Cliff shuddered at the thought of what that meant. For the rest of the time, he spent wondering how and what had led him to this, and he began to regret ever meeting Brenda.

Why the hell she had to have picked him that night? He lay on his bunk, fists clenched at his sides, as these thoughts ran through his head. However, his dreams while he slept were very different as visions of Brenda's face floated through them, and he'd wake very confused. So it was his feelings for Brenda ebbing and flowing as he sank into depression.

PREPARATIONS

Brenda got quite cross at the girls trying to get her to communicate with her family and talk about her life. Questions continued, like whether she'd she ever had a boyfriend, confessing to her that they doubted the story she'd told when she arrived, and why she hated the babies inside her so much. Brenda had become very mellow as the birth neared, and eventually, Silvie growled at the girls to stop with the twenty questions and leave Brenda alone to prepare for the birth.

Kevin took her up to meet the matron at the hospital. Matron was aware that the babies were being adopted. As Kevin and Brenda entered the huge foyer of the hospital leading into a wide hallway, all familiar smells wafted over Brenda, and she wondered if the Dubbo hospital had received her letter. Kevin walked briskly down the hall, making Brenda have to jog a little to keep up with him so she hardly had time to peek into some of the open doors as they passed. She was still trying to look, though, and ran into the back of Kevin as he stopped to knock on a set of ornate doors. A strong voice bade them to enter.

The office was very impressive, with a huge desk in front of a wall of glass looking out over the well-kept grounds. The light shining though these windows blinded Brenda monumentally, and it took several blinking seconds before she brought the room back into focus, noting that the desk was practically free of clutter. A blotter and several pens sat in front of an imposing lady in a nun's habit. This shocked her. She'd been unaware that the hospital was run by nuns. Kevin and the nun greeted each other as old friends before the nun turned her clear eyes towards Brenda and held out her hand as the introductions were made. Her gaze softened as she smiled and said her hellos, telling Brenda to call her Matron Jean.

For some unknown reason, for a moment, Brenda was reminded of her gran and mum, and a wave of sadness wafted over her. Brenda blurted out that she wanted to go back to nursing after she'd got rid of the babies. A look of sorrow flashed quickly across Matron's face as Brenda used the words "get rid of."

As Matron Jean discussed how far along Brenda was and to date the pregnancy, Brenda wandered over to gaze out the huge wall of glass. She really didn't take in their conversations. She picked out several familiar flowers lining the paths that wound round between the manicured lawns. As she shifted alone in front of the wide expanse of glass, a figure came into her line of sight pushing a wheelbarrow piled high with weeds. The figure paused and, removing his hat, exposed his face to her as he wiped sweat off his brow. Brenda sucked her breath in sharply and gasped as she recognized the lad—Tommy—who had been brought into the house as a skinny and sick boy. As she gasped, she stepped back from the window in an involuntary movement, bringing the attention of the others to her side.

Matron Jean glanced at the lad below, who was now heading down one of the paths, and she looked at Brenda with raised eyebrows. Brenda said, "I saw this lad when he was really sick before G—" She stammered, suddenly aware that maybe the matron wouldn't approve of what went on at the Silvie's house.

"Gary Evens is a businessman who helps homeless children, and we act as a stepping stone back into the real world for most of them." She indicated the disappearing figure and went on. "Tommy is a nice boy and is doing very well. He seems to have a green thumb. He has improved the gardens no end, particularly the herb and vegetable plot. The chefs are very happy with his effects." Matron paused and said, "He won't have seen you, luv. Now we better get down to the business of why you're here."

I wonder if she'd been one of Gary's cases, Matron thought *though never heard of Gary doing anything with girls* as she put her arm round Brenda's shoulders, leading her to a table and chairs off to one side of the office. She was surprised when Brenda tensed at her touch, thinking, *This lass has problems like that lad.* She sent up a prayer that she could help Brenda.

Brenda noticed several official documents on the table and sat trying to understand what they all meant, a form wanting all her personal information—one, a document detailing her charges of money for her stay in the hospital and for the birth and care of the babies, and two legal documents that the adopters of her babies needed to assume ownership of the babies. Kevin watched with knowing eyes as she answered the family name, knowing that all the names and places were false. Dealing with Doc H and the street people for a long time, he could recognize lies when he heard them. Matron glanced at him briefly when going through that document, indicating she also knew the names were false.

Matron went slowly through the adoption paper, explaining carefully in detail that they gave up all her rights to the babies, and while the hospital would record the birth in the name she'd given, Brenda Hay, the birth certificate would be issued in the names of the new parents. As Matron Jean went over all that again, looking earnestly into Brenda's face, she was forced to sit back in her chair and fall into a shocked silence as Brenda snarled, "I hate these things in my belly and can't wait to be rid of them so I can get on with my life. I hate them." The last statement was delivered with venom.

After Matron Jean and Kevin had recovered their composure from the stunned silence of Brenda's forcefully delivered statement, Matron stood and led the way out of the office, giving a running commentary of the various wards and areas as they passed them leading them to the mums-and-babies ward. There were two wards on either side of the nurses' station, containing several ladies some sitting in chairs and some sleeping. Brenda sucked her breath in and whispered, "This is the nursing I wanted to get into."

Matron's head snapped around at these words and she asked if she'd been a nurse. She was fascinated as Kevin answered that, with his help, Brenda had completed the first and second year theory of nursing, also that she done some nursing in Brisbane before … here, he waved at her swollen belly.

Matron stammered "You mean theory without ward time?"

Kevin, who knew that was the story they were going to tell Gary, nodded. "We had hoped that she may be able to continue with her career after the birth."

Matron nodded, indicating that it may be a possibility and swept them on to see the babies' nursery. Brenda stood outside the viewing window as one of the infants was brought over so they could see the tiny face and little hands. Brenda felt a wave of maternal feelings and gasped as the babies inside her kicked hard, causing her to clutch at her belly and give it a hard slap. She'd found that a hard slap usually stopped the kicking.

"Now this is the room that will be set aside for you after the birth." Matron showed her to a huge, well-lit room with windows overlooking the herb-and-vegetable garden. "The birthing room is next door. However, we can't go in there, as there's a lass giving birth." Right on cue, a scream of pain erupted from the room. "She's getting close now." Matron smiled.

Brenda turned and walked out of the ward, suddenly feeling frightened. Animals never made noises like that. Some soft moans were all they made, and not for the first time, she wished she could see her mum. She thought maybe that was how her mum had screamed when she had been giving birth to her, and she was frightened of what was to come. The others caught up to her, and Matron led them back to her office where a pot of tea and cups were on the table so they sit as a cup was poured for each of them. After a couple of silent sips, Matron cleared her throat and picked up the document pertaining to the costs, naming a sum that to Brenda seemed massive.

"Though this does not need to be any of your concern unless you decide at the last minute not to adopt," Matron said. She went on. "The babies will be kept here for a few days unless the adoptive people wish to transfer them straight away."

"Let's hope they do. I don't want to see them or have anything to do with the babies or the adoption people." Brenda had recovered from the visit to the mums' ward. She stood and held out her hand to Matron Jean, thanking her and turning to Kevin, demanding, "Let's g-go." Her voice still shook a little, and without waiting, she strode out of the hospital into the bright sunlight.

Kevin found her sitting with her head in her hands as Tommy was asking if she was okay. Brenda didn't answer Tommy but gave him a weak smile and a nod as she rose and she and Kevin walked briskly toward the road. They walked silently back towards the house, Kevin unsure what to say and Brenda unable to say anything as she had such a tightness in her throat she was unable to form words. When they arrived at the house, Brenda gave Kevin's arm a pat and rushed to her room while Kevin sat with Silvie, going over the events of the morning. Silvie was happy that she'd have some sort of a truthful story to tell Gary. She was happy to hear about Tommy. She rarely knew what happened to Gary's proteges and had deliberately kept out of that part of Gary's life, while being proud of him for doing it. She knew his dad would have been proud of him too.

Brenda slept almost right through to the evening meal. She was woken by the chattering of the girls, some finished for the day and others getting ready for a busy night in the rooms and a party or two. Silvie had managed to have made a start on tea, so Brenda had to add the finishing touches to the meal of salad and cold meat. She sat beside Silvie, who laid her hand on Brenda's leg, giving it gentle pats as they let the conversations flow around them. As the dishes were cleared away and the girls disappeared to work or study, Silvie pulled Brenda head onto her shoulder and let her sob her heart out. They disentangled themselves, and Brenda saw Silvie to her bedtime routine before lying down to fall into a deep, exhausted sleep.

MATTERS OF THE COURT

Cliff hadn't been able to reconcile his shattered of thoughts of Brenda and how she'd impacted his life. Against his better judgment, he had to agree that for the most part, it had been for the better. He could clearly see her face when they'd first met with the sun behind her and her fine hair waving in the breeze round her face. His heart tightened as he recalled that, and he said to himself, *You were a gone goose from then on, you romantic idiot.* Not for the first time, he wondered why she'd run away just because Pete had forced himself on her, unless she'd gotten pregnant. He finally decided that that had to be the reason she'd just up and left. He considered how he'd feel about raising a child spawned by Pete, but that became too hard to deal with. If she was pregnant, she'd be getting close to giving birth. He hoped that she was being cared for by decent folks.

His trial date came round quicker than he wanted. James had been busy shoring up witnesses to speak for him, including George Alwell, as he'd been the one Cliff had reported Pete's demise to, as he felt that he'd be the tipping point of the case. He received word, on the morning, from George that he was unable to attend proceedings. Brenden Forrest was speaking for the prosecuting counsel, and it would leave the Wilted station understaffed if George attended the trial as well. Apparently, there was no one available to stand in. James considered his options and let it slide. He felt he had enough people to stand up for Cliff. It would be a bit of a cakewalk, and he was confident that Cliff would get a suspended sentence. He asked

Cliff if he wanted to ask for more time, but Cliff was emphatic in his refusal. He just wanted it all over and done with. As he was led into the court room. Cliff glanced over the seated crowd, noting all the familiar faces including Cindy, and he felt a wave of nostalgia sweep over him. He thought, *I must talk to Cindy when this is done and dusted.* He'd developed a faith in James, so he never doubted that he'd get a suspended sentence.

The first time James realized that just maybe he'd misjudged this case when Phillip West, a big city lawyer with a string of successes against impossible odds, presented himself as the prosecuting attorney. A full day of what Cliff considered to be a gigantic waste of time was spent in the selection of a jury. Phillip, it seemed, had a particular type of person he wanted, so some time was spent with debates between Phillip and James.

Finally, at the end a long and confusing day for Cliff, the jury had been selected and sworn in. James was happy with the presiding judge, as he wasn't inclined to mete of long sentences. He listened as Phillip waxed on about what a hard-working man Pete had been, always willing to pitch in to help out on the farm when required while Cliff had left his dad and a sick mother to take a wild trip to the Northern Territory and Cape York, causing trouble wherever he went by drinking and fighting. These facts were reinforced by Brenden Forrest, who took the stand and read out Cliff's rap sheet that went back as far as his boarding school days. Phillip called a witness from Darwin, a young lass who'd been a barmaid at a place that Cliff had frequented in his wild spree. She told of numerous fights he'd been involved in. She looked decidedly uncomfortable on the stand, and upon cross-examination, she had to admit that in some of the fights, Cliff had been defending young, drunk workmates against bullies or coming to the defense of ladies.

Next, Sharon was called to the stand, and she told of how flighty and rude Brenda had been to her when she'd visited Lochlea at Pete's invitation, Brenda had gone off somewhere, leaving it to Pete to do all the chores around the property. James bounced on her like an angry bull, tearing down her story bit by bit. He had her in tears very quickly, and she admitted that, actually, Pete had done very little about the place while she was with him but that he'd told her the reason that Brenda had left them alone was because she was jealous of Sharon and wanted Pete for herself. All this left James a little put out—he hadn't considered this angle at all. Sharon said that Brenda had left as soon as she'd realized she'd get nowhere with Pete. She pointed out that Cliff had been jealous of Brenda's infatuation with Pete and that was why they'd fought. Sharon finished by saying she felt sorry for Cliff that he'd been led astray by Brenda. Cliff sat transfixed as Sharon went on with her web of lies, and though he tried hard, James couldn't make much good come out of Sharon's testimony.

After a lunch break, it was up to James to put up his defense. Several Wilted townsfolk had written letters of reference for both Cliff and Brenda. James had managed to get permission for George to give evidence over the phone, but he'd been instructed to keep his evidence to the time Cliff had presented himself to report the incidence regarding Pete's death. He spoke very slowly and clearly, not allowing his personal feelings into his statement. Each solicitor was allowed three questions. James had to interject several times as Phillip tried to twist George's words, and the judge admonished Phillip as well. George ended by saying he'd forwarded a request to Brisbane detectives as to how he was to proceed and also that Bill had presented him with a signed affidavit from the local magistrate quaranteeing that he stood up for Cliff, that he'd return from his quest to find Brenda. More jousting followed, as Phillip questioned the validity of the affidavit, insisting Cliff had simply run away instead of facing up to his actions and that he'd only returned home as he'd run out of money. James waxed long and lyrical against all these allegations. Phillips was getting more and more frustrated. He yelled on several occasions, and the judge reminded him to remember that he was in court and to conduct himself appropriately.

Both lawyers summarized their cases before the judge advised the jury to stick to the facts only as they considered their judgment and ended proceedings for the day. Cliff's head was spinning. He was very uncommunicative when Bill came to bring him a fresh shirt for the next day. After Bill left, Cliff lay awake on his bunk, unable to even look at his meal, his eyes staring unseeing at the blackness above him. He must have slept, because he was startled into wakefulness by pain gripping his belly. The pain waxed and waned, getting stronger each time. He twisted on his bunk but couldn't find a comfortable position. He tried to stand to walk, but the pain forced him back down onto his bed. He found that if he panted, it helped, and after several hours, the pain stopped as suddenly as it had started. His stomach muscles felt sore and bruised and standing was difficult. However, by the time morning came, aside from having to lean slightly forward, he was back to normal. His face showed the strain of the night and for what lay ahead.

The jury entered the court room, filing in silently. Cliff scanned their faces for signs of how they'd viewed his case. Nothing showed, as the judge called for the chairman to state if they'd a verdict. They replied in the affirmative. Cliff was asked to stand as questions were asked and answered. He was found to be not guilty of murder, not guilty of absconding to avoid charges, but guilty of manslaughter. Phillip was clearly not happy with the result as James patted Cliff on the back. A general sigh of relief swept through the gallery as the jury left. The judge called for a short adjournment before he handed out his sentence. Cliff and James remained seated for the thirty minutes, Cliff with his head in his hands, a feeling of hope rising in him.

After the adjournment was completed, the judge rapped his gavel and requested Cliff to stand. Taking a deep breath, the judge spoke quietly directly to Cliff. "A death has occurred, and that cannot be ignored. Plus, there are your previous misdemeanors from your youth, some of which you didn't atone for, which shows some disregard for the law. It is mainly for these that I feel I must hand down a custodial sentence." He cleared his throat. "For being instrumental in the death of Peter Chaffey, I sentence you to three years, and on the matter of not attending court re your fines in the Northern Territory, I sentence you to a further six months. Both sentences to run concurrently with a non-parole period of one year at a minimum security facility at which you will undergo a course in anger management. Think yourself lucky, sir, and use this time to reflect and learn."

With a flourish of his robes, the judge strode out to his chambers, leaving Cliff in a bit of a daze as to whether he was indeed lucky or not. James was delighted, Phillip angry, Bill was very relieved and scattered applause echoed through the room. He glanced back to see Bill and the Hays and Willows families, including Cindy. He managed a weak smile as he was taken to the prison van that was transporting him to his next home for that year. He straightened his shoulders and made a vow to himself that he'd put all his efforts into being able to get out at the end of this year.

TWIN TIME

Brenda found she was unable to walk as far as she could. Her belly bulged out in front, forcing her to have to walk with her legs farther apart. Baby would meet her most days at a bus stop seat not far from the cottage, where they'd chat. Brenda confessed her lingering doubts of being able to survive the birth as she kept dreaming of the poor cow at Bemerside and snippets her mum had said about her own birth. She found it hard to find a comfortable position to sleep, and she spent most nights in a lounge chair as these unwanted beings inside her wriggled and squirmed inside her. Although the girls and the minders moved in and out carefully, she still had a disturbed sleep. She'd become very restless in general.

Doc H had gone off on a bender, so Kevin had to take full responsibility for her. As she was into her thirty-eighth week, Kevin decided that it would be best if she went to the hospital till the babies arrived. Silvie and the girls had all made her cards of farewell and chipped in to get her a cake the day before she was to leave. Brenda was overwhelmed and burst into tears, something she'd found herself doing a lot. The evening before she was to go, she couldn't sleep, so she decided to go see if Doc H had come back. The street light showing a familiar lump was on the seat, so smiling to herself, she tiptoed over to him and, taking hold of his foot, said, "Boo."

Doc didn't flinch, and she realized that his foot felt very cold. Her heart felt as though it had lept into her throat, and she suddenly felt very frightened. As she stood staring fixedly at the prone figure, still holding his foot, she became aware of a putrid smell emanating from the body, and she dropped the foot and jumped back away. As she did, her foot caught on a stick, and she, not being very agile, fell heavily on her backside. Fluid ran out of her pants, and she was embarrassed to think she'd wet herself. As she sat catching her breath, she looked around to see what she could pull herself back onto her feet with. She came to the conclusion that the seat was all that was in offer. She edged along the ground on her bum, back towards the seat. As she put her hand on it to pull herself up, she glanced up and saw the head of a snake appearing from among the folds of clothing. Although she realized it was a python, light glinting off its skin, she let out an almighty scream and couldn't stop even after the reptile had disappeared.

A couple of the house girls were heading out, heard the commotion, and went to investigate. It took them a long while to calm Brenda down and get her on her feet. By then, Baby had arrived. Something had told her to go to train station. Baby offered to see her home, and putting her arm round Brenda's shoulders, Baby slowly walked her back toward the cottage, growling at her that she'd walked too far. Brenda blubbed that she'd wet herself as well. Baby gave her shoulders a squeeze. Even though she hadn't had children herself, she knew enough that the babies' birth had begun. The next few hours were an absolute blur for Brenda. Waves of pain swept through her body. She felt as if she was being pulled apart. At one point, with a lull in the pain, she thought, *This is worse than what Pete did to me.* This thought was lost in another wave of pain.

She didn't remember the trip to the hospital or the feel of the fresh sheets before they became soaked with her sweat. Neither the nurses and doctors milling round her bed or the fact that Matron Jean had taken it upon herself to oversee this birth bothered her. Matron Jean felt sorry for this pretty lass, who, finding herself in trouble, had found her way to this hospital and into her care. Besides, the adoptive parents were paying well to have their new babies delivered safely. It was Matron's call to alert the surgical staff that these babies would be need to be delivered by caesarean section. They were big babies and both in a rush to get out of Brenda's belly. By the time Brenda was wheeled into the theater, she was screaming constantly, so she never felt the anesthetic being applied, nor did she feel any of the procedures of getting babies out.

Brenda woke to the sounds of birds filtering through the window beside her bed. She lay very still for a time, hoping she was back at Gran and Grandads place and everything else had just been a nightmare. As she went to roll over so she could see out the window, she found she was hampered by a needle attached to her arm and a very sore tummy, and a wave of nauseousness overcome her. She felt an arm lift her up so she could be sick into the offered dish. It hurt so much as her muscles flexed to force whatever was in her belly out. Nothing came out, and she was let to lie back on the soft pillows. As she brought her eyes into focus, she looked into the kind eyes of Matron Jean.

"Easy, luv, anesthetic sometimes causes biliousness." Matron Jean patted Brenda's hand. :It'll pass. The babies are fine. Do you want to see them?"

Brenda shuddered and shook her head violently, which again caused her muscles to react. Brenda looked down at her now flatter belly and was surprised to find a wound there, all clipped together. Her hand lingered there briefly before withdrawing and reaching out to Matron Jean. Brenda asked in a trembling voice, "Is … is everything okay inside there?"

Matron Jean assured her nothing would stop her producing more children later on, and advised her to get some rest and let her body heal itself. Brenda slept a lot and managed to actually sit up after a few days. Nurses came and dressed her belly wound daily, trying to engage with her, but after a while, they gave up and worked silently. Baby came to visit her, relaying the sad news that Doc H had died. Indeed, he'd been dead several days before Brenda had found him and, no, the snake had nothing to do with his death—he'd chocked on his own vomit.

As Brenda was feeling very much better and with the thrill of having her friend visit, Brenda swung her legs over the edge of the bed and went to walk over to Baby, who was standing at the window. The effort of standing up quickly made her feel a little dizzy, and she fainted momentarily, hitting the floor with a thud. Baby rushed to help her back up, and as Brenda sat back onto the bed, Baby noticed blood seeping through Brenda's nightie and called for help.

Nurses and doctors were all summoned to her bedside. By then, Brenda was bleeding profusely. Brenda felt herself drifting into unconsciousness.

THE RECOVERY

Brenda could hear birds singing and the clutter of activity outside her room. The curtains were drawn so the room was lit by a single bulb emitting a faint glow above her bed. This was the first thing that came into focus as her eyes adjusted to the muted light. She sighed heavily and was startled by the nurse rushing to her bedside. Brenda realized that she had tubes in both arms and, when she moved her legs, a tube in that area as well.

"Welcome back, lovey," the nurse whispered, "You sure gave us a bit of a fright bleeding like that." As Brenda went to open her mouth, the nurse went on "You had to go back to surgery and have been out to it for a week. Now you lie still while I call Matron and the doctor."

The nurse came back with a handsome young man, whose name badge said Doctor Lochlan Auld, and the matron. They all fussed over Brenda, holding a sip cup for her to wet her dry throat, fluffing her pillows and brushing her hair while the doctor inspected her lower body, some of the inspection caused her to wince a little.

The doctor stood up and rearranged her nightie. He gazed at for a moment and spoke in a very deep voice. "Matron, I think that we have to get this lass up and moving, starting now, so let us get her over to the chair by the window."

"Her stitches," Matron said in a tentative manner.

The doctor frowned severely and assured her it was better for the recovery to have Brenda up and about as soon as possible. They all gently raised her to a sitting position on the edge of the bed, and

227

a walking frame was placed in front of her. Brenda felt a bit dizzy and was afraid she'd fall again, but the doctor put his arm round her shoulders, giving them a squeeze. Brenda thought it felt very nice. Plus, he smelt nice too, not at all like Cliff, who sort of smelt like dust and grease most of the time. She gave him a tentative smile. The slow journey of five steps went without incident, but Brenda gave a sigh of exhaustion as she sank into the chair. The doctor spoke directly to her, telling her that if she could get herself with or without help twice a day, she could get the tube from between her legs, that was there to take her wee away, and she could wee into a pan or walk a little further to the toilet.

Brenda frowned at his use of parts of her body in such simple terms and corrected him by saying the proper names. He instructed Matron to remove the needles from her arms. One was delivering penicillin, and she could have that as a pill, and the other a saline drip for her fluid intake. The doctor said that Brenda must drink lots of juice and water. "Got to get your poos happening again as soon as possible." He patted head as he left.

Brenda was left a bit bemused by the trip to the window chair, and the removal of the needles in her arms made the trip back to the bed quite easy. Her belly felt tight but not very sore. The routine to the chair continued, and after two days, she could do it by herself and had the tube from her fanny removed. She made her first trip to the toilet, where there was a large mirror so she could look at her belly properly. She was shocked at how thin she was first, her ribs visible, her shoulder and hip bones protruding from her body. But she was pleased to see her breasts were still pert and maybe a little bit fuller. Finally, she let her eyes examine the scar running down from just below her navel to just above her now almost non-existent hairline. Stitches were visible, and as she gently poked the area beside it, she found little soreness. A nurse who had come to see why she was taking so long startled her by saying, "He done a good job on that, girlie. Very fine work indeed. Youse will hardly have a scar."

Two weeks later when she returned to her room, Baby was there, and she jumped up and gave her a hug. Baby answered Brenda's questions and this and that before putting her hand onto Brenda's knee and producing some letters, mostly from the girls and a long one from Silvie, but she put them all aside to read the one from Dubbo. She read it twice and then again before she looked up at Baby with tears running down her cheeks.

"They want to give me an interview, but it's next month. Next month and I have to let them know if I can attend by today!" How? What do I do. Bugger! Bugger!" The last delivered was as she thumped her fist down on the bed. The two of them walked to the public phone at the entrance to the long hallway.

All the way to the phone and back, Brenda carried on about how could she get to Dubbo. She needed new clothes too, Baby stopped her and handed her a wallet filled with money. "Silvie's letter will explain more, but this money is for you. Five hundred dollars should be enough to get you there by bus, luv."

Baby hugged and kissed her farewell, leaving Brenda to read the letters. The notes from the girls stated they all missed her cooking and help with the housework, with most saying they were getting out soon. The only thing holding them there was Silvie, who'd had several falls and was now completely stuck in bed or in a chair. She needed help to look after herself, and Gary had employed a nurse to care for her. This nurse wasn't very friendly, and when no one was about, she was mean to Silvie. They'd all tried to tell Gary, but he only believed the nurse, so in general, they were all set to up and leave the minute Silvie was no longer in the house and bugger Gary. All this had Brenda sobbing because Silvie had been good to her and they'd become good friends.

After she'd settled herself down, she opened Silvie's long letter. Silvie told how she'd been trying to keep doing all the chores Brenda had done for the girls but had got very tired and fallen while doing the laundry and then again in the kitchen, spilling hot water on her arms and burning them badly and breaking some bones in her right foot, her best side too. Gary had put his foot down and gotten her a wheelchair, insisting that she wasn't to do anymore work round the house. Karen Howell, the nurse Gary had gotten for her, was very good when anyone was about, but became quite rough and negligent if they were alone. Like refusing to get her to the toilet quickly enough so she'd soiled or wet herself a few times. Very frustrating for her and no matter how much she complained to Gary, he'd hear nothing against this woman. She finished that particular bit of the letter by saying, "I think she is his mistress." She went on to the money she'd given to Baby to give to her as payment for all the work she'd done about the place, adding that the minders were keeping the garden going because the girls were back on the chore roster and unable to help out there anymore.

Gary apparently had gone to the hospital to see when she could start to be of some use to him, and had arrived while she was just out of the second surgery. He was very angry when he'd seen the long cut on her belly. He'd stormed out and spent several hours yelling at Silvie that Brenda wasn't going to be any use to him now and that she must never come back to the house. He'd then slammed the letter from Dubbo down on the table, stating that she may as well have it. He'd been hanging onto the letter for a while, assuming it was from family, and he hadn't wanted any interference from them before Brenda had paid him back for what he considered freeloading in his house. Silvie finished off by wishing her well, and she said not to worry about her, hoping all her dreams were realised.

Brenda folded the letters carefully and tucked them into the wallet with the money. Without any thought, she walked to the front of the hospital where there was a public phone she could maybe use to look into buying a bus ticket. She was a little out of breath, so collecting the phone book, she sat on the step to look up the number for the bus. She let her eyes drift over the neat garden and saw without really seeing Tommy and someone else walking towards her. She was snapped out of her dreamlike state by a familiar-sounding voice.

"Brenda? Brenda Willows, is that you? It's Jewel McGregor. Remember? From Bemerside? I was Harry's friend."

Brenda dropped the phone book and hugged her old friend. There ensued a lot of squealing and the girls talking over each. Tommy kissed Jewel on the cheek, saying, "Be back soon." The kiss stopped them both talking, and Jewel told Brenda that she was studying agricultural science and had met Tommy there. He was signing up to do horticulture in the next term. They were headed off to Dubbo for the holidays and so Tommy could meet her family. Brenda was silent for a brief time before asking if they'd take her to Dubbo, adding that she'd pay, as she had an interview at the Dubbo hospital in twenty days. Jewel agreed that she could and would come back in two weeks to pick her up.

Matron wasn't happy with letting her go. Matron called in Lochlan, who also voiced his concerns and told her she must look after herself and that her tummy was still delicate and must be let mend before doing any manual work. He set up some exercises for her to do in the meantime. He gave her another bottle of pills and some cream for the scar, reluctantly allowing her to leave. On the departure day, it took no time at all to gather her things, putting them into an old backpack Matron had produced. She strode out the front to wait for Jewel and Tommy. She didn't see the look of worry that passed between Matron and the doctor.

THE FUTURE, GET SET

Brenda

The trip to Dubbo left Brenda feeling very tired and flat. Most of what she'd been through was retold to Jewel, and in a quiet moment, Tommy confided to her that he hadn't told Jewel about his life on the street. He felt that as she came from not only a country environment and a stable and secure home life, she'd find it hard to comprehend how or why he'd ended up there. Brenda agreed with him. Jewel did most of the talking anyway, telling of her plans to help improve her parents' farm and get into the development of new verities of grasses and drought-resistant trees that could also be used as fodder in bad times.

Jewel's mum, Alice, noticed how exhausted Brenda was and sent the two young people off to find Jim. Jewel's dad took Brenda into the house, drawing her a nice warm bath before giving her a drink of milo. Brenda barely had time to finish the drink before sinking onto the soft bed, asleep before her head hit the pillow. Alice stood for a moment, gazing at this waif-like girl, taking in the dark circles under her eyes and how thin she was. Something made her bend down and place a light kiss on Brenda's forehead.

Over breakfast in the morning, Brenda advised Alice that she had an interview at the hospital in two days, and if she could get a lift into the town center, she'd try to find a room so she wasn't a nuisance. Alice insisted that she stay with them till after her interview, and then they'd take it all from there. Those days were heavenly for Brenda, getting about the farm, which was so different from Lochlea, only a few domestic animals, such as a dog and cat and a few chooks. The farm produced quality hay used primarily by feed lots where stations and farms sent their stock to be fattened before going to market. Brenda could see why Jewel was so keen to learn about grasses.

All too soon, her interview day arrived. Alice and Jewel spent an hour putting on her make-up and doing her hair. Jewel loaned her a dress, telling her they'd go shopping for some clothes after the interview. Alice told the girls where the best op-shop was, wished Brenda good luck, and sent them off in good spirits, which, for Brenda, dissipated as she got closer to the hospital. The hospital was an imposing building not unlike the one in Sydney, with wide steps leading to the double doors. So taking a deep breath, she forced herself to portray an air of confidence. She hardly heard Jewel's words of encouragement as she was directed to the interview room. There, she found three mature ladies sitting ramrod straight behind a large desk, several piles of papers stacked along the desk. A single chair was placed away from the desk in the center of the room.

As soon as the door closed, the three ladies smiled, which made Brenda feel a little better, and indicated for her to sit, not a moment too soon as her legs felt like jelly. Everyone was quiet for some time, during which Brenda looked at each of the ladies in turn. She felt sweat running down her back. Before she could get up the courage to speak, each of the ladies asked questions, allowing her time to consider her answers. Brenda explained that her late reply to their letter was she'd moved and had spent a time in hospital before getting home to find the letter. This was the only time her voice shook a bit. She didn't know Kevin had also written to them explaining some of her circumstances, including her pregnancy, so the ladies understood her reluctance to mention that. Kevin had also told them how bright she was, and had added she'd be an asset to any hospital.

Brenda was sent outside while they considered her fate. After what seemed a long time, Brenda was recalled to the interview room. The center lady spoke softly.

"My girl your record of study is incredible. You have completed theory exams to take you into second year. However, you do need to complete some on hygiene and cleaning practices. This is due to you doing the theory exams while not working in a hospital. We have contacted Brisbane, and they confirm that you work well in the team environment. They were stunned at your sudden departure, but we're aware of why you left." She held up her hand as Brenda opened her mouth to speak "Your mentor Kevin contacted us."

Brenda slumped a little in her chair.

"We would like to offer you employment for six to nine months at the end of which, providing you pass the hygiene and cleaning procedures, we could qualify you as an enrolled nurse. With this qualification, you can work in most hospitals and, of course, if you wish continue study to go further and become a registered nurse"

She had to stop as Brenda had started to sob, her shoulders shaking. All through this, Brenda had never lowered her eyes, though. A start date of two weeks from now was put forward, and Brenda was advised she could stay in the nurses' quarters or at a hostel close by that had reasonable rates and provided breakfast and dinner. Brenda thanked the ladies and walked out to Jewel, still crying.

Jewel assumed the interview hadn't gone well. She was excited when Brenda asked to be taken to the hostel so she could book her room. Jewel knew her mum would insist she stay at her place till she started at the hospital. Then they went to the library so Brenda could join and get the textbooks required for her couple of subjects. She was keen to get into the books. Buying dresses didn't come into the day's activities at all.

Alice was happy to have Brenda stay till she was to move into the hostel. Secretly, she wanted to fatten her up a bit.

··· ··· ··· ··· ··· ··· ··· ···

Cliff

The first week of his internment saw Cliff spend his first few days in the remand center, where all kinds of people were jammed in together—Shoplifters, driving offenses, break-and-enter people, and even those who had killed someone. He hated it because most of them were angry and would lash out at a moment's notice, usually over something as ridiculous as a glance their way. Cliff placed himself in a corner and tried not to draw attention to himself. A young chap squeezed up close beside him, whispering that he was scared some of the older, hardened criminals would bash him. Cliff shrugged his shoulders and, sighing, asked why would that be, and the young chap replied in a shaky voice, "I'm homosexual, and I've been arrested for prostitution."

Cliff didn't know what to say to that statement, but let the lad, whose name was Adam, sit beside him most of the time. He saw several of the older men watching them. It made him feel uncomfortable, but since no one came near them, he relaxed. On the third night, he was jerked awake by a hand being placed over his mouth. Adam was on the floor beside him, three men taking turns assaulting him. Adam had a rag stuck in his mouth and was gasping for air. They kept it up long after Adam stopped struggling, and flopped about with the assault. Cliff started to shake his head violently and bit into the hand covering his mouth and yelled, "Stop, you're killing him."

His yell drew the attention of the guards, so the ones abusing Adam stopped, and before leaving, one of them leaned in close to Cliff's face. "You saw nothing, you hear, or it will be your turn next." A hard slap was delivered to the side of his head so he fell back hard against the concrete wall, the words *You got that, gay boy?* echoing in his ear.

Only the guards arriving at the cell stopped him being hit again. The guards asked everyone to stand facing the wall while they checked Adam. Cliff was shaking so hard he found it very difficult to stand without swaying from side to side. The guards brought in a stretcher and rolled Adam onto it. One guards spoke softly to Cliff, asking if he knew what had happened. Cliff managed a slight nod. The guard put an arm round Cliff's shoulders, and they followed the stretcher out of the cell. As the cell door was slammed shut, the man who'd hit Cliff pointed at him and snarled, "I'll remember you, you dog, gay boy, and I'll enjoy meeting you again." And he spat on the floor.

Cliff shakily told his story and then found he needed to tell it several times. He asked about Adam, only to be told he'd died, and none of the officers seemed particularly sad. They just said he was a bloody homo and probably deserved what had happened to him. Cliff felt saddened by the attitude. No one deserved what had happened to Adam. The guards, however, realized that putting Cliff back into the cell would put him in danger, so he sat handcuffed to a chair till his transfer to the minimum security prison was rushed through, and he was whisked away that afternoon.

Cliff arrived too late to see the warden and was taken to a single cell for the night. In the morning, he was escorted to the warden's office where he was confronted by an angry-looking, overweight, short, balding man who had several strands of hairs plastered over his head in an attempt to hide his baldness. It brought and involuntary smile to Cliff's lips. The warden slapped a small cane onto the desk, causing even the escorting guards to jump. Taking a deep breath, the warden gave an hour-long lecture about what he expected from inmates and the fact that because Cliff was a convicted killer, he didn't think he should be at this prison at all. He said that Cliff had better keep his nose clean or he'd be bounced to a more appropriate prison. Then the warden dismissed him with a flap of his hands. The guards told him not to be too concerned—the bloke had stuffed up his previous job and really felt he'd been harshly treated by being sent here—and not to worry as he hardly ever ventured out of his office.

This prison was almost like being at home. He had a wide expanse of garden to propagate, both flowers and vegetables, He had a couple of horses that were used to pull ploughs for the other crops, like corn and potatoes, and several milking cows to care for. He became very fond of the horses and thought of ways he could make use of them when he got home. Home seemed so far away, and time dragged. The place was run like a normal farm, really, and Cliff started to enjoy his jobs. If it wasn't for the high wire fences, he could have forgotten he was in jail. There was a well-stocked library that the inmates were allowed to access for four hours a day. They were encouraged to participate in the short courses offered. Cliff opted for one in leather work and a self-defense course as he'd taken the threat to his body seriously and was sure that bloke would carry a grudge forever. He simply kept mostly to himself and actually enjoyed reading, learning both the intricacy of the leather work and the physicality of the self-defense course. Many of the inmates were there because they'd done dumb things like fighting and drinking in a public place, and had chosen to spend time in jail rather than paying the fines. Cliff found he had the longest sentence as most only had sentences of six-to-twelve months. Most of them were surprised to learn he'd killed someone and had only been sent to a low-security prison.

He'd only been at the prison for a week when Fred came to visit, voicing his sorrow that Cliff had ended up in jail. They talked of what his future would be, and Cliff was undecided really. So much of his past year had been taken up with Brenda and he was so unsure of those feelings now that he couldn't put any plans in place. Fred had left a suitcase with the warden with some street clothes and personal things, like a toothbrush and razors. It took a month for the personal items, minus the razors, and suitcase to be delivered to his cell. Among the items was a photo, taken at the show, with Brenda and Prince. This brought tears to his eyes, and deep inside him, he knew then that he still cared deeply for her, and for the first time for a long time, he felt the need to masturbate. He told Fred that he

B L Wilson

didn't want any visitors. He just wanted to get all this behind him so he could get on with his life, and he hoped that by then Brenda had returned and, yes, he did still want to marry her.

Day after day blended together. Inmates came and went so much that Cliff didn't put any effort into getting to know any others than polite conversation. Stories of drug taking had been on his mind, but the only evidence of that he saw was some marijuana plants in several of the garden plots. Most of these were started and left as that person left or found and removed by the guards. Never once did he see any of this reported. On the day he remembered was Brenda's birthday, he recalled how devastated he'd been when she disappeared the week of her birthday and their wedding. He wondered if she'd gotten pregnant after Pete raped her. If so, he wondered, what had she done with the babies? Just one huge lot of unanswered questions. He hoped to get out before Christmas so he'd be able to surprise everyone at Lochlea. He smiled at the thought. *I'll go to see Anna and Fred Hay first if that happens*, he thought.

One very bright moment was when the horses were put to work pulling the plow. After an hour's instruction, he was left to prepare the paddock. He found trudging behind the horses, watching their wide backsides swaying. The smell of the tilled earth crept tantalizingly into his nostrils. At that moment, he felt free and he felt compelled to burst into song, the breeze carrying the happy sound toward the prison walls and into the warden's office. The warden got up and slammed the window closed. He called a guard to go and shut that blasted fool up.

Cliff was hoeing at his garden plot when a guard told him he must go the warden's office. He washed his hands and made his way to the office, trying to think of what reason it could be. He couldn't remember any incidence that may have resulted in such a call. The warden glanced up as he entered and pointed to a chair. That in itself was unusual—inmates were always made to stand. After a finishing writing, the warden looked up and spoke, his voice angry.

"You've been given an early parole, lad. Think yourself lucky. You'll be escorted to Boggo Road Jail, where they'll finalize your release tomorrow. Go and pack your things now."

The words were spoken through clenched teeth. Cliff opened his mouth, but the warden flapped his hands at him and pointed to the door. Cliff walked back to his cell in a daze. He had all his meager belongings packed in the old suitcase Fred had brought to him just after he arrived, so now he could return it with thanks and be home for Christmas. *Beauty*, he thought.

GO

Brenda

Brenda had been summoned to the matron's office. As she walked quickly down the long hall, she wondered what she'd done. She was coming to the end of her many months of work. It had been marvelous after the first month, which had been difficult because of her sore tummy. She'd flown through the courses that were expected of her. She had several weekends with Alice and Jim. Jewel was doing well with her uni course apparently. Brenda enjoyed the postcards from Tommy and Jewel as they'd moved in together. Some cards from Silvie and Baby also came. The last one from Baby told her Silvie had gone to a nursing home as Gary had found out the nurse, Karen Howell, was being cruel to her. Baby said most of the regular girls had left, which Gary was upset about. Brenda shook her head to clear it before knocking on the imposing door.

Inside, she found the same group that had interviewed her initially, the same imposing desk, but this time with only one pile of papers. They bade her to take a seat, and as one, they linked their fingers together and leaned forward, placing their arms on the desk. Matron tapped the pile of papers. "These, young lady, are your marks up to date." She cleared her throat. "You've certainly done well and at some trying times, so I'm happy to present you with …" Here she glanced at the other two ladies, and they all stood. Brenda followed suit. They indicated that she should move closer to the desk as they all lifted a document and handed it to her saying, "Congratulations, you are now a qualified enrolled nurse."

Brenda felt behind her for her chair and sat down with a thump, tears streaming down her cheeks, stammering, "It's my eighteenth birthday today too."

After hugs all round, they advised Brenda that her tenure at the hospital had expired, and now she had confirmation of her skills she'd need to reapply to the hospital or any other hospital she wished to work at. And of course, she could continue improving her nursing by meeting more milestones. Though her tears, Brenda stammered, "I w-w-want to go see m-my mum."

Brenda floated out of the hospital into bright sunlight, which, as well as her tears, blinded her for a moment. She collided with a person skipping up the stairs. They both started to apologize before recognizing each other. It was Cindy. Cindy broke the spell of the moment, saying she had an interview and asking if Brenda could wait for her. Brenda agreed, thinking, *This most certainly is turning out to be a great day.* She hoped that Cindy was heading home and she could hitch a ride. She sat on the top step and let her eyes wander about while formulating plans for her immediate future. Although she was keen to see her mum, she felt she should go and see Gran and Granddad Hay, hoping against hope that Cindy would take her. Otherwise, it would be a long, lonely trip on a bus. She sighed as she heard Cindy's footsteps echoing down the wide hallway, and Brenda stood to meet her.

Cindy came back out of the hospital, smiling. "They're going to allow my transfer from Brisbane to here. Isn't that great!" she gushed. "Let's go have a cuppa. Goodness, how is that you're here? Where have you been? Everyone was so worried, and, no, I didn't tell anyone about your situation! Have you heard about Cliff?"

By this time, they'd reached a cafe, and Brenda asked her question while they waited for tea for Brenda and coffee for Cindy with a slice of cake for them both. "Cliff? Do you still go to Lochlea at all? How is Prince? How are Mum and Dad? My gardens?" She finished with, "Cliff?"

After they stopped trying to talk over each other, Cindy explained all the changes at Lochlea while Brenda keep mouthing "Cliff" at her. She hardly heard most of what was said, except the fact that Prince was a great and how he ran the farm, keeping an eye on everyone. Cindy eventually told her Cliff had gone to jail for killing Pete.

Good, Brenda thought and now had some understanding of why all the changes at Lochlea that Cindy had talked about and fancy her mum and dad working there too. Cindy said he most likely wouldn't get out till the new year. The information that Wilted had grown so much gave her hope that the hospital may be able to employ her even if they didn't offer further training. Brenda kept her story brief, brushing over the time at the house quickly and the fact she'd given her babies away without seeing them. She explained how she'd met Jewel there, and Jewel had brought her to Dubbo as the hospital had requested an interview, and she was now a qualified enrolled nurse. They chatted over a second cup of tea and coffee, and eventually, Brenda said, "I want to go home. I want to see my mum and dog. I don't know how Cliff will feel about me now, but I'll wait for him at Lochlea."

Cindy replied that she was indeed going to Lochlea after spending a night or two with cousins in Dubbo. After wards, she was heading to Brisbane for a few days before going to pick up her Aunty Linda and going to Lochlea. Plus, she'd be happy to have the company on the drive. All this suited Brenda, who skipped into the hostel and rang Alice to tell her the news. Alice was delighted and offered to pick her up for the night because Jewel and Tommy had just returned for their Christmas break. It was a fun night, full of laughter and much chatter. It was a tired Brenda who Jewel took to meet Cindy the next morning. One thing that surprised Brenda was that Jewel and Tommy were allowed to sleep together. Jewel told her most of the couples at the university slept together and were all taking birth control pills. Tommy had acquired some holiday work at a place called Wilted, working for the council there. And raising an eyebrow, Jewel asked "You heard of the place, eh?"

Brenda laughed and told her about the town, telling Jewel she too was going there to visit her mum and check on employment at the hospital, suggesting that, should Jewel come, they'd need to catch up. "Perhaps you can come and inspect some of the grasses being used at Lochlea."

Jewel and Brenda talked way into the night, so it was a very tired but excited girl WHO Cindy picked up the next morning. They shared the driving, even though Brenda didn't have a license yet, and it was quite late when they arrived at the Hays' Golda Avenue address. Brenda was surprised to find Gran and Granddad were still up watching the newly acquired television set. Anna wrapped Brenda in a huge bear hug.

Cindy declined the offer of a cuppa and drove off, saying, "See you in three days."

Anna led Brenda into the kitchen and kept hugging her, all the while telling her how bad she was to have just left like she did and not contacting anyone for so long. Fred brought up the subject of Cliff, and Brenda nodded that Cindy had told her he was in jail for killing Pete. Brenda had decided on the trip up with Cindy that she'd go back to Lochlea and wait for him there as she was unsure if he'd still want to be with her and she wasn't all that sure either. Finally, Anna noticed how tired the girl looked and tucked her into bed. The last thing Brenda whispered was not to tell the folks at Lochlea.

Brenda was up early and went to the chook house, where Dutchy fluffed his feather to attack mode till she spoke. Fred found her standing with the bird snuggled in her arms, emitting noises of contentment, and as she turned to greet him with a huge smile, Fred's progress was halted by the vision she presented.

My goodness, she truly is beautiful and no longer a child. She looks very like my departed mum. Together, they fed the chooks and returned for the special breakfast of bacon and eggs, after which Anna demanded that she and Brenda were going shopping

Cliff

Cliff's paperwork saw him spend the night in a holding cell. He couldn't sleep, with memories of his previous stay in this cell. Fortunately, there were only a few people in that night, but he was still very pleased to watch the daylight seep into the room. Finally, with all the boxes ticked and I's dotted, he walked out, only needing to report to a police station once a week. He nominated the Wilted station, knowing it would really piss Brenden Forrest off. He remembered which buses to take to get to the Hays' house.

He arrived mid morning and found Fred working his front garden. Fred stood, hands on hips, looking at him with an odd look on his face, which puzzled Cliff a bit. Still, he took the offered hand and shook it firmly. They went in to have the usual cup of tea while information was exchanged. Fred agreed he was a lucky lad, though he believed a bigger surprise for Cliff awaited as they heard the front door open and the sound of excited voices. Cliff turned his head toward the sound, his eyes unseeing because of the glare. As the figures came into focus, he found himself looking into the direct, blue-eyed stare of Brenda, who had been stunned into silence.

Cliff and Brenda

Fred took Anna's hand and led her out of the room, leaving Cliff and Brenda looking like a pair of statues, neither wanting to make the first move. Cliff broke the stand-off by crossing the few step between them and wrapping his arms round Brenda's slight frame. She felt taller and more rounded. Brenda tentatively put her arms round his waist before lifting her face to receive the gentle at first and then more passionate kisses. They broke off the kiss and stood for what seemed an age, their bodies welded together. Brenda broke it off by looking up at Cliff with twinkling eyes.

"Reckon I've got you going hay?" and she wiggled her hips They both stammered huskily, "I love you. I need you."

As Fred and Anna came back into the room, breaking another moment of passion, Fred, being the practical person he was, put forth a question. "What now, you two?" When Brenda tried to say something about the pill and it was okay to have sex outside marriage, both Fred and Nancy said together, "Not in this family!"

Fred, true to his word, rang the magistrate court to find out when or how they could marry. He was directed to a registry office and found there was an opening that afternoon. Anna managed to extract Brenda from Cliff and take her into her sewing room to try on her original wedding dress. It only needed very little adjustment as her breasts were bigger and her hips a bit rounder. Cindy was summoned to act as Brenda's bridesmaid Fred would stand up for Cliff. So it was. Brenda was sorry her mum wasn't there, but she knew they could have a church wedding for her later. Her insides were trembling at the thought of what was to come, and she silently thanked the house girls for all their tutelage in sex. Cliff was hoping her experience with Pete hadn't turned her off sex too much. He felt maybe he'd need to take the lead.

Following the ceremony, Anna produced a card, giving them a room in a motel for two nights to be their honeymoon. Cindy dropped them at the motel, and they suddenly realized they had no spare clothes as they stepped into the room and stood close together, facing each other. They burst into laughter, knowing they wouldn't need clothes. Slowly and very deliberately, they began to undress each other, folding each item of clothing neatly on the bedside tables. Brenda leaned forward as the last item was removed.

"Think I've got you this time," she breathed into his ear as she sank onto the bed, pulling him down beside her where she flipped him onto his back and straddled his body. She was surprised that there was no pain as when Pete had raped her, so she moved about watching Cliff's face. He was surprised to find that Brenda seemed to be very adept at guiding him to give her pleasure and where to touch him to drive him wild. The night passed quickly.

They lay close together for some time, as they'd done so many times, and slept. Brenda enjoyed the giving and receiving of pleasure that went on after the first and second frantic lovemaking. They lay close, holding each other, telling snippets of what had gone on in their lives in the time they'd been apart. There were several rounds of relaxed and gentle exploration of each others bodies. Neither was absolutely sure of the path their lives would take from here. They just knew that together they'd get through it.

It was a blissfully happy and contented couple that Cindy found when she came to collect them, bringing with her some travel clothes and a bag for the wedding apparel. After picking up Linda, they set off for Lochlea. It would be after dark when they arrived. Brenda wondered particularly if her dad would forgive her and if Prince would remember her. No one in the house took any notice of the car as they knew Cindy and Linda were coming to visit Albert.

Brenda need not have worried about Prince, for as soon as he heard her voice thanking Cindy for the lift, the dog came bounding over to her as they shut the house yard gate, a ball of happy, running round and round them as, holding hands, Cliff and Brenda walked toward the future. None of them saw the shaft of light from the doorway glint off the slithery form sliding off to the side of the doorway. None of the people, as they noisily greeted the young couple home, heard Prince yelp sharply as the serpent attached itself to the dogs leg. Prince retaliated by grasping the snake and shaking it fiercely to break its back. Prince dropped the snake and turned to lie, head on paws, watching his beloved Brenda as life faded from his body. Brenda smiled at the vision of her dog lying ever so still at the door.

ABOUT THE AUTHOR

Barbara has always been a dreamer so after some moderate success with 'Blood on the Bull Bar' set out on another literacy journey.

Barbara grew up on cattle station and became an amazing horse woman, commencing her horse training at 12 years old. She progressed form handling ponies to training their own country race horses, winning a trophy for the most successful trainer. She rode in one of the first Lady jockey races.

After moving to Atherton FNQ she continued to ride track work along with coaching junior soccer teams Barbara and her Mother joint owner a souvenir shop as well as Barbara bought into a late night pizza shop. This shut down when the late night hotels were forced to close due to general vandalism in the streets.

Barbara took a deep breath and as she child had finished school she headed back bush working as stock man and cook in western Qld and NT before ending up in Orange NSW where she worked in a factory building refrigerators while running a mowing business and putting out junk mail on the week-ends. While at the factory she assisted in compiling a manual for the track she worked on.

She returned to school studying first computing and then hospitality. After a year in Cairns she went to work at a mine, progressing to Bar manager and running the house-keeping. From there she went into Pest control, retiring in 2012.

Barbara has two sons and four grand children. She now resides in Townsville.

Printed in the United States
By Bookmasters